KENTUCKY SUMMERS

FOREVER THE PACK

Other Books by Tim Callahan
Kentucky Summers Series:

Others

KENTUCKY SUMMERS

FOREVER THE PACK

TIM CALLAHAN

TATE PUBLISHING
AND ENTERPRISES, LLC

Published by Tate Publishing & Enterprises, LLC
127 E. Trade Center Terrace | Mustang, Oklahoma 73064 USA
1.888.361.9473 | www.tatepublishing.com

Tate Publishing is committed to excellence in the publishing industry. The company reflects the philosophy established by the founders, based on Psalm 68:11,
"The Lord gave the word and great was the company of those who published it."

Book design copyright © 2015 by Tate Publishing, LLC. All rights reserved.
Cover design by Bill Francis Peralta
Cover Photography by Tim Callahan
Interior design by Jomar Ouano

Published in the United States of America

ISBN: 978-1-68164-946-7
1. Fiction / General
2. Fiction / Action & Adventure
15.10.13

This book is dedicated to:
my first grandchild, Savannah Rose.
May God bless her.
Born: March 30, 2015

In memory of:

Eleanor Holbrook.
December 26, 1937 - September 12, 2014

Contents

1   Old Age

2015

When most folks reach what people would call "old age", which I used to think was thirty—but now I believe to be over eighty, they look back at their lives and wonder what their life meant, what they accomplished, what legacy did they leave for future generations. I'm now quickly approaching that period in my life and wondering the same thing.

That skinny boy who was too weak to climb up a rope to get out of a cave is now a much heavier version, who again couldn't climb out, as a man in his sixties. Where did the years go? When I now go into schools to talk to classrooms of kids who have read one of my books I show them pictures of when I was a skinny nine-year-old and tell them, while I pat my large tummy, that I'm still as skinny as I was in the pictures. They laugh. I laugh with them, even though I wish I was still that young boy going on great Morgan County adventures.

I sit during the winter months and watch the birds feed from the seed I put out for them. They fight with other birds for their spot. They fly away when I go out to refill the birdfeeders, scared of me I guess, even though I'm the one who feeds them out of love. I wonder if they are thankful to the human who places the food there for them on those snowy days. That brings me to wonder if others are thankful that I was in their lives, or did they want to fly away when I approached? Did I make a difference? Did I make folks laugh? Did I do something to bless those I came in contact with? Was I a beacon of love? Am I thought of fondly?

Pretty heavy stuff, huh?

No matter what I've accomplished as an adult, the career I've had, or what little money I've earned over the years, I still look back at my childhood in Kentucky as my most cherished times. I'm sure not everyone feels the same about their childhood. I've met others who have said they hated their childhood, and I feel bad for them. But I was as fortunate as a boy could be when I was in Kentucky, and I'm thankful for every day I spent in Oak Hills.

Sure, I've had many other days that equal those as an adult—my wedding day, the birth of my children and others. It seems though I'm drawn to my childhood and the adventures I was caught in. I think of the Tattoo Man every week, at least. I think of the Wolf Pack, and the many things we experienced, as I drive down the roads. I sit in front of my TV and watch fictional adventures of different programs and think, *Too bad they don't put my childhood on a TV show, it would be a hit—talk about adventure.*

My buddies, the members of the Wolf Pack, have all lived their lives. All the members are still living, and I wonder if they have the same fond memories of those days that I do. I would bet good money they do. To me, we were a special group of boys, a unique collection of characters. I'm thankful for each of them.

As I entered the Oak Hills School in the fall of 1962 for my eighth grade year, we kids didn't realize it would be the last year for the one-room school. It would close after that school year. We were the last group of kids in the school. The twins blamed me. The following year we were bused to Wrigley for elementary and junior high. Times were changing. The one-room school building still stands, but in the form of a house. I used to see Eleanor Holbrook, our teacher at the one-room school, every year at the Sorghum Festival in West Liberty. I know she also had fond memories of the school, because we reminisced about those years.

Susie and I were talking one day in 2005 and she told me she thought it was time to get everyone together, a reunion of old friends from long ago, something we had never done. I quickly agreed, telling her it was a wonderful idea. We talked about dates, and soon settled on one, and she said she would send out invitations so people could make plans. We talked about who we should invite and we decided that we would invite everyone we could think of to invite including Sadie and Bernice, the skunk. I asked if that also meant the twins. I was disappointed with her response. I gave her any addresses that I had of our past companions.

After our discussion I began thinking about my friends and our many adventures and the moments we shared lying on the grass in the summers of the 1950s and −'60s, either looking up at the clouds as they passed by, or the stars and moon shining in the night sky. We talked about everything during those times. When we were younger we talked about insects, and pranks we could pull, and our friends. As we got older, we laid there and discussed God and sex, which we knew nothing about, and hopes and dreams and friends.

Then when I was even older, lying in the grass with Susie meant kissing and hugging, getting to second base, baseball, of course, and talking about not much of anything.

After talking to Susie about the reunion, I hoped everyone would be able to attend. I hadn't seen some of the kids since high school. Tucky left Morgan County after graduation to find a job and ended up not far away in Morehead. The entire Key family had left Morgan County by 1969.

All my thoughts about our gang of characters brought back memories of the Wolf Pack's last adventure. It happened in the late summer and fall of 1962 after we returned from our big canoe trip on the Red River. I'll never forget the events that led to—well, I guess I should start at the beginning and tell you exactly what happened.

2 HOT SUMMER DAYS

AUGUST 13, 1962

James Ernest turned on his radio which sat on the nightstand in our bedroom. We had just climbed into bed. I had literally climbed into bed since I slept on the top bunk. *Roses Are Red* by Bobby Vinton was playing on the national Top 20 countdown. It had dropped to number two. I wondered what the new number one song would be.

We had spent the day working in Clayton's tobacco fields. It was nasty hot work that had to be done. We spent the evening in front of the TV relaxing. We watched my favorite western, *Cheyenne*, and then *The Rifleman*. After the westerns, we watched *The Danny Thomas Show* and then *The Andy Griffith Show*. I was rolling on the floor laughing at the deputy, Barney Fife. I imagined he acted pretty much like Purty would if he was a deputy.

I told James Ernest what I was thinking, and we laughed all the way through the commercial.

We listened quietly in the dark waiting to hear the top song of the week. "This week's number one song is about love gone wrong..." I was hoping it would be *Twist and Shout* by The Isley Brothers, and James Ernest was rooting for *Ahab, the Arab* by Ray Stevens which was a crazy, funny song. "...

Neil Sedaka's *Breaking Up is Hard to Do*. It's up from number two last week," the DJ informed us.

"Oh man," I moaned from the top bunk.

"You just don't like it because you know it's true," James Ernest said and giggled.

I folded the pillow around the side of my head so I couldn't hear the sad, pitiful, crummy song. Even though Susie had forgiven me and taken me back as her boyfriend I didn't want to hear about how hard breaking up was. *What an awful thing to write a song about*, I thought.

The weather was unbelievably hot in the tobacco fields. The nights weren't much better. Mom had us put a screen in our window so Bo couldn't come in during the night. It also kept out the flies and bugs. We had a circular fan on the floor blowing some warm air around the room. It was too hot to even have the sheet over me. I was trying to fall asleep in a pool of my own sweat. I knew how Large Larry felt. I was sure his bed leaked from the bottom if he slept in a room this hot. It didn't help that I slept near the ceiling of the room. James Ernest had told me that hot air rose and I soon learned he was right. The fan didn't do much for me in the top—so I figured it was twenty degrees warmer in my bed than in James Ernest's bed.

When we finished in the fields around five earlier that afternoon, James Ernest and I headed straight for the swimming hole behind the lake. We even swam inside the Indian cave to soak up the cool temperatures of the cave.

After the song was over I said, "I can't believe we're working in the tobacco field again tomorrow."

"We should be able to finish tomorrow," James Ernest said optimistically.

"I wasn't worried about finishing—I'm worried about heat stroke before we finish," I told him.

"Better get used to it. There's going to be a lot of days in the fields before harvesting will be finished this fall," James Ernest said.

"I don't think I was born to be a farmer," I said as I stared at the dark ceiling.

"What do you think you were born to be?"

"A baseball player," I blurted out.

"A baseball player?"

"Yeah, I want to replace Vada Pinson in centerfield for the Cincinnati Redlegs."

James Ernest laughed, "You'd fall on your face the first time you try running up that terrace inside Crosley Field. Then you'll wish you were back in Morgan County working in the fields of your farm."

"Very funny. What do you want to do?"

"I'd be happy being a farmer and raising a family."

"I thought you'd be a preacher or maybe a singer on the radio. I could lie in my bed at night and listen to the DJ announce your songs," I said.

"Yeah, right. You have to be really good to be on the radio."

"You have the best voice of any singer I've ever heard, better than Neil Sedaka or Ray Stevens."

"Shut up. I'm not that good."

I wondered how James Ernest could think he wasn't that good. He was great. Everyone who heard him sing said he had the best voice they had ever heard, and it wasn't like

Neil Sedaka or Ray Stevens had great voices. I never even considered that James Ernest didn't believe it. Maybe he thought everyone was just trying to make him feel good, especially when I heard folks tell the twins that they did well after they sang at the Christmas service. It was the worst dog wailing I'd ever heard—and they got compliments.

I continued to stare above me. I would swear I could see beads of sweat falling from the ceiling in the dark. I always thought James Ernest was the most talented boy I'd ever met and I always thought he knew it. I guess everyone had doubts about themselves. Mom had always told me I could be anything I wanted to be. I didn't believe her. I figured it was something moms told their children. James Ernest had probably never been told that during his life. I knew there were certain things I could never be, but I really thought James Ernest could be anything—a singer, a preacher, a farmer, a doctor, a lawyer, or maybe even the president of the United States of America.

I wanted my best friend to know how talented he was. I whispered to him in the dark, "You are that good, James Ernest."

He didn't say anything. He might have drifted off to sleep.

I laid there in my sweat and thought of running headfirst up the terrace in Crosley Field and leaping against the wall and making the greatest catch the fans had ever seen. I went to sleep finally dreaming of my dream.

Tuesday, August 14

When I usually woke in the mornings I had to rush out to pee, but that morning I had no liquid inside me. I had sweated everything away during the night. I was climbing down the ladder, awakened by Mom, when a hand grabbed my leg in the dark, scaring the poop out of me.

"Gotcha," James Ernest said in his deepest voice.

"You jerk wad. You scared me to death."

"I succeeded then," he said and laughed. "Another fun day in the tobacco."

"You can do mine also then, since it's so much fun for you," I told him.

"You're beginning to sound like Purty. Complain, complain."

"Maybe Mom has made bacon and eggs," I said.

We walked into the kitchen and Mom was nowhere in sight. Instead there were boxes of cereal and milk sitting on the table. We took it as a hint.

I poured Cheerios into my bowl and added milk. I then sprinkled five heaping spoons of sugar on top and mixed it all together. James Ernest began cutting up a banana to put into his cereal and asked, "You want some?"

"Sure," I answered.

"Get your own, jerk wad."

I got up and went into the kitchen and got another banana. When I returned to the table my bowl of cereal was missing. "Where is it?"

"What?"

I turned and went back into the kitchen thinking I must have taken the cereal with me and forgotten it. It wasn't there. I went back again and James Ernest was gone. His cereal bowl was empty and he had disappeared. I looked under the table, thinking he was hiding. He wasn't there, but I did find my cereal bowl on the chair seat under the table.

"Big jerk wad," I said to the walls.

"What did you say?" Mom asked as she entered from her bedroom.

"Nothing," I said.

"Where's James Ernest?"

"Don't know. Don't care."

I heard the front door open. I figured it was James Ernest coming in. Then I heard Papaw's voice calling out, "Good morning." I looked at the clock on the wall and saw that it was five minutes after six. I wondered what was so good about the morning. It was already hot and muggy. My whole body hurt from the previous day in the tobacco, and I would be doing it all over again. If this was what it meant to be an adult I was all for staying young. Working in the fields made my chores seem like nothing.

"I need spring water before you head out this morning," Mom told me, as though she was reading my mind. After eating I went out the back door and looked for the water buckets. They were also missing.

"Mom, where are the buckets?" I yelled from the back porch.

Mom came to the door and said, "They should be right there on the sink."

"They're not here," I said. I looked around for Coty and he was nowhere to be seen.

"I think I'm going back to bed," I said.

"You had better find those buckets."

I shrugged my shoulders. How was I supposed to find missing buckets?

"I bet James Ernest took the buckets to the spring already," I yelled out.

"You had better go catch up with him then. He'll need help."

I jumped off the porch and headed down the gravel road toward the spring. Cars drove past me as I walked; throwing dust into the air so it could settle back down onto me. A car slowed down as it got to me and I looked over to see that it was Mud McCobb.

"Want a ride? I'm on my way to work." Mud was a dump truck driver for the quarry.

I jumped onto the front seat with him. "Where you headin'?" he asked.

"To the spring to get water."

"Where's your water bucket? Or are you carrying a handful at a time?" he said, and then laughed like he was the funniest guy since Red Skelton.

"I'm trying to catch up to James Ernest. He went for water."

"Let's catch him then," Mud said as he put his car into first gear.

Forty-five seconds later he stopped at the path to the spring. I opened the door to get out. "Thanks, Mud," I said.

"Stay cool," Mud laughed as he stomped on the accelerator and spun away, sending gravel and dust flying into the sky. How in the world could a fella stay cool on a day this hot? Mud's shirt already had sweat stains all over it, and all he was doing was driving. I hurried off the road away from the gray dust.

I heard Coty bark before I saw James Ernest. Coty ran up the trail toward me at top speed. He began whining and his tail was going a hundred miles per hour as I rubbed his head in greeting. I fell to my knees and he began bathing my face with his tongue. I finally saw James Ernest walking toward me carrying two buckets of water.

I quickly grabbed one bucket handle to help James Ernest.

"Why didn't you tell me you were going to get water?"

"I walked past the buckets and saw they were empty and just went ahead and left to fill them. No big deal."

"But Mom hadn't even asked us to do it."

"We are allowed to help out without being asked or told to," James Ernest said.

"Are you sure? That doesn't sound right," I said with a smile.

We made it back without a vehicle going past and covering us with dust. As we walked through the back door Papaw asked, "You boys ready to go to Clayton's?"

Mom walked in and said, "Thanks for getting water, James. That was sweet of you."

"Hey, what about me?"

"I had to tell you," Mom said.

"I thought that's how it worked." Everyone ignored me, so I headed for the truck. Coty stayed inside the house and found a spot in front of the floor fan. He was pretty smart for a dog.

3   STUPID RULE

We were in the fields by seven that morning. James Ernest and I were working with Clayton, Monie, Brenda, and Susie. The twins were probably still in bed getting their beauty sleep. They needed it. As I worked I thought of every mean thing I could. Mean thoughts ran through my brain. I thought of the twins. I thought of the Boys from Blaze and the Bottom Brothers, Zerelda, the self-claimed witch, Sadie and Bernice, the bootleggers, the Tattoo Man, and Billy Taulbee. I was chopping each one of them in half with my hoe as I made my way down the rows. Soon I was way ahead of everyone else.

"Look at that boy go," Clayton said out loud. "Looks like something got into him today."

After thirty minutes of the fast-paced hoeing, I began feeling the heat drain all my stored up energy and the rest of the workers soon caught up to me. Before long I was lagging behind.

"Looks like it's the story of the turtle and the hare all over again," James Ernest said loud enough for me to hear. Everyone laughed along with him.

As the day went on, the ground hardened as the sun baked it, making it harder to chop the weeds. We stopped often to drink water and rest. When noon came Clayton said that it was too hot for field work and we went to the house to have lunch. He decided the field work was done for the day. The thermometer on the porch read 102 degrees in the shade. I walked into their living room and collapsed on the wooden floor trying to soak up the coolness of the floor.

Delma stood over me and said to Thelma, "Maybe he'll die."

"He looks like he's dying," Thelma commented.

"He doesn't look like much of a field hand. Don't see much reason for him to live," Delma said.

"We know he's not much good at anything else. Good riddance," Thelma said with finality. They walked out of the room and into the kitchen.

Good riddance was my thought also.

Monie reheated some green beans and potatoes and she had cornbread ready for our lunch. I felt too hot to eat. I just laid on the floor while everyone else ate.

I thought it was a great afternoon to visit the swimming hole. Susie and Brenda thought so too, so Clayton drove us to the Washingtons' house and Raven, Junior, and Samantha came back to the store with us to go swimming. Within half an hour we were all jumping into the water. It felt better than I had ever remembered it being. This was so much better than chopping weeds in the middle of a field with the sun baking us like a potato in the oven.

We heard voices coming toward us and soon saw that Randy, Purty, Sadie and Francis were heading our way with members of the Key family—Sugar Cook, Tucky, Chero, and Rock. We greeted each other and soon the swimming hole was completely full of bodies being cooled off by the mountain water.

We had tremendous fun, splashing and dunking and, as always, laughing at Purty's antics. After being in the pool of water for three hours or so, we began to empty out of the pool. Purty climbed out, and we all quickly noticed that he was naked, his white butt in our full focus as he climbed over the bank. The girls began shrieking at the sight of his nudity. We guys either laughed or just shook our heads, used to it. Purty had been naked in the crowded pool the entire time, and no one had noticed.

Purty stood up and raised his hands to the sky and said, "What?"

Tucky splashed his way over to my side and whispered to me, "Too bad our group doesn't have a pretty girl version of Purty."

"Yep," was all I could say about Tucky's wish.

I suddenly heard a gasp and looked up to see Mom standing thirty feet from us staring at Purty in his full glory. She had heard about his nudity quandary but had never seen it firsthand.

Purty waved at Mom as though there was nothing unusual about him standing in front of my mother with no clothes on. Mom's face quickly turned red and shrieked, "Put your pants on, Todd. What's wrong with you? Did you lose the good sense God gave you?"

We all wondered that. I also wondered what Mom was doing at the swimming hole. She had never been here.

"I'm sorry to break up your swimming and nudity, but I need to tell everyone something."

I then noticed that Mom had tears running down her face. I figured Purty's nakedness some day would cause women to cry, but I was surprised it would be my mom. Everyone saw Mom's tears and quickly obeyed by hopping out of the swimming hole, and gathering around her.

We all looked at Mom as she tried to stop crying long enough to say whatever bad news she had come to tell us. She wiped her eyes and cheeks and took a deep breath and said, "Uncle Morton had a heart attack this morning." I heard gasps and moans in the crowd of kids. I immediately had tears well up in my eyes.

"Is he alive?" I asked.

"Yes. Homer and Ruby stopped by his house and found him stooped over on his porch. They rushed him to the hospital. That's all I know right now. Pray." Mom then turned and walked away. I ran to her and threw my arms around her. She turned and squeezed me and we cried together.

When I finally let go of her I asked, "Can I go to the hospital?"

"Sure, but we're waiting for a call from your papaw on Uncle Morton's condition. He went as soon as he heard the news. Your mamaw is at the store."

"Okay." I turned and ran to the swimming hole and gathered my stuff. I saw James Ernest and Susie doing the same.

Randy asked what they could do. I answered, "Do what Mom said. If you know how to pray, then pray. Thanks."

James Ernest, Susie and I then ran to catch up with Mom. As we walked with Mom to the store, all I could do was think about how important Uncle Morton was to me and to the community. I couldn't imagine him not being there telling his same stupid jokes over and over and everyone laughing each time they heard them. He had a way of making each of us appreciate what we had. None of us were rich. No one had a fancy home. But he had a way of showing us what was important in life—our friends and family and the nature around us that God gave. He taught me that the old adage was true—the best things in life are free. He loved his life even though he couldn't see it. I thought of his love for birds. I thought of the turkey baster that Geraldine used to remove the wax from his ears. I thought of our many talks about God's love for us and the many fishing lessons we gave each other. I hoped God wasn't taking Morton to Heaven for his own enjoyment. I felt as though we needed him more.

We arrived at the store and I quickly ran to Mamaw and hugged her and then asked, "Has Papaw called yet?"

"Not yet," Mamaw answered.

James Ernest and I went into the bedroom and changed into dry clothes. Monie arrived at the store with clothes for Susie. The three of us went out to the front porch and talked while we waited for the phone call. James Ernest suddenly bowed his head and began to pray out loud. Susie and I followed his lead and bowed our heads. He prayed for Uncle Morton's recovery and that God would hold him in His healing hands and protect and heal him. He then prayed for God's will to be done and that God would find blessings in whatever happened. I didn't totally understand what that meant at that time. I wondered why we would pray for Uncle Morton to be healed if he then asked for whatever God wanted to happen. Why pray? Why not just wait and see what His will was?

Uncle Morton was special to all three of us and I felt we were special to Uncle Morton as well. Mom and Mamaw were answering the phone constantly. I didn't see how Papaw would ever be able to call with information. They tried to get off the phone as quickly as possible without being rude explaining that they were waiting for a call. Then Loraine called. Mamaw finally had to hang up on her. Don't you know Loraine called back and said that they had somehow been accidentally disconnected. Mamaw told Loraine that something was wrong with her phone and hung up again. It was the first time I had ever heard her tell a white lie.

Pastor White drove into the gravel lot. He said that he was heading to the hospital and wanted to know if anyone wanted to go along. I knew I was going. James Ernest was already heading for the car. I went inside and told Mom I was going. I didn't really ask. I couldn't sit there any longer. Susie didn't ask permission either and the three of us climbed into the pastor's car.

Pastor White quickly put the car into gear and took off.

"Where are Miss Rebecca and Bobby Lee?" Susie asked.

"She left work early and she's staying home to answer the phone. We were getting a lot of calls from church members about Morton's condition."

"So were we," I said.

"I've never seen a community that cared for each other as much as this one. It's awesome," the pastor said. We had to agree.

"You wouldn't ever leave our church for another one would you?" I asked. I always worried about Pastor White going to a bigger church in a bigger town. I knew he didn't make much money here, and Miss Rebecca still had to work at the bank.

"I have to do what God directs me to do. If the Lord wants me to go somewhere else, that's what I'll do. I'm doing the Lord's work. But I do love it here, and I pray that God will leave me here for a while."

"How do you know that God wants you to go somewhere else?" I asked.

"Through prayers and His directing. He'll make it clear when He wants a change. Sometimes I can hear Him speaking to me in the quiet times. I believe you told me once that God had spoken to you. We were supposed to talk about it."

Uh oh! I had blurted out one day as I was leaving church that I thought God had spoken to me and now Pastor White suddenly remembered it. Susie and James Ernest looked at me in the back seat. I had heard a voice tell me "Duck, Tim!" as the Tattoo Man swung a large stick at my head. It was the only thing that saved me from dying that day. The only explanation of where the voice came from was that God or a guardian angel told me to duck.

"Yes," I finally answered.

"When?" Pastor White asked and then added, "If you don't mind talking about it in front of James and Susie."

Oh boy! I told the pastor the story as it happened. I explained that at first I thought it was James Ernest who had yelled it. "But he had told me he hadn't yelled it. He hadn't even seen the attack, so the only other voice I figured it could have been was from God."

I saw the pastor looking at me in the rear view mirror as I told the story. He hesitated before saying anything.

"Am I crazy to think that?" I asked.

"No. I agree with you. I don't want to put you on the spot, but we're among friends. You've never been saved, have you, Timmy?"

Oh gosh! "I've been saved lots of times. I was saved from the Tattoo Man. I was saved from the kidnappers. I was saved from the Devil's Creek cave. I was saved from the witch. I was saved…"

"Stop, stop, stop. I know you're smarter than that. You know what I mean. You know that's different from what I'm talking about unless you've not been listening during my sermons."

Pastors have a way of cornering you into difficult situations. Yes, I knew what he meant, and I knew it was different. I was scared of changing. How would I have to act if I got saved? I enjoyed my life and the way I was. Why change?

"Yes. I know the difference," I finally said.

"Well, I think God generally talks to folks who have been saved. Some Christians though never hear God talking to them. It depends on how close they get to God. But there are cases where God speaks to folks even though they aren't Christians. There are examples in the Bible. God spoke to Paul when he was a tax collector and Paul was converted and became one of God's greatest voices. I believe God speaks to folks when he has plans for that person. I think God spoke to you. You now need to ask God to forgive your sins and ask him to save you."

I sat there in the back seat and thought about what he told me. Susie took hold of my hand. James Ernest turned back around to face the road ahead of us. I thought about Uncle Morton fighting for his life in the hospital. I remembered the day Uncle Morton told me that he believed God was testing me for greater things in the future. I guess it scared me thinking that God wanted to use me and that I might come up short. I knew that if I became a Christian then God would expect something from me. That scared me—big time.

We rode in silence for the next fifteen minutes until we arrived at the Morehead Hospital. Pastor White parked the car and we hurried into the lobby and asked where we might find Uncle Morton. They directed us to the emergency room waiting area. We found Papaw, Homer and Ruby sitting there together.

Papaw stood when he saw us and said, "We still haven't heard any news–which I'm taking as a good sign. At least he's alive."

Pastor White asked, "Was he responsive after they found him, or on the way here?"

Homer answered, "No. 'Bout all I can say is that he was breathing. He was holding his chest."

"We haven't heard anything since they wheeled him into the emergency room," Papaw added.

There were enough chairs for all of us to sit down. I could see that Ruby had been crying. Homer spent his time stroking his long white mustache. Papaw fumbled with his hat, moving it around in his hands and turning it over and over as we waited for word. Pastor White went to the desk and told the nurse that he was Morton's pastor and that he would like to see Uncle Morton when he was able to be seen. The nurse said she would pass on his request.

I watched the second hand of the clock circle the face. Slowly the time clicked by. Susie would talk quietly with me and James Ernest. After around an hour Papaw finally got up and said that he should call the store. He headed for the phone booth at the end of the waiting room. I saw him begin to tell someone something when a doctor came into the room and asked who was there for Morton Collins. Papaw hung up the phone mid-sentence and ran over to where we all stood in front of the doctor.

"Morton is resting comfortably for now. He did have a heart attack. We will have to do tests later, but for now we need for him to rest and regain some strength. He was able to talk to us a little before he fell back asleep."

"Is he going to be okay?" I asked when the doctor paused.

"At this time we're unsure. The tests will tell us more. We're not sure if he'll need surgery at this time. Once he wakes up you can go in and see him—one at a time."

"Will I be able to see him?" I asked.

"I'm sorry, but kids are not allowed to visit."

"But..." I started to complain when Papaw placed his hand on my shoulder signaling for me to stop.

Papaw then said, "Hospitals have to have rules, Tim."

Papaw then asked the doctor to please let us know when he could see Uncle Morton.

"I will," the doctor assured us. The doctor turned and walked away.

I turned to Papaw and said, "You probably ought to call the store again. You hung up on them."

"Oh, yes, I should."

Papaw went to the phone and called again.

A few hours passed before Pastor White was told that Uncle Morton was awake and that he could go in and see him. Pastor White spoke to him briefly and prayed with him and returned to the waiting room. Papaw went in next to visit.

Pastor White told us that Uncle Morton had a hard time speaking but knew who he was and thanked him for his prayer. "He whispered to me to tell you guys that he was going to be fine and that he would see you soon. He said he still had some fishing lessons he hadn't taught you, Timmy."

We all laughed. It sounded just like Uncle Morton.

I was upset that kids weren't allowed to visit. What kind of stupid rule was that? What if he died? What if I never got to see him again? I wanted to tell him I loved him and how special he was. I wanted Uncle Morton to know how much he meant to me.

4   THE BIG FOOT THING

Four days later, Uncle Morton was still in the hospital. The doctors determined that with medicine Uncle Morton would not need to have surgery. They felt he should spend another week in the hospital before he could return home.

A light rain fell most of the morning, but it didn't stop fishermen from filling the banks of the lake. I went up to the lake to take lunch orders from the fishermen. The rain had stopped. Mud McCobb and Fred Wilson were fishing together and began giving me a hard time.

"Do you ever get to fish anymore, or are you just a delivery boy?" Mud asked me. Fred laughed like it was really funny, which it wasn't.

"Papaw told me I was catching too many of the fish and I needed to leave some for the pitiful fishermen. I believe he was talking about you guys."

"Well, lookee here. It looks like this pitiful fisherman is getting ready to catch a nice catfish," Fred said as he jerked the pole back to his shoulder to set the hook.

Fred began reeling the fish in. The fish didn't seem to be giving him much of a fight. I watched to see what was on the end of his line. He finally dragged the catch up the bank and it landed at his feet, which was a good place for it, because his catch was an old shoe. I began laughing so hard I nearly fell backward off the dam. Mud couldn't help but also laugh at his old friend. The look on Fred's face was priceless—from shock to embarrassment.

"How hard did that thing bite before you jerked? Did you use shoelaces for bait?" I questioned Fred, as his face turned beet red.

I went back to the store after taking all the orders and told Papaw what Fred caught. As Fred was leaving later that evening Papaw asked what size his big catch was. "Was it a ten or ten-and-a- half?" Mud and I laughed along with the other men sitting on the porch.

"Last time I'll ever fish this lake," Fred said.

"See you tomorrow," Papaw told him.

"See you then," Fred muttered.

As Fred was backing out of the lot, Robert Easterling ran down and handed him a dirty old sock and told him, "Here, Fred. This should go with your meal tonight." The men on the porch howled with laughter.

Later that evening Mom went on a double date with the sheriff and Pastor White and Miss Rebecca. Bobby Lee was staying at the Tuttle house to play with Billy. Susie and Raven had decided to throw a big party at the Perry house and invited most of their friends. They even invited Sadie, but not Bernice. Clayton had built a fire pit near the farm pond, and we were going to roast hotdogs and just have a fun time.

The entire Wolf Pack was there. Sadie and Francis came. Raven brought Samantha with her. Rhonda came, much to Purty's delight. Daniel "Spoon" Sugarman was even allowed to come. One of our classmates, Lisa Green, even came to the gathering, along with brothers Larry and Dudley Easterling. Rock, Sugar Cook, and Chero Key all came with Kenny and the Tuttle kids. Brenda was also there. There were a total of eighteen kids there, nine girls and nine boys.

James Ernest and Randy built a fire. We hung a lantern in one of the nearby trees for when it got dark. We had Kool-Aid and lemonade to drink and plenty of snacks, desserts and hotdogs and marshmallows to roast over the fire.

We were all standing around laughing and talking in small groups. Purty led a group that was roasting their hot dogs. Purty was cooking one for Rhonda. He kept running the hot dog over to Rhonda and having her check to see if it was just right. She kept sending him back to the fire to make it darker. He looked like a puppy trying to please its master. Tucky, Junior and I were watching him and laughing. I felt a little sorry for him. Purty loved Rhonda and Rhonda used him to do her bidding, which I didn't blame her for, because he followed her around like a puppy, constantly bugging her.

Soon Tucky saw Sadie sitting on a log alone and he left us to go sit with her. She smiled when he approached. I guess he was tackling his fears, because he always said she scared him.

I looked at Junior and asked him, "Do you have a girl picked out that you would like for a girlfriend?"

I could see him blush and look at the ground before he answered. "Nah. I really kind of, but just as a friend, like talking to Francis."

"Really," I said.

"She's always real nice to me at school. But we hardly see each other anywhere else."

"I've always really liked Francis." Junior's head whipped up and looked at me like I was trying to steal his girl.

"I mean as a friend. I've got Susie. I mean Francis is always sweet and she's awfully cute also," I said.

"She is, isn't she?"

"Now is your chance to talk to her and spend some time with her. She is sitting there cooking her hot dog all alone. Go on," I said as I gently nudged him her way.

He went and grabbed a stick and a hot dog and awkwardly approached her. Francis looked up and saw him and smiled. He carefully sat beside her on the log. I then realized I was standing alone at a party, so I hurried over to Susie.

Brenda had brought a transistor radio and she turned it on and turned it up loud because *The Twist* was playing by Chubby Checker. Sadie jumped up and started twisting, and then Rhonda joined her next to the fire. Before I knew it Rock and Tucky were with them—twisting the night away. I had never seen a guy dance like that before. Tucky was good. He would lower himself to a sitting position while still twisting his hips and then rise again. The girls began following his moves.

Susie and Brenda joined the fun, followed by Raven, James Ernest and Samantha. They were all twisting like crazy. When the song ended everyone began applauding the dancers and the song, I think. Then *Johnny Get Angry* began playing on the radio and the dancers began swaying and dancing to that song.

Dudley and Larry jumped into the pond, followed by Spoon. They tried to get everyone to join them. No one did. So we had dancers, hot dog roasters, couples talking and others just enjoying watching what was going on. It became the first of many campfire parties we would have over the next three years.

"This is so much fun, Timmy," Susie said as she placed her hand in mine.

"It sure is. Everyone is even getting along for once," I said.

We heard a couple of splashes and saw that Chero and Sugar Cook had decided to join the guys in the pond. There was a quarter moon shining above us, not giving us a lot of light, but enough to see what was going on.

Parents were supposed to pick up their kids around eleven. Near the end of the evening we heard a terrifying sound. I thought Purty had dropped a wiener in the fire pit, but the sound came from the field below. Everyone stopped what they were doing and peered into the dark to where the sound came from. Someone turned the radio off. Susie and I ran to the end of the pond to get a better look. Others followed us. I pointed toward a figure which looked to be seven to eight feet tall, crossing the field below us. It looked like a hairy large gorilla-like figure humped over and lumbering along. Several of the kids gasped when they finally saw it. The creature stopped and tilted its head to the sky and let out another bellowing cry, "Ahhhhhh. Ughhhhhh." I got goose bumps up and down my arms. The hairs on my body stood on end. Susie grabbed my arm and buried her head into my forearm.

James and Raven came over and stood next to us. Raven looked horrified.

"What is that?" I asked. I figured if anyone would know it would be James Ernest.

"I don't know," he answered, and then added, "But it looks like Bigfoot."

No one volunteered to chase it away or follow it to see where it went. The thing crossed the field toward the woods until we could no longer see it. I decided right then I would not be going with James Ernest on any of his nighttime roams in the woods when there were creatures like that around.

All eighteen of us quickly gathered around the fire. Everyone was talking at the same time about what it was, what they saw, and the sound that came from it.

When everyone finally quieted down Purty said, "I think it said 'Oh, boy.'"

"It didn't sound anything like that. It sounded like a wolf howling," Sugarman argued.

"What was it?" Sadie asked as she turned toward James Ernest.

James Ernest started to speak and then I think he realized that he had seventeen faces staring at him for an answer. Everyone there knew if anyone had an answer to this question it would be James Ernest. He said, "I've never seen it before, but I've heard rumors of a creature-monster-like-animal called Bigfoot. Some call it Sasquatch or even Yeti."

Most of us began murmuring about having heard of Bigfoot before. Could it really have been what we had seen?

It sure sent everyone home in an excited state. As parents came to pick up their kids, groups would run to the cars and begin telling the parents about the sighting. Most of the parents just grinned and said things like, "Okay. That's nice. Bet that was exciting."

I don't think any of the parents believed us. Papaw said it was probably Billy Taulbee gone crazy. It really wasn't a bad idea.

Around midnight I finally climbed onto the top bunk and wondered about what we had really seen. I couldn't stop thinking about the thing. I heard James Ernest slip into bed and I whispered, "Do you think it really could have been Bigfoot?"

"I don't know. I doubt it. But I don't have a clue as to what it could have been."

"The sound that it made was creepier than seeing it. I've never heard a sound like that."

"I know. I agree," James Ernest said.

"I thought you would be out in the woods tonight following its prints," I teased.

"I thought I would skip tonight. We have church in the morning."

"Could we go follow the tracks tomorrow afternoon?" I asked.

"Are you serious?"

"Yes," I answered, although I wasn't really sure if I was or not. When would I ever get a chance to follow Bigfoot again?

"I guess," was all James Ernest said before going to sleep.

I stayed awake all night thinking of the party, the fun, the thing. I wondered how anyone could sleep after seeing what we saw. I finally fell asleep a half hour before Mom woke us up for church.

Sunday, August 19

I fell onto the backseat of the car. James Ernest slid into the opposite side. Mom, Mamaw, and Janie scooted into the front seat. I laid there until the door opened at the Key house and KenTucky and Rock opened the door to get in. I was too tired to get up.

"Just sit on me," I told them. They did. Tucky sat on my chest and Rock on my legs.

"What is your problem?" Mom yelled to the back.

I didn't know how to answer, so I just ignored the question. With each bump of the road Tucky and Rock would fly into the air and back down onto me. They would giggle and James Ernest would laugh. By the time we arrived at the church, I had the wind knocked out of me, and my legs felt broken.

Everyone emptied the car, leaving me lying there in my pain. Mom turned to the open window and told me, "Get up and get yourself into that church building." Mom didn't understand that I had only gotten a half hour of sleep, and I don't think she would have cared if she had known. I opened the door with my foot and slithered out of the backseat. I slowly walked into the church as Pastor White was greeting everyone from the pulpit.

"We're especially happy to have Timmy joining us this morning," Pastor White announced. Every head turned to watch me walk to the row where Susie was sitting. She had saved a seat for me. I tried slipping into the pew while all my great friends blocked my way with their feet, knees, and legs. I saw Mom burying her face in her Bible.

Pastor White invited folks to come forward and kneel in front of the platform to pray for Uncle Morton. "You can also kneel at your pew," Pastor White directed. The front of the platform filled up quickly and most everyone was on their knees asking God to be with Uncle Morton and to heal him.

I prayed for my great uncle even though I wasn't sure God heard my prayers.

As everyone retook their seats James Ernest made his way to the platform and sang *How Great Thou Art*. His voice echoed around the room as though God Himself was singing to us. I especially loved the second verse. It reminded me of Morgan County. James Ernest sang:

"When through the woods, and forest glades I wander,
And hear the birds sing sweetly in the trees.
When I look down, from lofty mountain grandeur
And see the brook, and feel the gentle breeze.

Chorus:

"Then sings my soul, My Saviour God, to Thee,
How great Thou art, How great Thou art.
Then sings my soul, My Saviour God, to Thee,
How great Thou art, How great Thou art!"

I even yelled "amen" after he finished singing the verse. He took his seat once he finished and Pastor White preached on the difference of heaven and hell. I knew where I wanted to go. The service ended without me falling to sleep, probably because the sermon was so interesting. I didn't make the mistake of lying in the backseat on the way back home.

James Ernest and I were in our bedroom changing into our everyday pants and shirts. I asked James Ernest, "Are we going to go track the thing?"

"Maybe this evening. I need to do some work in my garden. I'll meet you at the Perry's house at six."

"I need to ask Mom." I hurried into the kitchen and found Mom and Mamaw cooking our Sunday meal.

I told her our plans and asked if it was okay.

"I don't think I should let you do anything but chores after that display of yours this morning," Mom threatened.

"I only got ten minutes of sleep last night," I told her.

"And what was the reason for that?"

I couldn't tell her that I had seen Bigfoot and that we were going to track it. I had a feeling she wouldn't like the fact that we had seen it or that we planned to track it down.

"I don't know. I just couldn't get to sleep."

"Is Susie mad at you again? What did you do this time?"

"No. We're fine." I was insulted that my mom assumed I had done something wrong—again. I got no respect—even from my mother, my flesh and blood, the person who birthed me into this world. I was her firstborn.

I then thought of something. "I guess I was worried about Uncle Morton." I hated to use Uncle Morton's heart attack as my excuse, but I was worried about him.

"Do your chores and then watch the store after you're done," Mom said, as she came over and hugged me. It had worked.

I took that to mean I could meet James Ernest later. I went to tell him and found that he had already left. Papaw told me James Ernest had said goodbye and walked out the door. Good grief. Papaw then told me to hurry and do my chores because he was going to the hospital to visit Uncle Morton.

I ran outside and up to the lake and cleaned up the trails and took orders as I was going around. There were a few fishermen, but not many. It was a usual Kentucky August day, hot and muggy.

I came back to the store and helped Papaw get the orders together and then ran back to the lake to deliver the orders and collect the money. I made fifteen cents in tips–cheap wads.

I then was sent to the spring for two buckets of water. It was rough carrying two buckets at the same time, especially without any sleep and being so tired. Coty stayed by my side as though he was urging me on. I returned home and took over for Papaw in the store so he could eat his dinner. I sat at the table eating also, but each time we heard someone enter the store I got up to wait on them. My fresh beans and potatoes weren't very fresh and warm by the time I was able to finish my meal.

I heard the door open again and when I walked into the store I was greatly surprised. My Uncle Jackie was standing there. I hurried over and hugged him. Jackie was my dad's younger stepbrother. He was always really nice to me and it was so good to see him.

"Boy, have you grown. And look at that hair." He began to laugh at my Mohawk which I still wore.

I grinned and then asked, "What brings you down here?"

"I came down to see Morton in the hospital and figured I might as well come visit you and Betty," he explained.

"You just missed Papaw. He left for the hospital. Come see everyone." I motioned for him to follow me and led him into the kitchen. Mom quickly got up and hugged Jack, followed by Mamaw. Mamaw then left to get Jackie a plate so he could eat.

"You look good, Betty."

"I am good. I like living back here again."

"I heard a rumor that you're getting married," Jackie said.

I heard the door open again and I left for the store. There stood Forest and Loraine. Loraine was gathering up supplies when she saw me. Forest took a seat in one of the wooden chairs next to the pop cooler.

Loraine began, "It is so hot and awful out there again today. I don't think we will ever have nice weather again. What do you think? It's got to cool off one day. I don't understand why you kids wanted to have a bonfire in this kind of weather. I think it was foolishness and then Todd coming home and telling us that you guys had seen a monster or something with big feet. I do not know where that boy gets his imagination from. Forest and I have no imagination. Never have and never will. We are just as boring as anything. Maybe an imagination is a good thing. Did you see the Big-foot thing? Of course not! Why did I even ask you something that crazy? Is Betty here? I bet she's in the kitchen. I'll just go on in and find her. Forest will talk to you for a while." She continued talking as she made her way to find Mom.

Forest looked at me and shook his head. I smiled, but I didn't want to say anything about his wife, even though he was thinking the same thing I was.

"Where's Martin?"

"He just left to visit Uncle Morton."

"How is he doing?"

"Pretty good. They said he might be able to come home in a week."

"That's good."

I agreed.

The door opened and Robert and Janice walked into the store. We all greeted one another, and Janice headed for the kitchen while Robert took a seat next to Forest.

I stood behind the counter and thought of Uncle Jackie and my other uncles. It made me think of my dad and how he was the first brother or sister to die in the family. Jackie had worked with Dad for years and had been wading creeks, fishing with him. He had all kind of tales about my dad, most of which was about him getting drunk and doing stupid things—not much of a legacy to leave behind.

Jackie left after a while for the hospital to see Uncle Morton. He told me he would be back one day soon and wanted me to take him fishing up one of the creeks. I was all for that. The afternoon went by fast as visitors and customers filed into the store and kitchen. Fishermen started coming in as evening approached

Papaw returned from Morehead around five. He said he had seen Jackie at the hospital. He said Uncle Morton seemed better today and was cracking jokes with everyone. The nurses were fighting over which one got to take care of him.

5 TWO HAIRY ARMS

Mom told me I could have the evening to do whatever I wanted. Uncle Jackie stopped by again later that afternoon and was leaving to go back to Ohio around five-thirty. I asked him if he would drop me off at Clayton's.

When he stopped to let me out I told him, "Thanks, and anytime you want those fishing lessons I'll be happy to do it."

"You take care of yourself, and I'll be back to see who gives the lessons," Jackie said and smiled. I waved as he drove back up the lane. I turned to see Susie running toward me.

"Hi, Timmy. I didn't know you were coming up this evening."

She grabbed my hand into hers as she turned back toward the house. "Hi. I'm supposed to meet James Ernest here at six."

"What for?"

"We're going to try and track Bigfoot," I told her.

"What? You guys don't really believe it was Bigfoot, do you?"

"Maybe. It was something we'd never seen before."

"So you guys think it's a good idea to try and find it."

"Maybe."

"I think you guys are out of your minds," Susie said as she stared at me.

45

"I thought you might want to go with us."

"Let me think. Do I want to go into the woods searching for Bigfoot?" Susie put her free hand to her chin acting as if she was thinking.

Before she answered I heard James Ernest yell out from the top of the gravel lane. We turned back to see him and Raven and Junior walking down the hill.

"Looks like we're going to have a whole posse searching for Bigfoot," I said as we started walking to meet them.

Junior yelled out, "Look out, Bigfoot, we're coming for you."

They began laughing. I noticed that James Ernest was carrying his .22 rifle that Papaw had given him for Christmas. I never even thought of bringing the one I got. All I had for protection was my pocket knife. I didn't think it would be of much use against Bigfoot.

We greeted one another and then Susie asked Raven, "Are you really going with these crazy guys to look for that thing we saw."

"I guess I am," Raven answered.

"I always thought you were smarter than that."

"I figure someone has to make sure they don't get in a mess looking for it."

"Hey, we guys are right here and we can hear you two talking," I said.

They ignored me and Raven asked, "Aren't you going?"

"Let me run and ask Mom." Susie turned and ran to the house. I figured she must have thought two of them could do a better job of keeping us from getting into a mess. Girls sure were funny.

Susie soon came running back toward us. "Okay, I'm going on this wild-goose chase."

"What did they say when you told them you were going to look for the thing?" I asked.

"I didn't tell them that. I just asked if I could go on a hike this evening with you guys. I don't want them thinking I'm as crazy as I am."

"Where are we starting?" Junior asked.

James Ernest pointed toward the spot we had first seen the Thing the evening before. We turned and headed down the hillside toward the spot in the field we had first laid eyes on Bigfoot.

"It rained a little yesterday morning, so I thought we might be able to see footprints in the field. Something that big surely left some prints in the field," James Ernest explained.

As we neared the location that James Ernest was heading he said, "It should be near here."

Raven said, "Wasn't it nearer than this?"

"I thought it was farther to the right," Susie said.

"I thought it was nearer to the woods," I offered.

James Ernest bent down and looked closely at the ground, "Look at this."

We all gathered around him as though we were looking at dinosaur bones. He was pointing at a track.

"What is it?" Junior asked.

"Deer tracks," James Ernest answered.

I began laughing. Raven pushed James Ernest so hard that he fell over and rolled down the hill. We all began laughing.

When James Ernest's roll ended he looked to his left as he was getting up and yelled, "Here it is!"

We had already been fooled once, we weren't about to be fooled again. I thought of the saying Uncle Morton once told me, "Fool me once, shame on you. Fool me twice, shame on me."

We all continued our own searches for the tracks.

"I promise. God strike me down if I'm joshing."

I knew James Ernest would never say anything about God if he wasn't serious. I ran to his side and was quickly followed by the others. Again we were standing over him looking down, but this time we saw an unbelievably large footprint that looked to be half human and half gorilla. It was imbedded into the dirt a good inch and was close to eighteen inches long. It was wider than a human foot and we only saw four toes. It looked to be its right foot and was heading in the direction we had seen Bigfoot walking. We moved ahead looking for the left footprint. We all saw it nearly at the same time.

"Stay here." James Ernest handed me his rifle and told us to stay there as he headed toward the nearest woods. We saw him running about the woods like a wild man, and then he came back toward us carrying a large stick. He was sharpening the end of the stick to a point with his pocket knife. When he got to us, he slammed the end of the stick into the dirt near the first footprint we found.

"I wanted to mark the spot so we can find it again." James Ernest then began following the deep tracks across the field. We followed close behind. My stomach was almost aching with excitement. I began to think about what would happen if we actually found Bigfoot. I hadn't thought of that before.

It had just been something fun to do on a Sunday evening, a hike in the woods.

We followed the tracks up to the main road. James Ernest crossed the road and began looking for signs on the other side of the road. "Timmy, look for signs on that side." Susie and I looked for footprints and broken weeds, which its large feet would have stepped on, as we followed the road to the east.

A couple of minutes later James Ernest said he had found it. The creature was heading across another field toward Homer and Ruby's farmhouse. It was walking between rows of tobacco.

Its body was so large that each of the two rows had been bent over as though its sides had hit each stalk of tobacco. We could see its prints in the dirt plainly.

Before we got to the house the tracks turned toward the woods, and you could see a path of destruction as it went through the rows of tobacco toward the forest.

"Bigfoot avoids getting too close to houses," I told the others.

"Wouldn't you if you were it?" Susie said.

We were soon in the woods. I knew it would be harder following it. The ground wouldn't be as soft as the plowed fields. James Ernest continued on a path he was sure followed Bigfoot. Every once in a while he would point to the ground at a partial print or a broken limb that had been hit by something. I was getting a look at James Ernest's tracking ability, and it was really neat to watch.

"This is a deer trail that we're following. The thing is following it also. It makes sense it would take the easiest trail it can," James Ernest explained to us. Every once in a while I would see a deer track that had been left behind after a heavy rain. I couldn't help but wonder if we would ever see Bigfoot again. Maybe it was just passing through, which was fine with me, or maybe it lived in the area. But I figured if it lived in the area there would have been more sightings that we would have heard about.

"What are we going to do if we find Bigfoot?" Susie suddenly asked.

"Nary one of us brought a camera," Raven said.

"I don't think we'll see it," James Ernest told us.

"Then why are we following it?" Junior asked.

"For fun," I answered.

"To see where it's headed," James Ernest added.

"But what would we do if we did come up on it?" Susie asked. We all looked at each other.

"I'd probably poop my pants," Junior said.

"I'd turn and run," Raven said.

"I'd ask it to come for dinner," I said, smirking.

"Instead, it'd have you for dinner," Raven said and laughed, joined by the others.

"Maybe it doesn't eat meat, like a cow or horse," Susie suggested.

"And maybe it eats nothing but meat, like a Bigfoot!" Junior added, which crept me out a bit.

The trail went deeper into the forest. The shadows the trees cast around us made it harder to see. It wouldn't be totally dark for another two hours, so we still had time to search, but it made the search a lot spookier and scarier.

"How much farther should we go?" Susie asked.

"We could still follow the trail another half hour," James Ernest answered.

Ahead of us I could see the outline of tall cliffs. As we moved closer we could see that there was no way up the concave walls. I looked to my left and right. James Ernest was hunting for a clue as to which way Bigfoot went. He pointed to the left and we followed. I had never been in this area before, but there were a lot of areas I had never been.

The dirt under the cliffs was mostly small slate rock and loose dry dirt. James Ernest pointed to the large footprints in the dirt. It was easy to know whom they belonged to. I then noticed that the left footprint had five toes. I didn't say anything for some reason. Suddenly they disappeared. The last print we saw had turned slightly to the right toward the wall. Large flat rocks blocked the entrance of a dark hole in the stone wall. I knew Bigfoot had entered the opening.

"It jumped from here onto that rock," James Ernest told us.

"How do you know that?" Raven asked.

"You can see how deep its toes bit into the dirt here," he pointed out the difference of the prints. "That's what a person does before they jump."

We moved cautiously toward the opening and peered inside. No one had brought a flashlight, and I didn't think anyone was going to volunteer to enter the opening without a light. I wasn't volunteering to enter even if I had car lights and I was sitting inside the car. No way was I going into a cave where Bigfoot might be hiding. For me—the search was over!

"Any volunteers?" James Ernest asked.

We all looked at him like he was the craziest person in the world. It was by far the dumbest thing I had ever heard James Ernest utter. "I didn't think so," he finally said.

He carefully went to the opening and called out, "Anyone in there?"

I picked up a rock and flung it past James Ernest's right shoulder and into the opening.

"Hello!" James Ernest yelled through his hands.

"Ahhhhhh–Ughhhhhh–Ahhhhhh–Ughhhhhh–Ahhhhhh–Ughhhhhh!" The answer seemed to echo inside the opening and then exited, sounding like a herd of Bigfoots was screaming out their displeasure of being disturbed.

Susie and Raven and Junior turned and ran back the way we came. I couldn't run. I was frozen with fear. I was standing so close to this thing. I was scared out of my mind, but I also wanted to see it close-up. I was unsure what to do. James Ernest had fallen back behind a tree. I just stood there looking at the opening expecting to see Bigfoot come lumbering out after me. "Ahhhhhh–Ughhhhhh–Ahhhhhh–Ughhhhhh–Ahhhhhh–Ughhhhhh!" The scream came at me again. But this time it seemed to be closer to the entrance. My feet began backing up as I stared at the dark entrance. I tripped on one of the large flat rocks and fell flat on my back. I knew I was going to be dead soon. My eyes were still locked on the entry when I saw two hairy hands and arms emerge from the entrance. Just then other hands grabbed me by my armpits and half-lifted and half-dragged me away from the flat rock to behind a large tree. I looked into his eyes and said, "Thanks, buddy."

"You're welcome," James Ernest said as we watched to see if Bigfoot was going to come all the way out to where we could see him.

We watched for the next twenty minutes. We saw nothing else and heard no other utterances. James Ernest said, "I'm going to spend the night here. You better take the others back home."

"No. You can't stay here," I begged.

"How often does a guy get a chance to see Bigfoot? I want to see him when he comes out in the morning, or if he leaves during the night."

"Then I want to stay with you," I said.

"You have to take the others back, plus Betty will get really upset if you don't come home."

I knew that was true, but I didn't want to miss out on seeing Bigfoot in the daylight. "I'll try to come back first thing in the morning."

"Okay. But if I'm not here that means he's already gone."

"Be careful," I said, feeling a little like Mamaw because that was always what she told me. I sure didn't want to leave James Ernest alone even though I knew he was always spending nights in the woods. I turned and left him there. I found the others about two hundred yards away on the trail. They couldn't believe James Ernest was staying.

6   WHERE'S JAMES ERNEST?

"What happened? Where's James Ernest? What was that screaming?" Raven bombarded me with questions when I caught up with them.

"The screaming was probably me." I answered their questions and told them about catching a glimpse of the thing. The girls were very upset over James Ernest staying during the night. They didn't seem all that upset about me almost dying, probably because I was standing there in front of them—alive and talking—with no blood showing. I would say that the hairs on my head were standing straight up but they were always standing straight up due to the amount of hair wax I put on my Mohawk. But at that moment I could feel the hairs standing up at attention.

I was afraid for my best friend, knowing that he was spending the night with what we thought was Bigfoot. Even if it wasn't Bigfoot, I wouldn't want to spend the night with the thing—whatever it was.

We all were looking back toward the wall as though we expected Bigfoot to come lumbering up the trail with parts of James Ernest hanging out of his mouth. I finally got everyone to head back home by saying, "Let's get out of here."

When we got to the main road, Raven and Junior left us and headed to their home. It was dark by the time Susie and I got back to her house. Mom's car was parked by the house. I was thankful I wouldn't have to walk home. I was unthankful for the scolding I received for getting Susie back home after dark.

We kids had sensibly decided not to tell the adults about following Bigfoot. We simply said we had hiked too far and lost track of time and couldn't get back before the sun set.

"Where is James Ernest?" Mom asked.

Instead of telling her James Ernest decided to spend the night in the woods with Bigfoot I quickly came up with another tale. "He walked Raven and Junior home. He said he may stay there tonight." The Washington family still did not have a phone, so Mom had no way to call and check on my story.

"Maybe we should drive over there and make sure he doesn't want to come home," Mom suggested. Oh no! Now what? I couldn't think that fast. Lying was hard.

"He told us he had some work to do in his garden in the morning and then wanted to get an early start making baskets with Raven," Susie said, saving my lie.

"I think Timmy should be punished for getting Susie home so late," Delma butted in.

"We were so worried," Thelma added.

"Small cute kids shouldn't have to worry so much," Delma said.

"You two are going to have a lot more to worry about if you don't go in the other room," Monie threatened them.

They turned quickly and headed for their bedroom. Delma looked at Thelma and said, "It was just a good suggestion."

"I agree. It was brilliant," Thelma told her.

When Mom and I were leaving, Susie walked with me to the car. Mom was talking with Monie about green beans or something like that.

"Thanks," I whispered to Susie.

She nodded and asked, "Do you think James Ernest will be okay?"

"Sure he will," I said a lot more assuredly than I really was. But, knowing James Ernest, he would end up petting the thing and becoming great friends as he had done with other wild things in the forest. I went to bed wishing James Ernest was in the bunk bed below me.

Monday, August 20

After midnight, James Ernest sat in the dark watching the opening in the stone wall for a glimpse of the thing. James Ernest told me later that as he watched for it he had decided to give the thing a name. He said he hated thinking of him as the thing, or a generic Bigfoot. He wasn't sure if it was male or female. He said his first thought was to call it Harry, but that seemed a bit juvenile and corny. He said, for some unknown reason, he settled on 'Charley'.

Around 1:00 a.m. that night he saw movement in the opening. Charley was looking carefully toward where James Ernest was sitting behind a tree and rock. James Ernest watched him from between them. Charley emerged from the cave and stood looking up at the almost half moon above him. James Ernest estimated that Charley was close to seven and a half feet tall and fairly thin but muscular. It was hard to tell with all the hair that covered him. Charley began scratching himself and rubbing the hair on top of his head. He pushed away the hair that had fallen over his eyes, and then grunted.

He took a few steps toward James Ernest's location and then stopped and smelled the air. James Ernest was ready to run. He figured Charley could smell a human. Charley then sat down on one of the flat rocks and searched the ground for a small flat stone, which he picked up and used to groom himself. He rubbed his hair that covered his body with the stone, fluffing it so that dust fell from the hair. When done with that chore he then began flattening his hair against his skin with the stone. It looked like Charley had his mid-section covered with something, maybe animal skins. James Ernest watched every little detail that Charley did and made mental notes of them. He watched Charley the same way he had watched farmers and outdoorsmen all his life, trying to learn from them by studying what they did and why they did it, storing away the knowledge he had learned in his brain until one day he would need the learning.

Charley rose from the rock and walked away from the cave. James Ernest wanted so badly to go into the cave and see if Charley made it his home or if it was just a one-night staying spot. But he didn't have a light with him and he could always come back with a flashlight, so he followed Charley.

I woke with the daylight and looked down to see that James Ernest's bed was still empty. I slid off my bed and dropped to the floor. I had dreamed all night, or at least it seemed to be all night. It was something about walking in the woods and staying on a trail. It kept going and going, never stopping. I was worn out by the time I awoke.

I knew that being a Monday morning we would probably not have any fishermen until that evening. I needed to get back to James Ernest. I wanted to take him some food and watch for Bigfoot with him, so I quickly threw my clothes on and made my way to the lake to pick up the garbage that had been left behind from the weekend fishermen. I peed on a tree as I ran around the lake.

Coty was leading me on the path and he was peeing on multiple trees as we went. I checked our drinking water when I returned to the store. We still had a full bottle in the fridge and a full bucket on the porch sink. Getting water at the spring could wait till later. I went to the front porch and swept it off. I then padded to Mom's bedroom door and knocked lightly. No answer. I knocked louder.

"Yes," Mom finally woke.

"It's me."

"Come in."

I opened the door and asked, "I've already done my chores and I wanted to go help James Ernest with his garden work. Is that okay?"

"What time is it? You've already done your chores? You want to do garden work?"

"Yes. We shouldn't have any fishermen this morning."

"Go ahead. You don't want any breakfast?"

She asked it as though this was going to be the morning she was going to fix bacon, eggs, pancakes and waffles instead of the usual cereal I had every other morning.

"I'll eat a banana."

"Okay."

She had asked it as though I was going to miss out on the greatest breakfast ever if I left. But I doubted it so I went ahead and left after grabbing the banana. I also filled a bag with some breakfast cakes and two RC Colas.

I knew a shortcut to where I had left James Ernest the night before. I ran around the pay lake to the stream and followed it toward the swimming hole. I ran past it and on toward the spot I had found Coty. I had made Coty stay at the store. He was upset at being left for a second straight day but I didn't want him battling Bigfoot. I ran past Robert and Janice's farm and finally slowed down once I got close to Homer and Ruby's farm. I saw Homer out in his garden gathering ripened vegetables.

I dipped into the woods to stay out of sight. I hurried to the spot next to the tobacco field where the trail had begun in the woods. I was close now. I was excited to see if James Ernest had seen the thing in daylight, whether he had gotten a good look at it. I was excited to make sure my best friend was still alive. After all the running I wasn't a bit tired. The adrenaline had carried me to this spot. I began running down the trail. I rounded the last bend and then eased to a quiet walk. I went to the spot where I had left James Ernest. He wasn't there. I searched the area and called out his name.

No answer. Nothing.

I walked to the opening and yelled inside, "James Ernest, are you in there?!" I had meant to bring a flashlight, but in my haste I had forgotten it. I yelled for him again. I stood there so disappointed.

⌒

James Ernest had followed Charley most of the night. He watched him walk into a stream and drink water by bending down and slurping it. He saw him catch small minnows and swallow them whole. He watched Charley chase a frog along the bank of the stream. James Ernest had to laugh at the big beast as he fumbled like a child to catch the frog. Once he had caught the frog, he ripped the legs off it and ate them.

Every now and then Charley would turn and look behind him as though he suspected something was following him. James Ernest's skill of silently moving and hiding was put to good use during the night. During the night Charley found an oak tree that had acorns lying on the ground beneath it. James Ernest watched as Charley cracked the nuts open with his fingers and ate the fruit of the nuts. Charley spent an hour eating under the tree.

During the night he also watched Charley eat green apples from an old apple tree at an old abandoned farm yard. James Ernest figured Charley knew these locations and had frequented them before; making him think that Charley did, in fact, make his home in the cave.

About an hour before daylight Charley went back to the cave and entered it. What James Ernest didn't know was how long Charley had lived in the area; must have been a while, James Ernest thought, with Charley knowing the different locations for food. James Ernest wondered why he had never come across Charley during his night hikes before. James Ernest stayed there after the sun came up and then left and headed back to the store. He was hungry, tired and sleepy. He would go to Raven's later in the day. He entered the store, grabbed a snack cake and orange juice and went straight to bed five minutes after I had left to find him.

I sat behind the same tree James Ernest had and ate two snack cakes and drank one of the RC's. I wondered where he was. I wondered if Bigfoot was still in the cave. I wondered if James Ernest was in the cave. I wondered if Bigfoot had killed and eaten James Ernest. After finishing the RC I decided to walk to the Washington farm. I figured that would be where he would go.

I made my way back to Homer's tobacco patch. He was still in the garden, but this time he was hoeing the weeds. I decided to go say hello.

"What the heck are you doing here this fine early morning?" Homer asked as I walked up to him.

"On my way to the Washington farm," I answered.

"I wouldn't have taken this shortcut, but to each his own," Homer said grinning.

"I thought maybe you could tell me how Uncle Morton is doing." It was the only thing I could come up with as to why I would be there.

"He's doing better every day. He misses seeing everyone." We laughed as we thought of his old joke. "I think he might be able to come home in around a week."

"That's great news. I sure do miss him. Well, I guess I had better mosey on."

"Have you had breakfast?"

"I had a banana."

"That's no kind of breakfast. C'mon, let's get you a sausage biscuit."

That sounded good, so I didn't argue. We walked into the front doorway and on back to the kitchen where Ruby was sitting at the table stringing and breaking the green beans that Homer had picked earlier.

"Well, as Gomer would say, Surprise! Surprise!" Ruby said when she saw me.

"Hi, Aunt Ruby."

"What brings you up here this early?"

"I came to get a sausage biscuit," I answered.

"You came all the way up here to get a breakfast sandwich?"

"Sure did. I heard they were the best made in the county."

Ruby smiled real big when she heard that and said, "Well, I think you had better take two then."

"I was hoping you would say that."

"G-o-l-l-y. It's just so nice of you to stop by. Did you bring Coty?"

"No. He stayed home."

"Well, shame, shame, shame. I had a sausage for him too."

Ruby must have been watching a lot of *The Andy Griffith Show* because she kept using Gomer's catchphrases from the show.

"Here, take this to him. He's such a good dog." She placed a sausage patty into the paper bag I was carrying along with my two sandwiches.

"Thank you. I appreciate it, and I know he will too," I said.

I said my goodbyes and headed down the lane toward the main road. I ate the sausage biscuits and drank the other RC as I walked. I figured James Ernest wouldn't need his if he had been eaten by Bigfoot anyway. It took almost a half hour to get to the Washington farm. Junior was in the front pushing a reel lawn mower in the front yard. Grass clippings were flying up into the air as Junior pushed the grass cutter. When he looked up he saw me approaching and waved.

I looked toward James Ernest's garden but didn't see him there. I heard Junior yell, "Timmy is here."

Within thirty seconds the porch had Raven, Samantha, Mark Daniel and Coal standing on it waving at me. Junior stopped mowing and ran to meet me.

"What's up?" Junior asked me.

"I was looking for James Ernest. But I guess he's not here."

"Nope, ain't seen him today." We began walking toward the house.

"I went back to the cave, and he was gone this morning. I thought maybe he had come here to work in his garden or to make baskets."

Junior shook his head. "What do you think happened?"

"I don't have any idea," I said as we approached the porch.

"It sure 'em nice to see you," Coal greeted me. "What brings ya'?"

"Just out for a walk."

"Nice mornin' for a walk," Raven said as she jumped off the porch and stood in front of me. I could tell that she wanted to know what was going on. I could see the worry in her eyes.

She turned back to Coal and told her, "We's going for a walk."

She grabbed my arm and pulled me away from the house. Junior and Samantha joined us. As we walked I told her about

James Ernest not being at the cave this morning and that I thought he might be there.

"Well, where is he?" she demanded, due to her worry.

"How would I know? No one knows where he is half the time."

"Do you think the thing got him?" Raven asked.

I looked toward Samantha to see her reaction. Raven then said, "She knows. I told her about it last night."

"No way, Jose. James Ernest wouldn't let himself get caught." I hoped I was right.

"What are you going to do now?" Junior asked.

"I guess I'm going back home."

"So I have to stay here and worry?" Raven said.

"You guys can go with me."

"We can't. Got way too many chores to do. Tell James Ernest when you find him to let us know he's okay."

"I will. And he is okay. I promise." I hoped it was a promise I could keep. Raven hugged me and they turned back toward their house as I walked away.

Almost an hour later I walked into the store where Mom was waiting on a truck driver and Mr. Smuckatilly was leaning against the counter drinking a Coke and smiling about something that had been said.

I greeted everyone and then Mom asked, "Did James Ernest come back with you?"

That answered my question. James Ernest hadn't returned home. I placed the two empty pop bottles I had drunk into a wooden pop-bottle case at the corner of the store. Mom asked me to go to the spring for water. I walked through the house and saw Janie playing on the floor with her dolls. I asked her, "You want to walk to the spring with me?"

"No. I'm playing with my dolls. I don't do chores."

"You're beginning to sound like the brat twins," I said.

"Well, that's just rude."

"That sounded like them too."

"Go do your chores."

So I did. Mom had already emptied the bucket that was full that morning, so I had to carry two buckets. Coty walked beside me after I gave him his sausage patty. He licked his lips as we walked toward the spring.

7 CHARLEY

I walked with both buckets toward the spring with Coty. I worried about James Ernest even though I would have told anyone else that I was sure he was okay. Suddenly, Bo flew onto my left shoulder. I hadn't seen Bo for a while. I was glad he was back.

"Have you seen James Ernest?" I asked him.

He cawed and bobbed his head up and down. I knew he had no idea what he was doing or saying. Coty came up out of the ditch he was searching and saw Bo. He began barking a greeting at the bird. Bo flew off me and lit onto the back of Coty. Coty pranced with the crow on his back, happy to see his friend. I walked off the road and down the path to the spring, filled the two buckets with the fresh, clean, cool water and began the trek back. The two buckets were heavy. I wasn't sure why I decided to carry two buckets.

I made it back to the house by stopping three or four times to rest my hands. It may have been six, or eight times. No more than ten.

Mom said a few fishermen were at the lake and asked me to check with them for snack orders. Mud McCobb was one of the so-called fishermen. He asked me how Uncle Morton was doing. I knew he had probably already asked Mom when he paid for his fishing and bait. I decided to be nice and tell him what I knew. "He'll probably be here next week giving you fishing lessons."

"That sounds like him," Mud said.

"You need anything?" I asked him.

"No, just a little luck."

"You need a lot of luck," I fired back–so much for being nice. No one else needed anything either. I went back to the store and waited on customers for the next two hours. Mom went to the kitchen to start supper. She told me the sheriff was coming that evening to eat with us. She was preparing fried chicken. I loved fried chicken.

The store got crowded with people stopping to pick up things on their way home after work, and fishermen arriving to fish in the coolness of the evening. I was busy. Mrs. Tuttle and Sadie walked through the door.

"Hi, Timmy, how is your Uncle Morton doing nicest man in the world I just hate to think about him laid up in that hospital when I know he would like to be here at the store or fishing up at the lake pulling in big catfish has anyone been up to visit him today I wish I was able to drive I would go visit him every day He is the nicest man and smart He is so smart did I say that already..." She was still talking a blue streak as she entered the living room heading toward the kitchen.

Louis Lewis was standing next to the pop cooler during her rant. He said, "She sure can gab. But I guess the good thing is a man doesn't have to answer her questions. Doesn't give you a chance."

Sadie and I and the other customers laughed at the observation. Louis left to go fish. The other customers paid for their goods and left, leaving me alone with Sadie.

"How are you, Timmy?"

"I'm okay."

"I have a new boyfriend."

"Oh yeah," I said, not really caring. I did wonder if this was another figment of her imagination or someone real.

"I'm courting Mr. Kenny Key."

"I thought Tucky was scared of you," I said.

"I'd like for you to refer to him as Kenny. It's not so primitive. Let's just say I tamed him."

"What spell did you have Bernice cast on Tucky to tame him?" I asked.

"You're impossible. He has better taste in women than you do." She turned and walked into the living room. The store was finally empty.

While I had a chance I went to my bedroom to change shirts for supper. I walked to my dresser and a deep voice said, "Is Loraine Tuttle here, or was I having a nightmare?"

I turned and saw James Ernest lying in his bed with the sheet up around his head.

"Buddy, you're alive!" I said before I went over and jumped on him. We went flying over the side of the bed and got jammed between the bed and the wall. We pushed and pulled and struggled with all our might to get out of our predicament.

Finally he was able to answer, "I think I'm alive. No thanks to you."

"I was excited to see you. I thought the thing had eaten you."

"What?"

I went on and explained how I had taken him breakfast, and he wasn't there. He said he would tell me all about his night later when we went to bed.

"Mom is fixing fried chicken for supper. Sheriff Cane is coming also."

"I'm starving," James Ernest said.

"I ate your snack cakes and sausage biscuit." I headed back to the store.

"You did what?" James Ernest yelled out as I closed the door.

Soon, James Ernest was dressed and in the store with me. Sadie saw him and followed him into the store.

I said, "She claims that Tucky is now her boyfriend."

Sadie started to say something, but James Ernest butted in, "Isn't he scared of you?"

"That's what I said." I laughed.

"His name is Kenny and I wish you would start calling him by his rightful name," Sadie exclaimed.

"What does KennyTucky have to say about this arrangement?" James Ernest asked.

"He's quite happy with it," Sadie boasted.

"You sure he knows about it?"

"You're an idiot. To prove it, you like a stupid Negro girl." She turned and hightailed it back to the kitchen.

"She insulted my taste in girls also," I told James Ernest. We both began laughing.

"I think we need to call for a Wolf Pack meeting and talk about Bigfoot, among other things," James Ernest said.

"I agree," I answered. "Maybe tomorrow evening."

That night when we went to bed after watching The Dick Van Dyke Show, Alfred Hitchcock Presents and The Red Skelton Show, James Ernest told me everything he had learned about Charley. I laughed so hard when he told about naming the thing 'Charley' that I nearly rolled off the top bunk.

"Are you two best buddies yet?" I asked through my laughter.

"Not yet."

⌒

As soon as I fell asleep James Ernest slipped from the bed, put his shoes on and slid the screen out of the window and climbed through. He reinstalled the screen, pulled the window back down to hold the screen in place, and left into the darkness.

James Ernest began running the same route I had taken to Charley's cave. He hoped to get there before Charley went out again searching for food. James Ernest figured Charley traveled mostly at night staying out of sight of humans who would want to hurt him. Maybe the thing had had run-ins with people before, maybe gotten hurt or even shot at. Thirty minutes later James Ernest stood between the large rock and the tree trying to catch his breath. He had run the entire way in the dark. He had trained his eyes to adjust to the dark much more than the average person. He could see the rocks and roots that littered the trails with danger of tripping and falling.

James Ernest smelled the familiar bad odor just before the rock slammed against his head. He didn't stand a chance of turning away from the blow. He fell and lodged between the two things that he thought hid him from the view of Charley.

TUESDAY, AUGUST 21

I dreamed that I was running from Bigfoot. Coty and Bo were laughing as they watched Bigfoot chase me around trees and rocks.

⌒

A splitting headache awaited James Ernest when he came to. He rubbed his head, and then rubbed his eyes trying to get them to open. They felt as though they were open, but it was pitch-black. He rubbed them again with the same results. He tried to stand to his feet without much luck. He relaxed to a sitting position. His back was leaning against a cold stone wall.

He then heard small clicking sounds against the stone floor he was sitting on. All kinds of thoughts ran through his brain trying to figure out where he was and what this sound was. He had never been this scared of anything in his life.

To his left he could see that the blackness held a small hope of some light. He wondered if that way led to the escape from this place. His head had never hurt so much. He then felt something on the back of his neck. He began scraping it off. He soon realized that it felt and smelled like dried blood. He touched the spot on the back of his head where the rock had been slammed. He jumped at his own touch. The pain almost knocked him out again.

⌒

I awoke when Mom began pounding on my bedroom door, yelling, "Boys, we have fishermen waiting on the front porch."

I would expect them early on a Saturday or Sunday morning, but not on a Tuesday morning.

"Okay, I'll take care of them." I then told James Ernest, "I'll take their money and you can get their bait." I climbed out of my bed and started to shake James Ernest, but he was gone again. I dressed and hurried to the grocery store door. There stood Phillip Satch and Sam Johnson.

"'Bout time you got your lazy butt out of bed," Phillip greeted me.

"What do you want? Uncle Morton isn't here for you to play tug-of-war with," I greeted back. Sam laughed. Phillip and Uncle Morton had hooked each other's line one day and at first each thought they had hooked a giant catfish. It soon turned into one of those stories men laugh about for years.

"We want to have our lines in the water when the fish start looking for breakfast," Sam explained.

"So you want some orders of eggs and bacon for bait?" I asked.

"Smart aleck. How is Uncle Morton?" Phillip asked.

After telling them what I knew, collecting their money, and getting their bait, they headed for the lake.

I went into the kitchen. Talk of eggs and bacon made me hungry. Mom had gone back to bed. I poured myself a bowl of Cheerios and wondered where James Ernest was again.

With the rising sun, light began to filter into the back of the deep cave. James Ernest again smelled Charley before he saw him lumber toward him from deeper in the cave. James Ernest heard the clicking sounds again. He squinted his eyes and looked to his right and could see the outline of a deer, a yearling, standing. His nerves make him shake. James Ernest could see lines in front of himself going down to the floor.

Charley came to the cage he had built and looked inside. His prey was still inside. The deer he would probably eat when he needed the protein. James Ernest was unsure what his fate would be. Was he being held captive for the same reason as the deer? James Ernest couldn't believe he had been so careless. He knew he had only himself to blame.

I spent the entire day watching the store, doing chores, and stocking the shelves with new cans and boxes, which were being delivered by big trucks. Pop vendors would arrive and take away the empty bottle cases that were full and bring in new cases of pop. Tuesdays were always busy with deliveries and store activity. James Ernest never did come home during the day. I began to worry about him and went into the bedroom to make sure he hadn't snuck into his bed again. It was empty.

That evening Mr. and Mrs. Washington brought the family down to visit. Soon we found out that they hadn't seen James Ernest all day either. Raven said that James Ernest had told her he would be up there early to help her make baskets. It wasn't like him to not do something he said he would do. They were worried. I wasn't sure if I should say something about James Ernest following Charley, the Bigfoot, or not. Perhaps James Ernest had gone back to the cave to spend another night with Charley, but hadn't returned. We were also going to have a Wolf Pack meeting, but he had left without organizing the meeting. That wasn't like him.

I knew that the adults would panic if I told them about Bigfoot. I was the only one who knew that James Ernest had spent the night before following him. I decided to keep it to myself—for now. Raven and Junior were looking at me as though they thought I should say something. I wondered if they were going to spill the beans and tell our parents about us tracking Bigfoot.

"Maybe I should call Hagar. I'm getting really worried," Mom said.

"Mom, we know how James Ernest is. He's probably just out following some deer or coyote over a mountain," I said, trying to ease her mind.

"Well that makes me feel a lot better, James out with a coyote on some mountain. I'm going to have to lay down some ground rules with him," Mom started to cry.

That didn't work too well. I wondered what she would do if I told her the truth—that he was probably following Bigfoot across the mountains. But truthfully, I was also getting worried. It wasn't like him to be gone all night and all day. I was worried that something might have happened to him, but I wasn't sure what time he had left during the night. I knew if he was going to follow Charley he probably left as soon as I had fallen asleep.

"Let's wait 'til morning before we involve Sheriff Cane. I'm sure James will be back," Mr. Washington suggested.

I could tell that Raven was bursting at the seams, wanting to say something. But she held it in. I could also see that she was ready to cry with worry. James Ernest had never stood her up before. He always did what he said. Raven suddenly motioned for me and Junior to follow her. Samantha started to follow, but Raven motioned for her to stay.

We went out to the front porch. "I think we'uns should say something. We should tell them about Bigfoot. James Ernest could be in big trouble," Raven said.

"Do you know how grounded we'll be if we tell them we were tracking the thing?" I said.

"Stop thinking about yourself, Timmy! Think about helping your best friend!" Raven said, almost screaming. "Susie told me about how you didn't want to tell anyone 'bout the Tattoo Man and lookee what almost happened. You near got yo'self kilt!"

I had thought about the incident. I still wondered what might have happened had I told Mamaw and Papaw about the Tattoo Man. I still wasn't convinced that they may have been killed had I told them about my suspicions. The way I had done it was scary and I was nearly killed but it all worked out in the end. I looked into Raven's eyes and saw the worry and tears that were forming, and I knew that this affected way too many people besides me.

"Okay, let's go tell them." Raven hugged me. Junior said he thought it was the right thing to do.

We walked back into the living room, and I proceeded to tell our parents about seeing the thing at the bonfire party and then how we had tracked it the next day. I thought Mom and Coal were going to drop dead right there on the couch.

I then went on and told everyone what James Ernest had done the night before. Raven and Junior didn't even know about how he had followed Charley and watched him all night. The kids' eyes lit up as though I was telling the best fantasy story they had ever heard. Mark Daniel quickly jumped into Coal's lap and wrapped her arms around his body.

"I suspect that's what he did again last night and today. I think that's why he isn't home," I said.

"Why didn't you tell us this earlier?" Mom questioned.

"I think he's probably okay. I didn't want you to worry."

"You think he's probably okay in the woods after following what you kids think is Bigfoot? No telling what kind of monster or lunatic man he's out there with. I can't believe you guys would do such a thing, tracking … whatever it is… into the mountains. I've got to call Mom and Dad and Hagar." Mom rose from the couch and went to the phone and began dialing. Within minutes the three of them were inside the store. We moved everyone into the store so there was enough room. Mom had me tell them what I had just told everyone else. Mamaw stood there with her mouth open. Henry quickly got her a chair to sit on.

"I've heard of other people here in Morgan County seeing what they thought was Bigfoot. But one of the reports was from Roger Smuckatilly. And that was when he was on the moonshine, so no one paid him much mind."

Sheriff Cane finally spoke, "How good of a look did you get of him, Timmy?"

"We all saw his footprints. I saw his hands and arms sticking out of the cave. But James Ernest told me all about what he looks like."

"Tell me how he described it."

I took a long sigh while trying to remember exactly what I had heard. I was tired of talking, of answering questions. I began rethinking my decision to tell them about it, but it was too late to take it back.

I began, "James Ernest said it walked humped over, but still was close to seven feet tall. No telling how big if it stood straight. It was covered with hair and had a choppy-looking beard. He said it smelled awful. He saw it eat raw minnows and frogs."

"Yuck!" Mark Daniel screamed out. Everyone agreed with him.

"It would be like eating sardines," Junior said.

"What else?" Hagar urged.

"It ate acorns by crushing the nuts with his fingers. James Ernest said Charley was as strong as an ox."

"Charley?" Mom questioned.

"James Ernest named him Charley." That broke the tension as nearly everyone laughed. "I don't remember anything else."

⌒

Earlier in the day James Ernest had watched Charley go a little deeper into the cave and lie down on a bed made from pine limbs and fall asleep. James Ernest reached into his pocket for his knife. It was gone. Charley must have taken it. James Ernest spent the day trying to find a way to escape. The cage was built from strong limbs and sugar cane stalks. It had four walls and a ceiling and was nestled up against the ceiling of the cave. James Ernest couldn't believe it had been built by Charley. Someone with intelligence had to have built it, and it had to have taken a long time to build.

James Ernest pondered a question in his mind, *Was Charley an animal, human, or a mix?*

Six hours later Charley woke and lumbered back to the cage. He dropped some grass and leaves into the cage for the deer to eat. It was so dark in the cave it was hard to see any of Charley's details. He then went back to his stash, where he had been sleeping, and brought back a handful of acorns for James Ernest. He dropped them inside the cage. They rolled around on the stone floor before settling.

James Ernest spoke to him, "My name is James Ernest."

Charley turned and stared at him and tilted his head to his left. He then started toward the cave entrance.

"I was only watching you to learn from you, and about you. I never wanted to hurt you." He stopped as Charley turned to face him.

"I like watching animals and humans hunt and work. I learn so much from watching," James Ernest told Charley. He wondered if his deep voice scared Charley. "I don't know your name, but I call you Charley."

James Ernest heard something that sounded like a chuckle. Surely it wasn't though.

Charley turned and left the cave.

James Ernest prayed.

Pastor White and Miss Rebecca and Bobby Lee arrived at the store after getting a call from Mamaw. Pastor White led the group of worried folks in prayer for James Ernest and his safe return.

⌒

At that time James Ernest sat against the stone wall and petted the yearling which had settled next to him and nestled its head on his leg. Charley was sitting near his bed, making something out of twigs and grapevines.

James Ernest began quoting verses he had memorized, "For God so loved the world that he gave His only begotten Son..."

Charley listened as James Ernest recited a Bible verse. They were words that were familiar to Charley, but words he had not heard since he was a young lad.

⌒

"Can you lead us back to the cave?" Hagar asked me.

"Yeah," I answered.

"We'll go at sunrise. I'll have two of my deputies go with us. Hopefully James Ernest will return during the night," Sheriff Cane said.

Papaw declared, "I'll go also."

"You will do no such thing. You go out there hunting for Bigfoot, don't even think about coming back home after doing something that stupid," Mamaw argued.

Sheriff Cane decided to stay out of this argument. The Washington family headed for their truck. Miss Rebecca hugged Mom and told her, "Everything will turn out okay. It always does."

"That's what worries me. Sooner or later it won't."

Once everyone had left I went to the phone and called Susie. She actually answered the phone. The twins must have already been in bed. It was a little after ten. I told her everything that had happened.

"Why didn't you call us earlier?" Susie asked, sounding upset.

"Everything happened so quickly, and Mom said she didn't want to upset the community again."

"Hopefully James Ernest will be there when you wake up in the morning."

"I hope so."

⌒

As Charley walked past the cage, James Ernest told him, "I have a large garden two farms from here. It still has a lot of vegetables in it. You are welcomed to whatever you need. I can show you where it is."

Charley never looked back and left through the opening of the cave, going on his nightly hunt.

James Ernest stood up. The deer's eyes followed his movements. James Ernest stood against the stone wall and then pushed himself from it and hurled himself against the wood structure that held him captive. The wood gave a little but then sprang back into place. He backed up against the wall again and did the same thing, listening for cracks as he slammed into the cage. The deer had risen and backed into the corner as far as possible. James Ernest slung his body against the wooden poles until his sides were turning black and blue and his muscles felt like jelly. The walls were the same—strong and sturdy.

James Ernest settled back down on the cold stone floor. The yearling came over and licked his hand and nestled against him again. James Ernest had all but given up hope that he would be able to escape.

⌒

Mr. Washington pulled into the long gravel driveway that led to their farm. The truck's headlights lit up the lane and the fields that surrounded the lane. Charley saw the lights coming toward him and started running from the garden. Henry saw something move to his left but didn't get a good look before it disappeared in the dark. Raven, who was standing in the bed of the truck, had seen Bigfoot when the lights first brought him into view. She saw him run off with his hands full of vegetables. She jumped from the slow-moving truck and landed hard on the dirt. She rolled into a standing position and then ran toward the spot where Charley had disappeared.

She stopped when she knew it was useless and began screaming, "Where is James Ernest?! Where is he?!?" Tears were streaking her face as Henry and Coal caught up and pulled their sobbing daughter close to them.

Mr. Washington dropped his family off at the farmhouse and then went to Papaw's house to tell him what they had seen. He felt as though the searchers the next morning should know.

⌒

I looked down from my top bunk at the empty bed below. I don't believe I had ever in my life felt so alone. I missed James Ernest terribly and worried about my best friend. I'm sure I was feeling the same things that James Ernest had felt when Susie and I were kidnapped. The difference was that James Ernest had spent every moment he had searching for me—while all I was doing was lying in my bed hoping he'd return.

WEDNESDAY, AUGUST 22

James Ernest woke up around four that morning and waited for his eyes to adjust to the darkness. He could hear the yearling crunching on something. James Ernest moved to the sound and then saw vegetables lying on the stone floor of the cage. The young deer was munching on a head of lettuce. James Ernest saw that cucumbers, lettuce, cabbage, corn and tomatoes had been placed inside the cage. He began eating one of the ripe tomatoes.

James Ernest knew what this meant.

⌒

Mom woke me up before the Tuttle's roosters crowed on their mountain that morning. I was to lead the sheriff to Bigfoot's cave. I heard the voices of Mamaw and Papaw already in the store. I then heard the voice of Henry Washington. I slipped on my shorts and T-shirt and shoes and joined them. Mr. Washington was making a phone call apparently to his boss at the quarry. He asked him if it would be okay if he came in late and promised to make up the time. He told his boss about James Ernest being missing and how he needed to help with the search. His boss agreed.

At daylight Sheriff Cane and two of his deputies arrived at the store. Hagar took Mom in his arms and hugged and then kissed her cheek and said, "He'll be okay. We'll find him."

"Bring him home," Mom told him.

Papaw told me I had better tie Coty up.

"He could help search," I told him.

"We don't want him getting in a tangle with this thing." I didn't argue, even though I thought Coty could help.

Mamaw stood wringing a dishcloth in her hands. The last drop of water in it dripped onto the store's wooden floor. Clayton drove up at the last instant and told Hagar he was going along. Hagar knew better than to argue. I rode in the police car. Clayton followed with Papaw and Henry crowded into the cab of his truck with him.

Sheriff Cane drove to Homer and Ruby's farm lane. Halfway down the lane I pointed to the spot on the other side of the tobacco patch where we had tracked Bigfoot into the woods. The sheriff pulled off the side of the lane. Clayton pulled in behind him. A minute later Homer came driving up the lane from his house and stopped in the middle of his lane. He hopped out of his truck with a rifle at his side.

Sheriff Cane told him, "Homer, why don't you sit this one out? We have plenty of help and guns." Looking around I noticed that each of the men had a searchlight or a flashlight and a rifle of some kind. I wondered why I had forgotten mine again.

"This is my land. I have a right to go if I want to. Try and stop me," Homer told Sheriff Cane.

The sheriff just shook his head and said, "Let's go then."

"You're a stubborn old fool," Papaw told Homer as we began our walk through the tobacco.

"I notice you're going too," Homer shot back.

"The sheriff could throw you in jail for disobedience," Papaw told him.

"I'd tell Betty on him. She'd straighten him out," Homer threatened. The men laughed.

"You're as stubborn as Honeycomb," Papaw said, referring to his mule.

I stopped the men in the middle of the patch and knelt down. I pointed to the footprint in the dirt. The men all gathered around and they each murmured and gasped at the size of the print. The men all seemed more nervous after seeing the print, making this hunt more real. They weren't just searching for a missing boy; they were looking for Bigfoot. I led the men into the woods and down the same deer path where we had tracked Bigfoot.

The woods were still fairly dark, the trees blocking the morning light. Men used their lights to keep from tripping on the trail. When we got near the cave I stopped and told them the cave was just ahead. We silently went forward and I motioned for them to follow me off the trail to the same spot James Ernest and I had watched from before.

"That's it," I told everyone, pointing to the dark spot in the stone wall.

"Let's go," Sheriff Cane told the men. "Timmy, I need for you to stay here and keep watch."

Sheriff Cane pulled his pistol from his holster and handed it to me. "If you see Bigfoot while we're inside, fire a shot in the air as a warning. I don't want us to have a sneak attack in case he's not in there."

I was disappointed I wasn't going in with the men, but I also agreed with the sheriff's plan.

Sheriff Cane led the way into the cave. The seven men, armed and ready, entered the cave in hopes of rescuing James Ernest. They went farther and farther back into the cave. They saw signs that something had been there. They found a pile of dead pine boughs that could have been a bed at one time. They moved on back through the cave until they came to a dead end. The cave was empty. There was no Bigfoot in the cave. James Ernest wasn't in the cave. They couldn't even find footprints inside the cave.

The men came out of the cave with their heads hung in disappointment. I ran up to them and they told me what they had found.

"That doesn't make sense," I said.

"Are you sure this is the cave?" Sheriff Cane asked. It reminded me of the time Sheriff Grizzle had searched the cabin for the Tattoo Man and found nothing and had accused me of lying and making the whole thing up to get attention.

"This is it. I swear it is!" I told him.

"I believe you, Timmy. Do you know of any other caves around here?" he asked me.

"No."

He turned to Homer and asked the same question.

"No. I didn't even know about this one," Homer answered. "Never been much of an explorer, especially after buying the farm."

"Should we search the area since we're already here?" Clayton asked.

"Wouldn't hurt," the sheriff said. "Let's meet back at the trucks at eight."

It was six-thirty. They then split up in twos and began combing the area. We went in four different directions. I went with the sheriff.

James Ernest knew that Charley understood English since he had gone to get the vegetables that he had told him about. James Ernest tried to figure out what Charley was. If he was Bigfoot did that mean that he was the one and only, or was there more than one Bigfoot. Were they like a bear or a lion, a type of animal? But Charley understood English. Did all Bigfeet understand English? James Ernest didn't think so.

Something was odd. Something was off. He wasn't even sure he believed in Bigfoot, especially one that understood English.

I followed Sheriff Cane, my future stepfather farther into the woods. We tried to keep quiet as a way of maybe sneaking up on Bigfoot. We looked along cliffs and around large boulders which stood fifteen feet high. We followed streams thinking it may want to be near a water source. After almost an hour the sheriff sat down on an old log. I sat beside him.

"I'm looking forward to being your stepfather," he said.

"Thanks," was all I said. I didn't know what to say.

"I'll try to be the best father I can be to you and Janie, and James Ernest."

"I know."

He drummed his fingers on the wood awkwardly as we sat there on the rotting log. He scooted his foot on the ground making a smooth spot with his boot.

"I guess we better be heading back to the trucks," he said.

"Are we giving up on finding James Ernest?"

"We need to meet up with the other guys to see if anyone found anything. We haven't given up."

"James Ernest searched for me and Susie for two solid days without stopping. He probably saved our lives."

"We'll meet with the other men and come up with a new plan," Hagar told me.

⌒

James Ernest could hear Charley sleeping somewhere deeper in the cave. He wanted to talk to him some more, but didn't want to wake him from his rest.

James Ernest thought about people who might be worrying about him. He knew that I and Betty and the Washington family would all be worried. He hated being the one to cause them the heartache. He wondered if anyone was looking for him. James Ernest knew that I would lead people back to the cave first, so he couldn't figure out why no one had come to the cave to rescue him yet.

What James Ernest didn't know at the time was that Charley had another cave, which was well hidden. And after he had hit James Ernest in the head with the stone, Charley had taken James Ernest to the well-hidden one and placed him inside the cage with the deer. James Ernest thought he was inside the cave to which we had tracked Bigfoot.

James Ernest also knew that people were used to him disappearing for days at a time before, and that they may not even be worried about him yet.

9 THAT'S MY GRANDSON

About ten minutes after eight we arrived back at the trucks.
We were the last to arrive.

Papaw was first to speak, "We all didn't find anything.
What about you guys?"

"No luck," Sheriff Cane told the men who had gathered
around us.

"What we do now?" Henry Washington asked.

The sheriff rubbed his forehead with his left hand and
shook his head. "I just don't know. Hasn't James Ernest been
gone for days before?"

"Yes," Homer answered. Papaw, Clayton, and Henry agreed.

The two deputies, whose names were Derek Clouse and
Linny Stutts, stood silently looking at their boss.

"I believe we need to give up the search for now. We
have no idea where he could be, and he might show up any
time." He turned his head toward me. I was so mad I could
hardly speak. I couldn't believe after a two-hour search he was
giving up.

"But-"

I was going to say more when Papaw put his hands on my
shoulders. I stopped. I probably would have said something I
would have regretted.

"We'll give it another twenty-four hours," Sheriff Cane said.

All the men began getting into the vehicles. I didn't want to ride back with the sheriff, so I hopped into the back of Clayton's pickup. Sheriff Cane looked at me but didn't say anything. I noticed a disappointed look on his face. I was sure his disappointment wasn't nearly what mine was. Two minutes later we pulled into the gravel parking lot of the store. I hopped out and ran into the store where Mamaw and Mom and other folks were gathered and talking about James Ernest.

"Did you find him?" Mamaw asked.

"No! And he's giving up."

"Who?" Mom asked.

"Your fiancé, Sheriff Cane, that's who." I went straight to my bedroom and flopped onto James Ernest's bed.

The next thing I knew, Mom flew into a rage. I jumped up, went to my bedroom door, opened it a crack and stood there listening.

Mom had flung the screen door open and met the sheriff on the porch steps. "You're just giving up the search?! You haven't even been gone two hours!"

"Betty, we've done all we can do for now," Sheriff Cane said calmly.

"This is your future stepson we're talking about! You've done all you can do? Well, I think I've done all I can do! Don't come back!" Mom turned away and stormed back into the store and through the house, past me, and on to her bedroom.

The other men stood around in the gravel lot silently looking at their shoes. Sheriff Cane swallowed hard and then turned toward his cruiser.

Papaw walked over to the sheriff and put his hand on his shoulder and said, "You know she doesn't mean that. She's worked up because she's worried. You need to go to her. Explain your decision."

The sheriff tilted his head up and said, "I can't explain my decision. I just don't know what to do. There's no handbook for searching the mountains for a missing boy and Bigfoot. Maybe I did give up too soon." He opened the car door and slid in. He led the two deputies back to West Liberty.

I went outside and untied Coty. He licked my face and followed me to the front porch where Papaw and Clayton were sitting. They said Henry had headed off to work. Pastor White came walking out of the store. He and his family had been in the store when we got back.

No one said anything. We all sat in silence as though each of us was thinking of what to do next. Bobby Lee opened the door and came out onto the porch. He looked at each of us as he petted Coty and then said, "I think you should get the Wolf Pack together. You guys could find James Ernest."

"Bobby Lee, that's a good idea."

I knew he was right. Why was I just sitting there? I hopped up from the edge of the porch and went inside to the phone. I called the Tuttle house. Sadie answered on the second ring. She must have been in the outhouse or something to be so late in answering.

"Hello. Tuttle residence."

"What took you so long?"

"I tripped and fell over Francis."

"This is Timmy. I need to talk to Randy. Please, it's important."

"What's so important?"

"James Ernest is missing."

"And Bigfoot has him," Sadie said and then laughed and laughed.

"Let me talk to Randy," I begged.

"He's out in the barn doing chores."

"What about Purty?"

"He's out there also."

"Would you go out there and tell them I need to talk to them right away?"

"No. I'm doing chores also."

"What are you doing?"

"Answering the phone, stupid!"

I gave up. How do you talk to a crazy girl? I hung up the phone.

I opened the cooler and took out an RC Cola and got a pack of peanuts from the counter. I opened the bottle and the bag and carefully poured the peanuts into the bottle. The brown foam quickly rose to the top of the bottle and began to spill over. I stuck the bottle in my mouth and let the foam collect there. It tickled. I went over to the snack rack and grabbed a moon pie and went out to the porch.

"Would you drive me around to collect the Wolf Pack?" I asked Papaw.

Papaw looked up at me and smiled. "That's my grandson. Let's go."

Coty and I jumped into the back of the pickup. We first drove up to the Tuttle farm. Papaw parked in front of the barn. He honked the horn and I jumped out and raced inside. Randy and Purty stood inside facing each other with hay covering each of them.

"What are you guys doing?" I asked.

"We got into an argument. Purty was slacking off, and I was doing all the work. It turned into this," Randy explained. Purty was trying to uncover his head of the hay.

"What are you doing here?" Randy asked as Purty gagged.

"You guys know that James Ernest is missing?" I said.

"Yes. Isn't he back yet?"

"No, we need to find him."

Finally, Purty was able to speak, and he said, "But we have chores."

"Not that you're doing any," Randy said to him.

"I'm really worried. We need to get the Wolf Pack together and search for him. Papaw is outside with the truck," I explained.

"Okay. We can finish this later."

"We may need your gun and Purty's sling-shot," I told him.

Randy ran to the house while Purty was still cleaning all the hay off which still clung to him. Randy must have covered him with it and then rolled him around the barn.

"It will blow off in the back of the pickup," I told Purty.

When we came out of the barn, I saw Loraine at the truck talking at Papaw. Papaw was nodding politely as he listened and listened to her non-stop jabbering. Randy returned and we three boys jumped into the bed of the pickup.

"Where are you boys going?" Loraine asked.

"To help find James Ernest," Randy answered.

"But you have chores and why do you need a rifle?"

"We'll finish chores later." Randy didn't address the reason for the rifle.

Papaw put his truck in reverse and began to back away. Loraine hung on to the window, walking along and talking, "Well, I ain't ever seen such a thing. Are they going to be okay, Martin? Are you going with them? Are they looking for James Ernest? He's the best kid in the world. I sure do hope you find him. Are you going to look for that thing? I think they saw a bear. I've heard of bears being around here. I think…"

Papaw put the truck in first gear and hit the gas. Loraine's hand was jerked off the window and she kept on talking as she waved to her boys. I could still see her lips moving as we disappeared over the hill toward the creek.

"We need to get Tucky now," I said to Papaw as I leaned around the cab. I turned to look at Purty and saw hay flying out the back of the truck. It was as if we had a hay-filled scarecrow with us.

As soon as we pulled into the driveway of the Key's house, Tucky came running out of the house and jumped into the truck bed. Papaw backed up and headed back toward the store. I leaned over and told Papaw I needed to stop at the store before going to get Henry Junior. At the store I jumped from the truck and went inside to get my rifle and a pocket full of bullets. Mom saw me as I came out of my bedroom and followed me to the porch.

"Timmy."

"We're going to find James Ernest. I can't stop looking. He would look for me no matter what."

Mom hugged me close to her and kissed my head and said, "You boys be careful."

She let go of me and then I had a thought. I ran back into my bedroom and found one of James Ernest's dirty shirts hanging on one of the bedposts. I grabbed it. I then remembered my binoculars and my pocketknife. I also thought of a flashlight. As I got into the store Mamaw gave me a sack of snack cakes and sandwiches she had made. She had stuffed them into my backpack. I smiled at her and said, "I love you."

"Be careful," was all she said. That was her way of telling me she loved me.

When we got to the Washington farm I saw Susie standing with Raven and Junior. Coal was on the porch with Samantha and Mark Daniel. Coal came off the porch while Junior and the two girls climbed into the pickup.

"What are you two doing?" Randy asked.

"We're going with you all. He's our friend too," Raven answered.

Randy started to say something, but, before he could, Coal confronted Randy and said, "This isn't a Wolf Pack meeting. This here is looking for someone we all love. You can't tell Raven and Susie they can't go. They have to help look."

Randy looked at the rest of the Wolf Pack and then said, "Okay. You're right. The more help, the better."

"God be with ya'll," Coal said as she reached out and grabbed Randy's hand.

"Where to?" Papaw asked.

"Back to Homer's," I answered.

10 FUNNY LOOKING DOG

It was nearly eleven that morning before we began the search again. I carried my rifle. Randy carried his. Purty had his slingshot. Susie carried the binoculars around her neck. Tucky said he wanted to carry the backpack even though Purty offered to carry it. We were scared Purty would sneak and eat all the food before anyone else had anything.

Papaw wished us luck before he drove away. He instructed us to have someone go to Homer's and call with an update later in the day. "Don't leave everyone worrying about you guys also." We promised.

"Where do we start?" Randy asked after Papaw drove off.

"I think we should go back to the last spot I knew James Ernest was. I brought one of his shirts. We can let Coty smell it and see if he can pick up his trail."

"That's a good idea. I should have brought one of Dad's bloodhounds," Tucky said.

"I didn't think of that," I said.

"We can try it if this doesn't work," Tucky told us. "Coty has a good nose. Remember, he's part coyote, and James Ernest's scent should be familiar to Coty."

We took off across the tobacco field. The path was beginning to get well worn. The sun was high in the sky, and the heat was beginning to rise into the nineties. Everyone had on shorts except Randy, who had on bibbed overalls for working in the hay. He had taken off his shirt in the truck. His muscles were well shown off without his shirt. Everyone wore tennis shoes or boots except for Tucky, who was barefoot as usual.

It wasn't long before we were at the cave entrance.

"Let's go inside," Purty quickly said.

"The men have already searched it. It was empty," I told them.

"They may have missed something," Purty argued.

"I don't think they would have missed James Ernest or Charley."

"Who's Charley?" Tucky asked.

I then had to explain to everyone who Charley was and I went ahead and told them everything that had happened that morning and everything James Ernest had told me. Once everyone was caught up on everything I took the shirt and had Coty smell it. "We need to find James Ernest, Coty. Find James Ernest."

Coty began sniffing the ground. I led him over to the tree that James Ernest and I had been standing behind. Coty acted as if he recognized the smell and began following the scent down the trail away from the cave.

⌒

James Ernest was softly singing Hank Williams' *I'm So Lonesome I Could Cry* to pass the time and because it reminded him of the way he felt there in the cage. James Ernest cherished his freedom, his freedom to come and go whenever he wanted. It was nearly killing him to be locked up in the cage.

He could hear Charley stirring deeper in the cave. He continued to sing but sang a little louder. James Ernest could hear Charley walking toward him. He kept singing the song. Charley got to within twenty feet of the cage and stopped and leaned against the cave wall and listened to the angelic voice that James Ernest had. James Ernest still could hardly see Charley at all due to the darkness of the cave, but he knew he was there by sound and smell. Something seemed different though.

Suddenly, James Ernest stopped singing. It was eerily quiet. James Ernest heard Charley sigh.

Out of the darkness came one word, "More."

James Ernest started the song once again.

We seven kids followed Coty as he sniffed the trail and led us down a narrow path. The trial zigzagged up a hillside and then made its way around the mountainside. When it looked like we were going to cross a small stream, Coty turned left and followed the stream back down the mountain. We were moving farther and farther away from Homer's farm and getting closer to the Cumberland National Forest.

We finally decided to take a break. Purty had been whining for the past half hour about being tired and hungry. I went to the stream and dipped my hands into the water and poured it over my head. Susie followed me and wiped her forehead with the water. Soon most of the others were doing the same. Tucky waded into the water and sat in it.

"Timmy, what's you think has happened to James Ernest?" Raven asked.

"I don't know."

"You think he's still following Bigfoot? You think Bigfoot caught him? You think he killed James Ernest?" After Raven asked these thoughts she began to cry.

"That's why girls shouldn't have come," Purty said.

Raven walked up to Purty and slapped him. Purty grabbed his face and fell to his knees.

"Why did you do that?" he cried out.

"Even I knew better than to say something like that," Tucky said as he lay in the stream.

"I know he's alive. I'm just not sure where he is, but I know he's alive," I assured Raven. I did believe it, because I knew God had great things planned for James Ernest. Uncle Morton had taught me that. Uncle Morton thought God had plans for me too, but I knew God had bigger plans for James Ernest. Plus, he was my best friend. He had to be alive.

Raven came over and hugged me tight. We got up to continue our search.

⌒

James Ernest finished the song again. He heard Charley move to the back of the cave.

"Charley. Hey, Charley. I have a group of friends that I'm sure is out searching for me. You need to let me go before they find us." James Ernest hesitated, searching for the right words to say. "I can help you. Come and talk to me. I know you understand me. You went and got the vegetables from my garden that I told you about."

The yearling paced inside the cage as though she was upset by all the talking. Her feet clicked on the stone floor. James Ernest went to her and stroked her head, calming her.

⌒

Coty again sniffed the shirt and then picked up the trail. We followed Coty into the Cumberland National Forest. The sun was high in the sky, meaning, it was past noon. We kids were tired and hot. Sweat was dripping down our bodies and arms. Tucky's water-soaked clothes dried out quickly but were now soaked with sweat. I was uncertain whether Coty was following James Ernest's smell or the scent of Bigfoot. The problem was—we weren't certain James Ernest was with Bigfoot.

What if James Ernest was already home? That meant all we were doing was tracking Bigfoot, which could mean big danger if we caught up to him.

For the next hour we hiked over hillsides and a mountain, and then we came to the bottom of a tall cliff. Purty was complaining about his feet hurting as Coty began going wild over the area he had led us to. There was a strange-looking patch of tall canes growing in front of the wall. It was nearly ten feet by twenty feet thick. Coty went back and forth along the front as though he was looking for an opening. I began searching with him. Soon everyone—except Purty, who was rubbing his stinky feet—was looking for whatever Coty had found.

Coty began barking and, even at one point, howled to the sky.

James Ernest woke up when he heard the barking sounds of a dog. When he heard the howl he knew it was Coty. He began screaming, "Coty, Coty!"

We couldn't hear James Ernest's cry, but Coty could.

Coty went around the patch of cane and found a path along the wall, which went behind the tall patch and slipped along the rock wall to a cave opening. I watched Coty disappear along the wall and followed.

"Follow me, guys!" I yelled out.

The gang quickly fell in closely behind me, except for Purty. He was yelling for us to wait. I wasn't waiting. I scooted along the wall until I nearly fell into the opening, which was dark, due to the canes covering it. I turned on my flashlight and we all followed the light. Coty stayed close to me.

"Should we yell out for James Ernest?" Raven whispered.

"No. We don't know where Bigfoot is," Randy said. He had his rifle pointed down the corridor of the cave just in case.

I could hear Purty screaming outside the cave, "Where is everyone?"

Susie held onto my arm as we made our way slowly, deeper into the cave. Raven held onto Susie, and Junior held onto Raven. We turned left around a bend, and Coty took off running ahead. I then shined the light on the cage, and there stood my buddy inside. We all ran to him. Coty was jumping up against the cage, trying to get to James Ernest. The yearling backed up against the wall.

I didn't know what to say. I wanted to say 'hello'. I wanted to ask what had happened. I wanted to know if everything was okay. Nothing I wanted to say seemed appropriate. I watched as James Ernest reached out for Raven. Raven was crying. Randy was looking at the cage trying to figure out how to unlock it. There was no door to it. Therefore, there was no lock to break or undo. The walls were continuous all the way around. There had to be a way inside. How did James Ernest and the deer get inside?

"How did you get in there?" I asked, finally having thought of something to say.

"I have no idea. He knocked me out, and I woke up in here with the deer."

"Where is Bigfoot now?" Susie asked.

"I fell asleep. He was deeper in the cave. He may have left while I was asleep—or he's still back there."

I quickly moved the light around to shine farther back in the cave. We didn't see anything. We all huddled together.

We were starting to move toward the deeper part of the cave when James Ernest said, "Don't. Help free me. Let's leave him alone."

"Why?" Tucky asked. I was sure Tucky wanted to shoot Bigfoot and see what he tasted like.

"He can talk and understand English," James Ernest said.

We stopped in our tracks. "Did you talk to him?" Susie asked.

"Yes."

We all had questions, but first we needed to get James Ernest out of his prison. I shined the light all over the cage. We tried pulling the cage from the wall. It wouldn't budge.

When I was about to give up I noticed something three feet up from the stone floor. All the vertical slats were solid pieces except for four slats that were side-by-side. They looked to be hinged with grapevine. The bottom of the doorway was tied by grapevines to the adjoining slats. I took my pocketknife and began cutting into the vines. The others came over to see what I was doing. Within ten minutes I had cut through the vines, and I lifted the bottom of the door upward, creating a doorway where James Ernest could crawl out. He dropped to the stone floor and crawled through the three-feet by three-feet opening. James Ernest coaxed the deer to follow.

Once the deer was out she went to James Ernest and stood beside him. Susie and Raven carefully went over and petted her. Coty stood watching the deer.

"Let me have the flashlight. I'll be right back." James Ernest moved carefully to the back of the cave looking for Charley. When he returned, he knew for sure what he expected—Charley was human.

James Ernest returned without saying anything, and we hurried to the cave's exit. We slid along the wall between the stone and canes that hid the entrance. When we got to daylight we looked for Purty. He was nowhere in sight.

"Don't tell me we now have lost Purty," I said.

"Purty! Purty!" we all began yelling.

"Where are we?" James Ernest asked.

"We're in the Cumberland National Forest," I answered.

"I thought I was in the cave where we first saw Charley," James Ernest said.

"We searched there first. Then Coty led us to you," I told him.

James Ernest reached down and patted Coty's head. We continued our search for Purty.

"Here he is," Tucky yelled out.

We ran to the spot. Purty was lying on the ground behind a fallen log. He looked to be asleep. Randy began shaking him. Coty began licking his face. Purty finally came to.

Randy helped him sit up. "What happened?" Randy asked.

Purty shook his head trying to clear the cobwebs inside his head. "I remember yelling for you guys, and I remember something grabbing me, and that's the last thing I remember. James Ernest, we found you!"

We laughed at the look on Purty's face when he realized James Ernest was there with us. "That's a funny looking dog," Purty said, looking up at the yearling. Purty was still kind of out of it.

"I think his head is still swimmin' like a nest full of hornets," Tucky told us.

"How can you tell with Purty? It's always like that," I said.

We opened up the backpack and took out the snacks and sandwiches. I handed James Ernest a couple of each. I was sure he was starving. The yearling reached out to the low trees and ate the leaves.

Everyone had something as Purty's head cleared up. We then began our trek back to the store.

"Let's go home, Coty," I said.

Coty led the way. We all followed, including the yearling.

11   A Freak

It wasn't long before James Ernest recognized where we were. Coty was leading us back to the stream that led to the pay lake. It was a long rough walk back to the lake. Around four that afternoon we finally were walking across the empty dam. Janie was playing in the backyard with the twins and Bobby Lee. Janie ran into the house and yelled out that we were coming. The adults came storming through the back door. They applauded and lifted their hands in praise that James Ernest was alive and well. When we made it to the yard, we were swallowed up with folks hugging us and patting our backs.

Delma and Thelma just stood there, shaking their heads, acting like we were the dumbest humans on the earth.

Mom hugged James Ernest first, and then Susie and then me.

Papaw told me that he was sure we would return with James Ernest. I told Papaw, "Well, there's no doubt that I had doubts."

Papaw laughed and said, "You did it, though."

I looked toward the lake and saw the yearling standing at the bottom of the dam. She was shaking with fright. Bobby

Lee yelled out, "Look at that deer!" He pointed his finger at it and pretended to shoot it. The deer turned and walked away.

Within an hour folks had left for their homes. It was suppertime. Clayton took Raven, Junior, and Susie. Randy, Purty, and Tucky walked home, and James Ernest and I went to the front porch and sat with Papaw and Pastor White. They began peppering James Ernest with questions about Bigfoot.

"I'm not sure what Bigfoot is supposed to be or even if there is such a thing, but Charley, I figured out, is a human."

"What?" Pastor White and Papaw both said at the same time.

"I never did get a good look at him because it was always dark. The cave was almost pitch-black," James Ernest told them.

"It sure was," I agreed.

"It was dark when I was following him outside the cave so I never got a good look at him then either. But he spoke to me, and he understood English."

"What did he say?" I asked.

"I was singing in the cage this morning. I had quit, and he said, 'More.' So I sang another verse. I had told him about my garden and that he could have some of the vegetables. The next morning he had placed vegetables inside the cage. I was rescued before I was able to talk to him again."

Papaw grinned and said, "James Ernest's voice is so good he could get Bigfoot to ask for more. Now that's saying something. That's some pretty good singing."

We all laughed. James Ernest seemed embarrassed.

"He could put that on the front of his album," I said through my laughter. "A voice so good it soothes the savage Bigfoot."

We all laughed.

"How do you explain the other stuff you guys have told us about him, covered in hair and gigantic?" Pastor White asked.

"I don't know. All I know for sure is that he knows how to talk and he understands," James Ernest said.

We sat there on the porch for the next hour retelling the story from the beginning to the end—James Ernest's version and my version. Miss Rebecca came to the porch and told us supper was ready.

During supper Bobby Lee and Janie asked us a million questions from "Did Bigfoot try to eat you?" to "Why do you guys smell so bad?"

After supper I went out to give Coty the leftovers. He was lying on the grass near his doghouse with the yearling. Bo, the crow, was sitting on the doghouse. Apparently we now had three pets.

I was surprised that Sheriff Cane hadn't come back for supper. I guessed Mom's yelling at him scared him off.

Later that night I climbed to my top bunk. My bed never felt so good. Our window was open and a cooling breeze blew in. Papaw said he thought we might get a good rainstorm during the night. James Ernest was in the bed below me.

"I'm glad you're here," I whispered.

"A lot better than being in a cage."

"Were you scared?" I asked.

"Of course I was. But I never got the feeling that he meant to hurt me. I think he didn't like being followed. He was scared, so he locked me up."

"So do you think Charley is an animal that talks–or a human that looks like an animal?"

"I pretty much know he's human. I think he was wearing furs that made him look like an animal."

"Why do you think that?"

"When he told me to sing more I thought I could barely see a glimpse of naked skin in the dark."

"Why didn't you tell Papaw that?"

"Because I'm not positive. I'm going to try to find Charley again."

"You're what?" I said a little too loud.

James Ernest didn't say anything else. I stared at the ceiling thinking about what a strange life I was living. That summer I had encountered the Bottom Brothers, their mom who thought she was a witch, a possible Bigfoot, all the good people of our community, but no one that was more interesting than my best friend, James Ernest.

Thursday, August 23

I awoke the next morning to the sound of rain pinging on the tin roof. I leaned over my bed and looked down to see James Ernest staring back at me. "Boo," he said.

"What are you doing this morning?" I asked.

"Thought I'd help you in the store. I saw boxes sitting on the floor of the store that haven't been opened and put on the shelves yet."

"I saw that too."

"Can't do much else in the rain."

"You could go play with your friend, Charley," I teased.

"I don't like the way he plays," James Ernest said and then laughed.

"You mean it's not fun playing sheriff and prisoner?"

"Especially when I'm the prisoner."

I lay on the bed and listened to the sound of the rain and smelled the odor of wet gravel the summer rain always brought with it.

"Let's take Raven and Susie on a canoe trip," James Ernest said.

That got my attention. I was always ready for a canoe trip. "That sounds great. Where?"

"I was thinking we could have Martin take us up to where Devil's Creek begins and we could float back to the store. It would be about an eight mile trip. We could take a picnic with us and make a day of it," James Ernest suggested.

"I'm ready. When?"

"First day we have free."

I slid off the bed and quickly slipped on my shirt and shorts and went out the back door. I peed off the back porch before Mom got up. She would get upset if she saw me, but I didn't want to go out in the rain. I went back into the kitchen and poured myself some Cheerios and even fixed James Ernest a bowl.

We ate our cereal and then started emptying the boxes in the store, putting the cans and boxes of goods on the shelves.

An hour later Mom came into the store after sleeping late.

"It's so good to see you boys here in the store instead of worrying about you," Mom said.

"I'm sorry I worried you. Are you and the sheriff okay? I'd hate it if I caused trouble between you two," James Ernest said. I didn't even know James Ernest knew about their disagreement.

"We'll be okay. Don't worry," Mom told him.

"Mom," I said.

"Yes, dear."

"James Ernest and I were talking about taking Raven and Susie on a day-long canoe trip down Devil's Creek. Is that okay with you?"

James Ernest offered, "They've wanted to go on one ever since we returned from the Red River trip."

"I don't see why not. When do you want to do this?"

"Maybe Saturday or Monday if the weather is good," I said.

"Monday probably would be better since we're getting this rain today. That will give the creeks time to clear and we can help here at the store and lake Saturday," James Ernest told her.

"Check with Monie and Coal. Monday is fine with me," Mom said and walked out of the room.

I high-fived James Ernest.

The rain fell most of the day. James Ernest and I stocked and reorganized some of the cans. We cleaned the store by dusting the cans and washing down the shelves. We straightened all the boxes behind the counter. We waited on customers, made sandwiches for truckers from the quarry, teased our mailman, Roger Smuckatilly, when he brought in the wrong mail, and even loaded a pickup with some bags of feed that a customer bought.

It was a fun day working with James Ernest. Toward evening I called Susie and told her about the canoe trip. She said she would ask and call us back later. James Ernest said he would be seeing Raven the next day when he went up to weed his garden. He also said they needed to work on their baskets.

FRIDAY, AUGUST 24

Susie called back the night before and said she could go on the canoe trip. We were trying to take the trip on Monday, since school would be starting soon. James Ernest got up early to go to his garden and weed it. Most folks let their gardens go to weed by this late in the year, but James Ernest had planted stuff later in the year to try and get a second crop in.

I headed to the lake to get it ready for the busy weekend I knew we would have. Papaw had the lake stocked again and the forecast was for the weather to turn cooler. The fishermen would be lining the banks.

Later that night James Ernest told me what happened as he was working in his garden. I could hardly believe it.

⌒

James Ernest was hoeing down through a row of green beans when he heard a voice coming from the edge of the woods. He stopped to listen closer. The yearling had followed James Ernest and was lying at the edge of the garden. The deer's head rose to look at the sound.

"Hey, hey," the voice called out.

James Ernest turned toward the voice. He saw a hand waving at him from the edge of the tree line. James Ernest moved forward trying to get a better view. He was around twenty yards away from the movement.

He again saw the waving hand and noticed that it was large. He knew whose it was, Charley. James Ernest stopped in his garden and watched to see what Charley would do. He certainly didn't want to get captured again.

"What do you want, Charley?" James Ernest called out.

Charley didn't speak at first. James Ernest knew Charley wouldn't come out of the woods and into the daylight, for fear of being seen by others. James Ernest waited minutes for Charley to say something again. Finally he turned to go back to his hoeing.

"James Ernest, can we talk?" Charley said as James Ernest turned away.

James Ernest turned back around and went closer to the woods and then said, "How can I trust you? You might try to lock me up in your cage again."

"I won't," Charlie simply said.

"You stay there. I'll move a little closer and sit down so it looks like I'm taking a break. We can talk," James Ernest explained.

He moved within fifteen feet of the tree line and then collapsed onto the ground. The yearling paced behind him, nervous.

"Who are you?" James Ernest asked as they began the conversation.

"Been long time since I talked out loud," Charley said after a minute pause.

"I know you aren't Bigfoot."

Charlie chuckled and then said, "Is that what you guys thought I was?"

"Yes, at first. That was why we followed your footprints."

"I am not Bigfoot. I wear fur for protection; better than being naked."

"Then who are you?"

"A freak," Charley answered.

"Why?"

"I am big and ugly. I do not look like others. I was always twice as big as kids in my class. I was born big. I had only four toes on my right foot. I was ugly and freaky. I was made fun of."

"Where did you live?"

"Alabama."

"How did you end up here?"

"It is a long story."

"I have all day."

12 Amen, That's Over!

Charley eased down to the ground and leaned against a tree as he told James Ernest the first part of his story.

James Ernest could see him a lot better in the daylight despite the fact that he stayed in the shadows of the tree limbs. Charley had a scraggly long beard and long hair, which grew past his shoulders. All James Ernest could see of Charley's face were the eyes that peeked out. The fur that he wore looked like a mixture of different animals that had been sewn together somehow to form his clothing.

Charley's neck and head hunched forward, making him look as though he was extremely uncomfortable. He carefully chose the words he spoke, as though searching for them from his memory, having not spoken them for a while.

"I was not going to hurt you. I did not like you following. I was scared of what you might do to me."

"I understand," James Ernest told him.

The yearling continued to pace on the other side of the garden. James Ernest tapped the ground by his side. The deer stopped, raised her head and looked at the spot, as if she was considering the offer. She turned her head slightly and stared at Charley.

"My dad took me out of school when I was eleven and I never returned. They kept me in the house as I grew taller almost every day. By the time I was ten I was over six feet tall. I was seven feet tall when I turned fourteen. Dad took me to the circus for my sixteenth birthday. I was seven feet and seven inches tall by then. He left me with the traveling circus. A man gave him a pouch that was full of money. I became 'The Tallest Man on Earth'. They made me carry a deer leg of meat and a giant club. Families would shriek and scream when they saw me enter the tent. Many thought I was walking on stilts. A midget would appear and lift my pant legs to show the crowd my legs were real and then pull the hair on my legs, bringing forth laughter from the crowd.

"I stayed with that circus for ten years. They became my family, and I became even taller. My spine began to bend to where I couldn't straighten up to my full height. This upset the owner. They would make me lie down and try stretching me with ropes and pulleys to straighten me out. It hurt."

"James Ernest! James Ernest!"

James Ernest looked toward the Washington house and saw Raven walking toward the garden. He looked back around and Charley was gone. He called out, "I'll be back in the morning." He was unsure if Charley heard him or not.

⌒

Coty and I were sitting on the slanted rock as I tried to catch a mess of bluegills for supper. Mamaw and Papaw were coming down to the store to eat with us, and Papaw told Mom he felt like having a fish fry. So it was up to me to provide the fish even though we had frozen fish in the freezer. But we all liked fresh fish better. Bo was perched on a low-hanging limb above the rock. I had to make sure not to hook him when I went back to cast, or Bo could become the bait. I had never tried crow meat before.

Every time I cast my worm into the water he would caw as if upset at that possibility. Coty would then bark as though he was trying to tell Bo to shut up and let him nap. I looked toward the stream which ran into the back of the lake, and when I looked back James Ernest was sitting there beside me. I jerked my pole due to being startled, and I had a bluegill on the line.

"Where have you been all day?" I asked.

"I hoed the garden and then Raven and I made baskets all day. I have to tell you what happened today." James Ernest proceeded to tell me the entire conversation he had with Charley.

"So you were right. Charley isn't Bigfoot."

"Nope, he's not."

"That's disappointing," I said.

"You think so?"

"Yeah. Aren't you a little disappointed we didn't find Bigfoot?"

"I guess so. But maybe we can help Charley."

"Maybe we could teach him that it's not nice to capture people and put them in cages," I suggested.

James Ernest laughed and said, "That would be a start. But I feel bad for him. It's not his fault he's so tall. He shouldn't have to live like Bigfoot."

"You're right. It's awful that his dad sold him to the circus. I've heard of boys running away and joining the circus, but never of being sold to the circus."

"I know," James Ernest said.

"I wonder if they had a bearded lady. Do you think that's real? I heard of a mermaid lady also, half girl and half fish. That would be something to see," I told James Ernest.

"I'd like to see a half boy and half crawdad. He could have pinchers instead of hands, a long crawdad tail, and long whiskers sticking out," I went on. "You think there's such a person out there somewhere?"

"I think you're strange. You got a bite."

I looked toward the bobber and saw that it had disappeared while I was thinking of crawdad boy. I jerked the pole and lifted a large bluegill to add to my stringer.

"I think we've got enough for supper. Let's go clean them," I said.

"Okay, bluegill boy. Are those gills growing on the side of your neck?" James Ernest said as I was gathering my stuff.

I reached up and touched my neck. He laughed all the way back to the house. I didn't think it was that funny.

During supper I asked if a circus was going to be coming to the area.

"Why do you ask that?" Mom questioned.

"He wants to see crawdad boy," James Ernest said.

Janie began laughing and then asked, "What's that, James Ernest?"

"It's a boy with pincher hands who likes to pinch girls," he told her.

"Oh, you mean Bobby Lee." We all laughed.

Saturday, August 25

There was a line of men on the front porch before the roosters crowed at the Tuttle farm. I opened the front door, and it was like I opened up a lid to a full nightcrawler box. Men began spilling into the store. James Ernest was gone when I woke up, and Papaw hadn't arrived yet. Mom was still in bed, I guessed.

"I ain't never seen a store that made good customers wait outside the door. I ought to go someplace else," Mud McCobb complained.

"You'd never go anywhere else. You enjoy complaining too much," I told him.

"You got that right," Louis Lewis agreed.

Fred Wilson said, "While they're arguing get me a dozen nightcrawlers and a box of chicken livers."

"I was here first," Mud yelled out.

"It doesn't matter when you get to the lake. You'll be the last to catch a fish," Sam Kendrick offered, and all of the men laughed.

"I'll bet a two-dollar bill on who catches the first fish over two pounds," Mud challenged them.

"You're on," the crowd yelled out.

Mom walked into the store as I was returning with tubs of nightcrawlers and boxes of chicken livers.

"Everyone calm down," Mom said as the place fell silent. "That's better. Good morning, gentlemen."

The men all removed their hats as if the Queen of England had walked into the store.

"I hope we didn't wake you," Fred said to the floor.

Mom took over the register as I passed out the bait to the fishermen. I knew what bait most of the fishermen wanted. They usually always got the same every time they came to fish. It was hard to teach old dogs new tricks. As I was handing out the bait Papaw walked in. A hint of sunlight was just beginning to rise over the hillside.

"I thought something important was going on with all the trucks in the lot," Papaw said as he entered.

"Are you saying we're not important?" Mud muttered.

"Important to my wallet," Papaw said, and laughed.

"Is that all we are to ya?" Mud asked.

"Pretty much," Papaw answered.

"He doesn't mean that and I don't feel that way," Mom said, flirting with the men, making them happy. Mom could tell them anything and they would slop it up like biscuits and gravy. "You guys are like family."

"Yeah, like creepy uncles," I volunteered.

The men began laughing. I looked at Mom, expecting to see her angry face, but was surprised to see a grin forming.

Before the fishermen left for the lake Louis asked, "Speaking of creepy uncles, how is Morton doing?"

"He's doing well. The doctor said yesterday that Morton may be able to come home in a few more days if all goes well. He'll stay with Corie and me for a while when he returns. I've got tobacco that needs cutting and hanging," Papaw said.

The men all laughed. The men were happy with Papaw's report. I was especially happy to hear that Uncle Morton would be back soon. I missed him.

I was worn out that evening when my head finally dropped to my pillow. It had been a long and busy day. The fishermen drove me crazy, and Mom had me doing chores between serving my so-called "creepy uncles."

"Anything new with Charley?" I asked as I leaned over the bed and looked down toward James Ernest.

"He came back to the garden this morning. He told me more about his life."

I waited and waited.

"Tell me, James Ernest. Did you fall asleep?"

"Nope. I was just thinking."

"About Charley?"

"It's really sad. His height and looks aren't his fault. A person doesn't have a say in how they're born. We could have been born just like him. He told me that he finally couldn't take the abuse any longer. The circus was doing a show in Knoxville. He could see the mountains in the distance. He said it was like they were calling him. So that night he snuck away and went into the mountains. He's lived all alone in the mountains for the last twelve years."

I tried doing the math in my head. I figured that made Charley almost forty years old.

"He told me that I'm the first person he's talked to since he left the circus. For twelve years he's been alone."

"You and him have something in common. You also went years without talking."

"Not quite the same, but kind of."

"What else did he tell you?"

"He told me that he's lived off the land all those years. He said that every once in a while a person would catch a glimpse of him. He even said he's been shot at a few times. He was even shot in the arm once."

I thought about all that James Ernest told me. I often had dreamed of being a mountain man and living in the woods. I had thought it would be cool, building a small cabin and hunting for food and living off the land, like Daniel Boone or Davy Crockett.

"Is he going to stay around here?"

"I don't know. I never asked," James Ernest said before falling asleep. I looked up at the ceiling and wondered if I was dreaming this whole thing of James Ernest being captured by an eight-foot-tall circus man and Uncle Morton having a heart attack.

Sunday, August 26

I woke up to the smell of bacon frying. My first thought was *Mamaw must be here.* I jumped down from my bed and stumbled forward and crashed into the wall. My elbow banged into the dresser. James Ernest wasn't in his bed. I was glad. He would have laughed and called me a doofus. I felt like a doofus.

I walked into the kitchen while rubbing my hurt elbow. The kitchen table was all set with dishes and a bowl of biscuits, jellies, and butter. Mamaw had eggs frying and the bacon was draining on a paper towel. Mamaw was stirring the gravy. Everything looked wonderful. Oh boy!

"Morning, Mamaw. The kitchen smells great," I said.

"Good morning, Timmy. You hungry?"

"Sure am. What's the occasion?"

"Nothing. I just thought we could use a good breakfast before church."

I agreed, and then I thought of Charley. I figured he could use a good breakfast. I walked into the store and there stood Papaw, James Ernest, and Sheriff Cane. I was surprised to see the sheriff.

James Ernest was in the middle of telling them about Charley. I listened carefully. I didn't know James Ernest was going to tell the adults about Charley.

"That's sad," Sheriff Cane finally said.

"Maybe we could get some clothes and food for Charley," I said.

"Where would you get clothes to fit an eight-foot man?" Papaw commented.

"I think we have to remember that he still captured you and locked you in a cage," Sheriff Cane said. "He can be dangerous."

"I don't think he's dangerous unless someone starts it," James Ernest told us. "He's not looking for trouble at all."

Mom came walking into the store with her best Sunday dress on, and her face and hair all made up. "Breakfast is ready," she said.

The sheriff followed us to the table. Apparently Mom and Hagar had made up. Papaw said grace and we dug in. I ate until nothing was left on the table to eat.

"You act like you haven't eaten in a month," Mamaw said.

"It's been a month since I had a good breakfast," I said as I leaned back and rubbed my full tummy. Mom shot me a dirty look. I suspect she didn't like me saying she wasn't feeding us very well. Cereal was okay, but it wasn't anything like Mamaw's cooking.

Papaw changed the subject by asking, "Is tomorrow when I'm supposed to take you guys up Devil's Creek?"

"What are you doing?" Sheriff Cane asked.

"We're taking the girls on a canoe trip down Devil's Creek tomorrow," I answered.

"That sounds like fun. Should be a good day for it," Hagar said.

"Can I go?" Janie asked

"Maybe you're not nourished enough for another canoe trip," Mom threatened. Everyone ignored Janie's question.

"I'm nourished plenty now after this meal," I said.

Mom huffed and rose from the table, grabbing her plate and coffee mug and headed for the kitchen. I was oblivious to her being insulted.

Later we pulled into the parking lot of the church. James Ernest and I rushed into the building looking for Raven and Susie. They were already sitting in a row with Randy, Purty, Rock and Tucky. Of course Susie was sitting at the end of the row next to the wall and window. I had to climb over all the legs and feet to be able to sit next to her. No one made it easy. I wondered why they didn't grow up. Of course, I would have done the same to them.

I smiled at Susie when I had finally sat down beside her. She smiled back. She was so pretty. Her freckles danced across her face as the sunlight from the window lit up her smile. "I'm so excited about the canoe trip," she said.

"What canoe trip?"

She playfully poked me in the ribs with her elbow. I heard Raven say the same thing to James Ernest. I was also ready for the canoe trip. I had really been working hard around the store and helping in the gardens a lot since coming back from the Red River canoe trip. I needed a day to have fun and there was no one I'd rather enjoy the day with than Susie.

The church filled up fast, and it wasn't long before Pastor White was opening the service in prayer. Then two women came forward and kind of sang a song. It was half dog-wailing and cow-bellowing, but the adults yelled out "Amen" when they were through.

I thought, *Amen, that's over!*

But the nightmare wasn't over. Pastor White asked Delma and Thelma and Janie to come forward and recite the verses of the day, the verses Pastor White was going to preach from. I didn't even know Janie was doing this.

Pastor White told the congregation that each of the girls would recite one verse. Delma began by slumping her head into her hands, having forgotten how the verse started. Janie went around Thelma and whispered into Delma's ear. Magically, Delma began quoting the verse. She closed her verse by saying she didn't know what it meant. Thelma was next. She cleared her throat and then started repeating the first verse. Janie shook her head and then whispered into Thelma's ear after getting her attention. Thelma started over.

When Thelma finished she said, "Delma doesn't know what that one means either."

Delma gave her sister a look of wishful death.

Janie then quoted the third verse with no problems. The church began applauding as Janie returned to her pew while

Delma and Thelma bowed to the crowd, soaking up the applause. Pastor White ended up having to gently nudge the twins off the stage.

I thought, for the pastor to be such a smart man, he sure made some bad decisions. The verses had been about taking communion. A few of the elders went forward and passed around the bits of crackers and the grape juice for those who would take communion. The pastor gave directions that everyone would take, drink, and eat at the same time.

Only those folks who had become Christians were supposed to take communion, so I passed on them. Purty grabbed the cracker and threw it into his mouth and began chewing it and then washed it down with the juice before the plate had been passed down to me. He then looked around and saw everyone still holding theirs with their heads bowed in prayer. As the plate was passed in the row behind him, he reached back and took a second helping. It was the first time I'd ever seen anyone go back for seconds at communion.

We were standing around outside the church after the service was over and Randy suggested we have a Wolf Pack meeting that evening. We ended up deciding to have one Wednesday evening at the cabin. We told them about the canoe trip, and of course Purty said he wanted to go. We all said, "no!"

His feelings got hurt, and so we explained that it was a double date, and that was why we didn't invite everyone else to go. Plus, we said we didn't have enough canoes for everyone. He seemed to be okay after that.

James Ernest went home with the Washingtons, and I went back to the store to do more chores. I went for spring water, I cleaned the banks of the lake, I swept the front porch and I waited on fishermen and customers. Whatever happened to not working on the Sabbath?

That evening I went to bed in deep anticipation for the morning to get there. James Ernest told me it would be here quick enough.

13   Canoeing

Monday, August 27

I stood in the slow current of the water watching Susie as she placed her bag in the canoe. The early-morning sun had risen in the sky high enough to shine on her freckled face which I loved so much. Her tan arms and legs glistened with the light upon them. She had on her one-piece swimsuit with blue shorts covering the bottom half.

In her tight-fitting top I couldn't help but notice that Susie had begun to change over the summer. She had curves now where she hadn't had curves before. Her whole body had changed. Before this summer, she was thin, small, and short like I was. But now she had changed into a different body, kind of like a tadpole to a frog, or a caterpillar to a butterfly. She had grown taller, as I had. I liked the change, but for some reason it scared me at the same time. But I knew she was still the prettiest girl I had ever seen.

I knew I had also changed. Mom had a full-length mirror hanging on the inside of her bedroom door. One day last week I was in her room taking a bath. It was the only place we could find privacy, so we placed the washtub in Mom's room and filled it with water. After taking my bath I stood naked in front of the mirror. I was no longer the skinny nine-year-old that I used to be. My arms and legs had muscles that I could see. I flexed my arms into a weight-lifter's pose and saw the bulging muscles pop up—maybe not bulging, but I did see muscles where it used to be just skin.

I had hair where I had never had hair before. I was getting older and stronger. Susie and I were growing up. I was now a teenager and Susie would be soon. It seemed like only yesterday when I was the weak kid who had lowered himself into the cave and gotten trapped because I wasn't strong enough to climb out.

So much had happened since then, and here I was standing in Devil's Creek ready to begin another adventure with Susie and my best friend, James Ernest, and his girlfriend, Raven. They were placing a cooler and bags filled with other stuff into the other canoe.

Papaw had driven us eight miles up Devil's Creek to where a road crossed the water. We were going to canoe back to the store. Susie had wanted to go canoeing ever since we had returned from the Wolf Pack's Red River adventure. We would only be gone for the day and it was a perfect day for it. The temperature was supposed to get into the nineties. The water and shade of the trees and cliffs would be welcome relief from the heat that had enveloped the county over the past week.

"Are you just going to stand in the water–or help us?" James Ernest cried out.

I didn't say anything. I just smiled.

"I think he's peeing in the water," Papaw told everyone.

"Is that why you're standing in the water up to your waist?" Susie asked.

"No. I'm standing here because it feels so good," I answered.

"Maybe we'uns could know how good it feels if you would help us," Raven said.

"Okay. Okay. You could just ask me to help."

I waded back to the bank and walked up to the truck and asked, "What else do we need?"

"Nothing now, we've got it all. Thanks for offering," James Ernest said in a tone that I thought sounded sarcastic.

So I added my own sarcasm by saying, "I thought you guys could manage without me."

"We could probably manage the canoe trip without you," James Ernest said.

He cut me to the bare bone. My best buddy in the whole world raggin' on me. Not really. We ragged on each other all the time—just like brothers.

"There is one positive thing you guys have going for you," Papaw offered.

"What's that?" Susie asked.

"You don't have Purty canoeing with you," Papaw told us.

We hadn't told Purty about the trip until he found out about it at church. We knew he would want to come and bring Rhonda. Rhonda would have told him no and then Purty would have been upset, so we saved him all the heartache by not telling him about the trip. At least that was how we justified it. We also decided not to bring Coty. He didn't like the water, and it wasn't a Wolf Pack trip, so we left him at the store. I did feel bad about it. He had stood there beside the truck looking up at my face in the cab window as we drove away. His brown eyes looked so sad and betrayed.

I didn't bring fishing poles. I didn't bring anything except some snacks. All I needed was a paddle—but the girls insisted on bringing a picnic lunch with food and drinks. They also brought towels to dry off with when they got wet. I had decided that boys and girls were totally different. Not in the way our bodies were made, but in every way. Never in a million years would I have thought about bringing a towel on a canoe trip.

They even brought a hairbrush, toilet paper and a book. A book! Books don't do well when they get wet.

I guess they thought we were going to paddle them down the creek while they brushed their hair, tanned themselves, and read their book in the front of the canoe. No wonder the Wolf Pack had a "no-girls" policy. But I had learned enough over the years to not say anything about the stuff they brought. Susie could have placed a chicken coop in the canoe and I wouldn't have said anything about it.

We were ready to hop into the canoes and take off. I shoved the front of the canoe into the water and told Susie she should go ahead and get in. She waded out into the water and then stepped into the canoe. I shoved it off the bank and hopped into the canoe. James Ernest and Raven did the same.

"You kids have fun. I'll see you this evening. Be careful!" Papaw yelled out as we began paddling down the creek.

Thelma and Delma began writing the eulogy for Susie's funeral when they found out Susie was going canoeing with me. I remember the stunned looks on their faces when Monie told Susie she could go. Delma began crying. Thelma looked at Delma and saw the tears, and then she began crying, although real tears never ran down her face.

"You look awfully pretty this morning," I said to Susie when she turned to look at me.

She smiled her pretty smile. Her freckles sparkled in the morning light with the sun hitting them. "Thank you. This is going to be fun."

I wanted to make my way to the front of the canoe and kiss her on the lips, but I didn't want to be the Purty on the trip and tip us over.

She turned back around and we floated down the creek. It seemed as though the forest animals had all awoken and were looking for their breakfast. Birds were flying up and down the creek, singing their songs. Turtles were basking on fallen logs already. I saw fish swimming by as we moved down the creek. Susie pointed to a doe and her fawn drinking from the creek when we floated around a bend. We saw a pair of mallard ducks swimming in the creek. They kept ducking under the water in search of food.

When the creek changed direction, the hills and cliffs would block the sunrise, and we would be in semi-darkness. The water became spooky and dark. Fog was still lifting in sections of the creek, especially where the sun hadn't burned it away. The sights were new to me. Moss-covered ledges reached out from the banks beckoning us to move closer and feel the softness of their covering. I hoped we would find one like them when it was time for our picnic.

Ferns spouted up around the large rocks and forest floor. August summer flowers speckled color into the green of the trees. I looked back to see James Ernest and Raven also taking in the beauty that surrounded us. They were no longer hiding the fact that they were boyfriend and girlfriend. When they were together they were usually holding hands—unless they were in town. Some of the stores in town still had "No Coloreds" signs on their windows.

Most of our community had decided to stop frequenting those stores and had asked Papaw and Clayton to let the owners of the stores know of the community's decision. The news left some owners flabbergasted while other owners acted as if nothing would change their minds. A few owners took the signs down.

I was so proud of the farmers and families in our little section of the county for taking such a strong stand against racism and hatred. Blind Uncle Morton had said during the decision, "You're telling me I have colored folks living around here? I've never seen any. I sure couldn't tell the difference." The community laughed, especially the Washingtons.

The creek's water was low that time of the year. It wasn't long before I had to jump from the canoe and push us through a shallow spot. I knew there would be many spots where I would have to do the same during the trip. I hopped back into the canoe and we were off floating again.

"I can't imagine what it was like to be on a four-day trip on a river," Susie said when she turned to look at me.

I stared at her when she turned around, unsure how I had such a great girlfriend. I was so happy to have Susie back as my girlfriend. I was going to try my best to not do anything stupid from then on to upset her or cause her to break up with me again. If I was down at the creek and saw girls coming I was going to hightail it out of the creek, up the bank, and back to the store. I was going to watch what I said from now on—thinking before I spoke. I was going to be the perfect boyfriend. I hoped I had gotten smarter.

I thought about what she just said about the four-day trip on Red River. Then I said, "It was great fun, but I really missed you." I figured that was what Susie would want to hear.

"But I wasn't even your girlfriend—Rock was."

I thought about that before saying anything. "Yes, but I still missed you. I thought of you a lot." It was true.

"That's sweet."

This thinking before I spoke seemed to be working.

James Ernest and Raven paddled up beside us. They both had huge grins on their faces as though they were having the time of their lives.

"Have you been canoeing before?" I asked Raven.

"No. My first time," she answered. "We just started, but I already love it."

"She's a natural," James Ernest said.

"I guess Junior told you all about his canoeing experience," I said.

"Yeah, he loved it. He said it was the best time of his life."

"It would have been the best trip ever if we hadn't met the Bottom Brothers."

"Junior said he was actually more scared he was going to have to canoe a day with Purty than he was of the Bottom Brothers," Raven told us. We all laughed.

"How many times did Purty turn his canoe over?" Susie asked.

"Probably a hundred," James Ernest exaggerated. Or maybe it wasn't an exaggeration.

The creek was small where we started and got wider as we floated along. We knew the creek flowed through the mountains and the forests of Morgan County and would not come close to a farmhouse until we were near Susie's farm. If anything bad happened it would be a long walk to find help.

We rounded a bend in the creek and Susie pointed to a tree that looked like it was bloomed out in blue flowers. I had never seen a tree like it before. The limbs stretched out over the creek. When we got closer I saw that the blue wasn't flowers at all but rather a party of blue jays. The birds began squawking as we neared and then they all flew from the tree one after the other until the sky was filled with blue on blue. There must have been a thousand of them that flew away.

We *oohed* and *aahed* at what we were seeing. I didn't know what to say. It was one of those moments that left a person speechless. What could I say to match what I had seen?

We all watched as the jays disappeared over the mountain. James Ernest then said, "Wow! That was something."

We drifted under the tree that had been filled with blue jays and looked straight up through the massive limbs

Susie said, "I could do a four-day canoe trip. This is so peaceful and fun."

I agreed, but this was nothing like the trip down the Red River. This was so much different. We floated leisurely along the moss-covered banks letting the current take us. All I did was steer with my paddle—no paddling was necessary. We didn't want the trip to end too soon so James Ernest and I took our time.

As I was staring at Susie in the front of the canoe, Bo landed on my left shoulder scaring me half to death. I would never get used to a big black bird attaching itself to me from out of the blue—no matter how many times it happened. Bo then cawed. Susie turned around and saw Bo sitting there. She smiled her beautiful smile. "Hi, Bo," she said.

"Caw!" Bo screeched into my left ear.

James Ernest and Raven quickly paddled up beside us to see Bo and say hello. Bo rocked up and down in excitement. He had probably never been canoeing before. Bo hopped down from his perch on my shoulder and landed on the gunwale of the canoe. He then began pecking on the silver sides of the aluminum canoe. After having no luck at removing the silver from the sides of the canoe, he hopped along the gunwale to the front deck and claimed the front point as his perch.

We looked like a Viking ship with a carved black crow leading our canoe down Devil's Creek. Susie reached forward and petted Bo. He seemed to like her touch as much as I did when she would hold onto my hand as we walked. I was jealous of the stupid bird.

I had never been this far up Devil's Creek before. It was pretty much what I expected it to look like: a smaller version of what the lower part of the creek looked like. It was a beautiful creek with overhanging tree limbs and shelves of rock that shot out from the creek banks above the water. Tall trees lined the banks when the tall stone walls would disappear.

We came to another shallow portion of the creek and I climbed out of the canoe and began pulling the canoe through the sand, gravel, and silt. I wasn't making much headway and Susie said, "Wait. I'll get out and help." James Ernest and Raven also had both gotten out of their canoe. Bo flew into the air. Then the canoe easily floated through the shallow water.

Before we reentered the canoe Susie walked up to me and wrapped her arms around me and gave me a big kiss. She then said, "Thank you for taking me canoeing."

I should have been thanking her for coming with me. I should have been thanking her for taking me back as her boyfriend. But all I could think to say was, "Ah, that's okay."

I looked around as we were getting back into the canoe and saw Raven and James Ernest kissing. It was the first time I had ever seen them kiss on the lips. I wondered if they kissed a lot. We canoed for around another hour and then came to a good area to stop and swim and eat lunch. A large flat rock hung out over the water and it was easy to climb onto it. We tied up the canoes and unloaded everything we needed and I quickly jumped into the creek. It wasn't but five seconds before Susie was splashing in beside me.

Raven and James Ernest joined us in the cooling water, and we splashed and dunked one another. We ended up just floating on our backs in the gentle moving water, the warm sun on our faces. The sunshine lit up Susie's freckles, dozens of beauty marks on her face. Bo perched himself high in a dead tree and watched us as we played in the creek. He would "caw" every so often as if shouting out a warning cry.

Later we sat on the flat rock eating lunch and relaxing, our legs dangling over the rock, our toes and feet in the sparkling water. Bo was walking around on the rock looking for scraps that fell from our food. We ate sandwiches, which Susie had made, tomatoes, snap peas, which Raven had picked from

James Ernest's garden—and snack cakes I had brought from the store.

"Tell me about Bigfoot," Susie said, looking at James Ernest.

"You know he's not really Bigfoot?"

"Yes, I know that much."

James Ernest went ahead and told Susie everything he knew about Charley, including his escape from the circus.

"Is he going to stay around here, or move on?" Susie asked.

James Ernest hesitated before answering, "I don't know. I honestly don't. I don't even know what would be best for him."

"I'd think staying here and having a home would be best," Raven said.

"But he's been living in the woods so long—the woods and caves are home to him," James Ernest explained.

"Have you told him he could stay?" Susie asked.

"How can I tell him that? I can't give him a home, or a place to stay, or a job."

"He could stock the highest shelves in the store," I said and laughed. The other three just looked at me. Apparently they were having a serious discussion.

"Surely there's something he could do," Susie then shot a quick look at me before finishing the sentence, "besides stock high shelves."

"He could hang tobacco without climbing into the rafters?" I offered. Again, they just stared at me. I was being serious.

"I don't know. I'm in no position to help him other than giving him some vegetables, and he won't talk with anyone else. It's really up to him," James Ernest explained.

I knew there wasn't much demand for old circus freaks or Bigfoot impersonators in Morgan County. I decided to keep it to myself, thinking maybe I should go back to thinking before speaking.

We sat in silence for a few minutes. I figured everyone else was thinking about Charley. I had begun thinking about how nice the water felt on my feet and whether there were fish under the overhanging rock.

"School starts in eight days," Raven finally blurted out.

"This will be our last year at the one-room school. It's kind of sad," Susie said.

"The high school is different, but I got used to it quickly," James Ernest told us.

"At least we won't have to put up with Purty being in the school house this year. He drove everyone crazy last year acting like he was 'the man' all year," I said. I then added, "I guess I get to be 'the man' this year."

"Especially since Bernice won't be there either," Raven said. We all laughed.

"Sadie will be lost without her," Susie added.

"You can be her best friend at school this year," I said without taking the time to think before I spoke. I was leaning over the rock edge looking for fish when Susie shoved me and I fell flat on my face in the creek water just after I had placed a snack cake into my mouth.

I could hear laughter from the rock above.

14   Bo's Hide-away

I watched the rest of the soggy snack cake float down the creek. Small fish attacked the cake as it made its way in the water. Suddenly, one big splash and the cake disappeared. I was sure it was a big old bass that engulfed it. Maybe I had accidentally found a new fish bait—banana-flip snack cakes.

The others gathered up our picnic stuff and met me at the canoes. We loaded everything and headed down the creek. I looked over to see James Ernest paddling with a Moon Pie lodged halfway in his mouth. I guessed he hadn't said anything stupid. It made me hungry for one.

The weather had warmed up and Susie was now just wearing her swimming suit. Boy! She was so pretty sitting there in the front of the canoe. I decided to tell her so.

"You sure do look pretty up there!" I said.

She turned and smiled back at me. My heart did a leap of joy seeing her smile at me like she had. Bo yelled out, "Caw," from his perch on the front of the canoe. Maybe he was agreeing with me. We drifted on down the creek past giant sycamore trees, their white bark shining like snow on the banks. Summer wildflowers grew between the rocks and crevices and hung over the edges as though trying to reach for a drink. Large ferns covered the forest floor lifting their petals as if in praise of their Creator. Everywhere I looked I saw beauty around me, and I smiled to myself.

For the next two hours we slowly floated down Devil's Creek, getting out every once in a while to cool off in the water. During one of the stops, I took advantage of it to kiss Susie. I still wasn't sure how this all worked. I mean, was I allowed to kiss her any time I wanted to since we were boyfriend and girlfriend? Or did I need to ask her if I could? Or should I kiss her only at special times? I wanted to kiss her all the time, but I figured she would get tired of that. I was as confused about that kind of stuff as a boy could be.

Another thing I wasn't sure about, where to put my hands when I was kissing her, especially when all she had on was her swimming suit? I was okay with touching her and grabbing her all over when we were dunking each other or when I was throwing her in the water or when we were wrestling. But I wasn't sure what to do with my hands when I kissed her so I just let them hang at my sides. I figured I looked like a doofus. Susie would put her arms around my neck as we kissed. Would she get upset with me if I put my hands on her bare back? I could have asked, but that seemed so dorky. So my choices were to either look like a doofus or seem like a dork.

When we were nearly two miles from the store we heard voices. Susie and I looked down the creek and saw people wading up the creek toward us. From our distance I couldn't tell who they were. I hoped it wasn't the Boys from Blaze. From behind us I heard James Ernest ask, "Who is that?"

I then recognized Purty's laugh among the people coming toward us.

"One of them is Purty," I answered.

"Is it too late to turn around and paddle back upstream?" Raven asked. We all laughed.

Bo called out, "Caw! Caw!" He then flapped his wings and flew away.

I knew that our peaceful trip was coming to an end—so much for our romantic quiet canoe trip. As they got closer I saw that Tucky was beside Purty. Behind them were Rock, Sugar Cook, and Chero. I had told myself that anytime I was in a creek and I saw girls coming toward me I would run. But this time—I couldn't very well run. I was with Susie in a canoe. We stopped paddling and floated toward them. We weren't in a hurry getting to them. Finally Purty yelled out, "We were beginning to think you guys went the other way."

What other way? There's only one way down a creek. I didn't say anything.

"Hi guys," Susie greeted them when we got to them.

Everyone greeted back.

"What brings you guys up here?" James Ernest asked.

"We came to the store to go swimming and they told us you guys were canoeing so here we are," Tucky explained as Purty tried to lift himself into our canoe.

I yelled, "What are you do-"

The canoe tipped over dumping Susie and me into the water. I was unable to finish my question. I came up and jumped onto Purty's back and threw him backwards into the creek. I began looking for a crawdad. I wanted to stick it up Purty's nose. James Ernest and Raven decided it was safer to go ahead and get out of their canoe. Everyone was standing there watching my battle with Purty. I decided to give up the battle.

"Why are you not at football practice with Randy?" I asked Purty.

"I quit."

"Why did you quit?" Raven asked. I already knew.

"They told all of us to run around the field four times. I made it half way and decided I didn't like football. So I quit."

"You made it farther than I thought you would. Half mile wasn't bad," James Ernest told him.

"I didn't realize half a lap was half a mile," Purty said.

"You mean you only ran half a lap and quit?" I questioned.

"Almost. I made it to the first curve. It was hard. I wasn't made for long-distance running," Purty explained. I had to agree with him on that fact.

Rock and Chero began asking Susie and Raven about the canoe trip and what all we had done. Purty asked if he could ride in the canoe since we weren't using it. "I'm worn out," he begged.

"Have at it," I told him. I knew if Susie and I tried to use it again, he would continue to tip it over. "Have fun turning it over."

James Ernest offered their canoe to the other girls.

"I've never canoed before," Chero said.

They got in, and James Ernest quickly explained how to steer the canoe.

"You can canoe with Purty," Susie told Tucky.

"I've served my time in a canoe with Purty on the Red River. Never again," Tucky swore.

"I'm doing better by myself anyway, jerkfaces!" Purty yelled out and then turned around to his right to look back at us. The canoe did a quick swerve to the left, and over it went, throwing Purty back into the creek water. We all laughed at him again.

The last two miles ended up being great fun. We played in the water, looked for animals and rocks and shells, made fun of Purty, and James Ernest told them all about Charley.

Bo was perched on my left shoulder as we waded the last portion of the trip. He seemed to enjoy the laughter and fuss being made all around him. Suddenly, he flew off to the high southern creek bank and disappeared into a small opening between two large rocks. I watched to see what he was up to.

"What are you looking at?" Susie asked.

I pointed toward the hole in the wall and said, "Bo flew into that opening. I was watching for him to come out."

"Let's go check it out," Susie suggested.

We splashed our way across the creek to the spot where Bo had disappeared. The others continued down the creek without us. They were watching Purty trying to get back into the canoe, which was quite a sight in itself.

The opening was two feet above our heads. I tilted my head back and called out, "Bo, Bo."

I heard Bo's familiar caw from inside what I assumed was a small cavern. Bo then poked his head outside the entrance and held a silver shoe in his beak. It took me a few seconds to recognize the thing he had stolen from Janie's doll.

"I had suspected Bo was taking silver things and stashing them. This proves it. I bet the nest is full of silver things he's taken," I said.

"Why would he take silver objects?" Susie asked. "You think he just likes shiny things?"

"Who knows why a crazy bird who sits on a person's shoulder would steal silver things and hide them in a nest. But that's what he does. He took Papaw's pocket knife. He's taken spoons, a silver dollar, and remember when he took the watch from the Boys from Blaze?"

"Oh yeah, I remember that. No telling what all he has in there," Susie said.

"I guess this is where he's been stashing the loot. He may be the richest crow in America. He's a thieving bird," I said as I grinned at Susie.

I turned away from the wall and Susie and I ran through the water trying to catch up with the gang.

Twenty minutes later we were standing in the water across the road from the store. Our trip was over. We pulled the canoes up onto the bank and we all headed toward the store. Coty was lying on the front porch. I saw his head pop up when he heard us and he quickly jumped up and ran toward me. We all gathered around Coty and petted him. Mom came out to the porch and waved to us, a smile spread across her face.

It was late afternoon and Purty and the Key kids headed to their homes. James Ernest changed clothes and Mom gave him and Raven a ride back to her farm. James Ernest wanted to check on his garden. Susie spent the rest of the afternoon with me in the store. Janie had gone with Mom and they were going to Mamaw's to help her can tomatoes and make tomato juice.

Robert Easterling came into the store and smiled when he saw us. He oinked knowing he would get laughter from me. Susie laughed and then looked at me as though I had to explain the oink. Before I could start to explain, Robert continued.

"So, how the heck are you two?" he asked. Before we could answer, not that he really wanted an answer, he continued his line of questioning, "You haven't dumped his sorry butt again? What do you see in this skinny half of a boy?" I was beginning to get insulted.

Before Susie could answer, he answered for her, "I guess he's okay. At least you don't have to worry about other girls being attracted to him. That's one thing."

I figured I was insulted again.

Before he could continue his barrage of insults, I forced my way into the one-person conversation. "What did you come in here for anyway?"

"Oh yeah, Janice sent me down for a bag of sugar, and I wanted a pop." He walked over to the cooler and slid the metal lid open. He searched inside, and his hand came out with a grape Nehi soda. He opened the bottle with the opener that was attached to the wall of the counter, and the cap fell into the metal container below. He took a big gulp, and the bottle was half empty.

"That sure is good," Robert said.

Susie gathered the bag of sugar and placed it in a paper bag. I totaled up the sugar and pop and asked, "Anything else you need, Robert?"

"No. I think that's all we need today."

Robert paid me the thirty-six cents he owed and left before insulting me again.

The rest of the evening was spent waiting on customers and fishermen. Susie went to the lake and took orders. She made way more tips than I ever did. She split them with me, a fact that I would never tell the grubby fishermen. They'd probably want my half of their tips back.

Clayton arrived around eight that evening to take Susie home. I relaxed on the couch watching the TV and the front door.

15 THE FLYING SQUIRREL

WEDNESDAY, AUGUST 29

Ever since the canoe trip with Susie I had been working at the store while Mom and Janie were at the farm helping Mamaw can the garden bounty. But finally that evening the Wolf Pack was having a meeting at the cabin. James Ernest was going to return around eight and we were going to the cabin together. Henry Junior was coming with him. Mom told me Papaw would come to the store to close up, so I could go. But I had to be back early the next morning to watch the store again. This was the last week before school started and it seemed as though my summer vacation was over.

I was working hard at the store and soon we would be helping in the fields cutting tobacco and picking corn. I loved the fall except for all the hard work. Plus I had to go back to school on Tuesday. Bummer!

I at least had the Wolf Pack meeting to look forward to. Papaw arrived around seven-thirty and Mr. Washington drove up a little later with Junior and James Ernest. Mr. Washington came into the store and sat with Papaw as the three of us went to the shed to get our tent and supplies ready for the night.

Mr. Washington offered to drive us up to the Tuttle farm. We took him up on it. The day was warm and the evening was still suffocating with the humidity and heat. I quickly called the Tuttle house to let them know we were coming up there.

Sadie answered and I quickly said, "Hello, this is Tim. May I talk to Purty or Randy?" I tried to use the phone manners I had been taught, thinking it might help.

"Why wasn't I invited to go on the canoe trip on Monday?" Sadie asked. I knew she knew the answer but I tried to appease her as best I knew how.

"It was only for James Ernest and me and our girlfriends," I answered.

"I don't think so. Todd and half of the Key backwoods clan went along," Sadie offered.

"They weren't invited either. They just happened to show up near the end," I tried to explain.

"So it's okay for me to show up during one of your lame dates," Sadie said.

"No, it is not, and my dates are not lame. Tell your brothers we're coming up to your farm. Tell them to wait for us," I said and hung up. I figured there was no way they would get that message.

I hurried out of the store and jumped over the tailgate and into the back with the others. Coty was sitting between James Ernest and Junior getting his ears rubbed. Mr. Washington drove to the Key house to see if Kenny was still there, but he had already left. When we drove into the Tuttle circular drive I saw Randy putting his backpack on as though they were leaving. Mr. Washington honked his horn and we waved.

Five minutes later the seven of us were walking across the field toward the path that led to the cabin. I heard a familiar caw just before Bo landed on my shoulder. It seemed as though everyone was going to the last meeting of the summer. Two minutes later Bo flew off and landed on Coty's back. He didn't seem to mind any longer. What a sight it was watching Coty prance along the trail with a large black crow on his back. The eight of us were a strange lot.

"How is football practice going?" James Ernest asked Randy.

"Hot and tough."

"What position are you playing?" I asked.

"I'm a linebacker on defense and a tight-end on offense," Randy told us.

"Are you going to start on both?" James Ernest asked.

"I think so, but I'm not sure yet. Our first game is next Friday against Johnson County High School."

"We'll all come and root for you," I said.

"That would be great."

I had never been to an actual football game before. My dad was never a football fan and my only exposure to football was watching the Cleveland Browns on TV and some college games. My favorite football player was Jim Brown, who was a running back for the Browns. He was great. He would get tackled and act as though he couldn't get up and take another step. But then the next play he would run over the defense again and again.

"Tell us how long you lasted again, Purty," I said.

The other guys began laughing.

"I felt bad for the other guys on the team. I didn't want to embarrass them with my awesomeness," Purty explained as we laughed. "I may try out for the wrestling team."

"If you rub some of that Brylcreem that's holding up your Mohawk all over your body, it would be like rassling a greased pig," Tucky blurted out.

With that, we all cracked up.

We made it to the cabin about a half hour before dark. We readied the camp while we still had daylight. Randy built a small campfire so we could cook. We definitely didn't need the fire for warmth.

This was our last meeting before school started. Our adventures were over for the summer of 1962. I figured we might come up with some ideas for a fall or winter adventure. The Wolf Pack meant so much to me, I didn't want it to end. I would do anything for the other members of the Pack, even die. Yes, die. They were fellow explorers. They were family. They were brothers. We had been through so much in the last two years or so—I couldn't imagine a day when we weren't anticipating our next adventure.

As the sky grew darker we began to gather around the campfire. James Ernest and Randy had placed the logs farther from the fire so we wouldn't melt from the heat.

"Where's the hotdogs?" Purty asked as he held up a bag of marshmallows after searching the packs.

"I didn't bring any. Everyone has already eaten supper," I said.

Purty whined and said, "But we always have hotdogs. I can always eat again. What's a meeting without dogs?"

"We'll have to make do with Coty," Randy said, making a joke.

"I don't want to eat Coty," Purty cried out, not quite understanding the joke.

Coty looked up at Purty and then moved closer to me, probably afraid Purty would take a bite out of him. Bo paced back and forth on one of the long logs that no one was sitting on. He seemed nervous. Coty peered out into the forest around us before lying at my feet.

"I'll have some of those marshmallows," Junior told Purty.

Purty threw the bag toward him. Junior caught the bag, ripped it open, and speared one onto his whittled stick. He then passed the bag around the fire.

"I'd like to open the meeting," Randy said as he stood and placed his right hand out in front of him. We all stood in a circle and chanted, "Wolf pack, wolf pack, wolf pack, wolf pack, wolf pack, wolf pack, wolf pack, forever the pack!" We then raised our faces to the sky and howled. We were having our meeting during a time when there was no moon. It was almost as dark as dark could be.

We took our seats and Randy began the meeting. "I think we've had a great summer. The canoe trip was really something."

"It was unbelievable," Tucky chimed in as we all agreed.

"We were able to have fun and save a girl from Zerelda, the witch that turned Purty into a toad," Randy said.

A deep croaking *ribbit* came from the direction of James Ernest. We all laughed.

"Don't forget that she turned me into a white boy," Junior said laughing.

"You should be so lucky," Purty said while sticking four marshmallows onto his stick.

"Not if she turned me into you," Junior shot back.

"Whoa! Deep shot! Hurt!" we all cried out as Junior cut Purty back.

"We've also helped in the fields, had swimming parties, a big bonfire party, and rescued James Ernest from Bigfoot. It's been a fantastic summer. But, does anyone have any thoughts about the fall or winter?" Randy threw out.

We all stared either at him or at the dancing flames before us. "Or maybe we should wait until next summer?"

"We still need to build the tree house," I said, not knowing if there was still interest in building it. We still had a pile of lumber lying in wait.

"I think that would be fun," Junior said.

No one else offered any comments on the tree house. I figured most of the guys were too big for a tree house, but I still thought it would be neat to have and spend time in. I was sure it would be fun to build.

We spent the next hour talking about past adventures and laughing and ripping on each other. Some of the guys did another kind of ripping. It was around eleven, and the laughter was dying down. Guys were getting tired.

Suddenly, out of the darkened woods, came a loud voice, "We warned you guys to stay on your side of the crick!"

We all turned toward the voice. I knew who it was. I wondered if they were going to attack us. A shot then rang out. I could hear the bullet whiz over our heads and land in a tree twenty feet from us. We all hit the ground. I hid myself behind the log I was sitting on. Bo flew off into the trees. Coty began barking at the intruders.

"This is your final warning!" Hiram yelled out. Another shot rang out with the bullet again flying over our heads. We then heard running footfalls heading up the trail toward Blaze.

I stayed behind the log as others began to retake their spots on the log. Tucky stood up and said, "C'mon, let's go get them."

"Are you crazy? They have a gun," Purty said.

It was one of the few times that I had heard Purty say something I agreed with.

Randy seconded Purty's concern, "We can't go after them in the dark with nothing to defend ourselves."

"We're going to let them get away with this?" Tucky argued.

"They're not getting away with anything. We'll get even in time," James Ernest said.

Just then something flew over our heads, and we all dove to the ground. Coty began running after it.

"What was that?" Purty yelled out.

"I don't know, but it scared me to death. Especially after having bullets fly over our heads," Junior said.

"I'm pretty sure that was a flying squirrel," James Ernest answered from behind the log he had been sitting on.

"You mean like Rocky?" Purty asked.

"What's Rocky?" Junior asked.

"Rocky is the flying squirrel on *The Rocky and Bullwinkle Show*. It's a cartoon. Bullwinkle is a big moose. Haven't you ever seen it?" I asked.

"We've never had a TV. The only time I've ever watched TV is at your house," Junior said.

"That wasn't a flying squirrel. That's made up. There's no such thing," Purty said and then laughed about it.

"You big doofus, there's flying squirrels all over Kentucky. They taste just like regular squirrels," Tucky said.

"Is there anything you haven't eaten?" I asked.

"Otter. Because you were going to cry if I'd shot one," Tucky answered.

"You're unbelievable," I said.

"Thank you," Tucky came back.

For most of us it was the first time we had actually seen a flying squirrel. Tucky was the only one to ever taste one. James Ernest later said that he had come across them while taking his night walks through the woods.

The invasion by the Boys from Blaze and the flying squirrel had livened up the meeting and now no one was ready to climb into the hot tents for sleep. We stayed up until two in the morning talking and planning and deciding what we could do to get even and be able to keep our meeting place.

I knew that our rivalry with the Boys from Blaze could really turn very ugly, like them. Someone could get seriously hurt or even killed. I didn't want that to happen. I still didn't know why we couldn't settle it with a game of wiffleball or football. Or a fishing contest?

I knew that everyone would have a hard time sleeping that night.

THURSDAY, AUGUST 30

Mom and Janie were again helping Mamaw with canning, James Ernest was making baskets with Raven, and I was home alone watching the store. I had gotten very little sleep during the night. I had tossed and turned in the tent from worry and possible heat stroke. As soon as I saw a glimpse of daylight I was out of the tent.

The other Wolf Pack members weren't far behind me as they dragged themselves from the tents, stretching and shaking, and then looking for a tree to pee on. Within a half hour we were packed and heading back to our homes. Our last meeting of the summer hadn't accomplished a whole lot.

It was that Thursday afternoon around four when I heard footsteps on the front porch. The screen door opened and in walked the boys from Blaze. I froze behind the counter. I knew this couldn't be good. They were never up to any good, and they had never before set foot inside the store that I knew of.

Last to enter was Hiram. The other four spread out as he walked between them and up to the front of the counter. He stopped at the counter and stared at me. He looked at the giant glass containers and then opened one of the big glass jars and reached inside for a gum ball.

"That's a nickel," I said.

"I thought we made ourselves clear about staying on this side of Licking Creek. Did we not?" he said as he popped the gum ball into his mouth. I decided not to say anything. Silence was golden—wasn't it?

He tried to say something else but the big gum ball muffled his words to the point that everyone just stared at him. He then spit the gum ball back into his hand. The blue color of the gum ball began coming off on the palm of his right hand. He shifted the gum ball to his left hand and wiped the blue goo on his pants. He then reached down into the rear of his pants and pulled out a handgun.

My first thought was to duck behind the counter and grab the shotgun. But I didn't. I was outnumbered five to one, and they also had at least one gun. I figured I was dead.

"Grab him!" Hiram ordered the others.

The two biggest goons came from opposite ends of the counter and grabbed me by my arms and forced me out into the open room.

Hiram got into my face and said, "I guess we have to teach you a lesson so you can let the rest of the Oak Hill gang know we mean what we say."

"I didn't know you knew enough about anything to teach anyone anything," I nervously said back to him.

He laid the gun on the counter and then socked me in the stomach as the two goons still held my arms. I slumped over and thought I might throw up. If I did, I wanted to be able to throw up in Hiram's face, so I straightened back up, just in time for him to punch me in the eye.

I then knew that I had been right. Silence was golden. Why hadn't I stayed silent? The vomit that I thought I was going to throw up had now been knocked back down my throat. I heard a whimper. I think it was me.

"So you think you're so smart, do ya!?" he yelled into my face.

I decided to go back to the silence is golden thing. I didn't answer, although I wanted to say that I was ten times smarter than he would ever be. The two big goons held me up again so Hiram could get another shot at my stomach. He twirled his arm over his head twice and then, with all his force, knocked the breath and vomit out of me. I was so bent over that the vomit came out and landed on his pants and shoes. The two goons released my arms and I fell to the floor.

At that moment I heard one of the smaller guys say, "A truck just pulled into the lot."

I had a hard time hearing anything. My ears were ringing, my stomach was tumbling, and I felt as though I was gagging as I lay on the wooden floor.

Hiram then told the others, "Let's get out of here."

The Boys from Blaze ran back through the house and out the back door to make their escape.

I yelled out the best I could, "You owe us a nickel!" I opened my eyes to see the gum ball lying on the floor in the middle of the remaining throw-up that hadn't landed on Hiram.

I heard men stomping on the wooden steps and then across the porch. The screen door opened, and I heard Fred Wilson call out, "What in the world!?"

He ran over and bent down beside me. Soon Louis Lewis and Mud McCobb were also leaning over me.

"Don't smell too good in here," Mud stated the obvious.

"Are you okay?" Fred asked as I lay there moaning.

"Who did this to you?" Louis asked. "There's no telling what we'll find when we walk into this store."

"When did this happen?" Fred asked.

"Whose gun is this?" Mud asked as he picked up the handgun that Hiram had forgotten and left behind on the counter in his hasty getaway.

Fred went into the kitchen and found a towel to wipe my face and mouth. They got me off the floor and took me to the couch in the living room where they laid me down.

"We'd better call Martin," Fred suggested.

I started to say no, but then decided not to protest. I was lying there in pain as I heard Fred's phone conversation with someone. It wasn't two minutes later that Mom, Janie, Mamaw, and Papaw were all hurrying into the store.

My eye was already swollen and turning black. My stomach ached as though I hadn't had food in a month. My head pounded in pain. I had never been beaten up like this before. The injuries I sustained from my fight on Devil's Creek with the Boys from Blaze were nothing compared to these.

"What happened, Tim?" Papaw asked.

"The Boys from Blaze came to teach me a lesson."

"What did you say to them?" Mud asked.

"I told him I didn't think he knew enough to teach anyone anything."

"That's our Timmy," Fred yelled out.

Everyone laughed and patted one another on the back.

"It's yucky in here," Janie said about the smell.

"Go into the living room," Mom told her.

I tried to explain what had happened. It was hard talking. My stomach still felt as though a flying squirrel was trying to claw its way out through my throat. Mom went to the phone and called Sheriff Cane. Mud was showing Papaw the gun that had been left behind by Hiram. Papaw was shaking his head.

Janie walked up to the couch and looked down at me lying there and said, "Why did you throw up in the store, Timmy?"

"Some guy punched me in the stomach," I answered.

"It looks like he punched you in the face also," Janie said and frowned at my face. She then asked, "Why didn't you punch him back?"

"Two other guys were holding down my arms," I told her.

"You should have kicked him," Janie said.

She was right. Why hadn't I kicked him in the gonads? Probably because I was too busy trying to catch my breath.

I've found out over the years that it's always easier to think of what I should have done after it's over. Like, I knew I shouldn't have climbed down into the cave by myself after I'd done it. And when the Key girls took turns kissing me in the creek while trying to resuscitate me, I should have stopped them. That suddenly dawned on me after Susie stomped on my stomach and I rolled back into the creek. I wondered if everyone was like me.

Ten minutes later the Perry family arrived. First ones in the door were Delma and Thelma. They saw Mamaw mopping the wood floor where I'd thrown up. They pinched their noses shut as they carefully made their way around her.

I heard Delma tell Thelma as they entered the living room, "It's too bad they didn't finish him off and put him out of his misery." Susie, Monie and Clayton were close behind.

"You're right when you're right," Thelma agreed.

They then walked over to the couch and Delma said to everyone in the room, "It looks like they rearranged his face. He's never looked better."

"But it's still not too good," Thelma followed.

The twins then continued around the couch and into the kitchen. The men in the room tried not to laugh—but not too successfully. They decided to head to the front porch, I guess so they could laugh without being in front of me.

Monie came up and shook her head side-to-side and said, "You poor child. Something is always happening to you." She then followed the twins to the kitchen leaving me alone with Susie.

I noticed that Brenda didn't even bother to come see me. Clayton had taken one look and went out with the men.

Susie sat on the couch and let me put my head on her lap. It made me feel better. I then told her what happened at the Wolf Pack meeting and about the beating I took.

"Maybe you guys should stay on this side of the creek," Susie said.

I started to argue but decided it wasn't worth the breath. I looked up into her worried face and knew an angel was holding me. Maybe I had died and gone to heaven. I just wanted to look at her. The freckled face with the soft green eyes smiled back down at me. Maybe she was right.

Sheriff Cane, mom's fiancé, walked into the store a while later. He asked me about what all happened, and I told him about both incidents, at the cabin and at the store. Papaw gave Sheriff Cane the handgun Hiram had left behind. The gun meant that he had evidence to use against the Boys from Blaze. He told us he was going to go to Blaze to round up the five boys. I also told the sheriff about Hiram taking the gumball without paying. I figured he could also charge him with burglary.

Mom was beside herself with worry. It seemed to her that no matter what she did she couldn't keep me out of danger. When she heard about the gunshots at the Wolf Pack meeting, I thought she was going to blow a gasket. I heard her tell Sheriff Cane, "What do I have to do, lock him in his room until he's twenty-one?"

I hoped it wouldn't come to that. Even though I was tired of being in danger myself, I still wanted to be able to live the life I loved. By that evening, word had spread throughout the community, and the store, rooms and porches were filled with families showing their concern.

James Ernest and Raven walked into the living room where I was sitting with Susie. He walked over and looked at my face. I saw true anger in his eyes–something I'd never seen in James Ernest.

He paced the living room. "I can't believe they did this. I'll get even," he said out loud.

Susie and I looked up at him with surprise.

"Calm down. He's okay," Susie said, trying to compose him.

He turned and left the room. I then heard clapping and laughter fill the front porch. Susie and I and Raven hurried to see what was happening. I opened the screen door and saw Uncle Morton standing beside Homer and Ruby in the parking lot, bowing to the applause. He was soaking in the response to his return. I was so happy to see him. I didn't care that I was hurting. I ran down the steps and hugged him.

"I've really missed you Uncle Morton. It's great that you're back."

"It sounds like the whole community missed me," he said through a gigantic smile.

I didn't want to tell him they hadn't gathered for his return so I said, "Everyone missed you."

I looked back to see James Ernest standing there on the porch, applauding along with the others. Raven stood beside him.

The gathering took a very sudden turn to a welcoming party for Uncle Morton. I wasn't sure if anyone knew Uncle Morton was coming home on that day or not. I hadn't been told he was. He looked like himself. He may have lost a couple of pounds, but it was hard to tell because he had a lot of pounds. He acted like himself, though, and he looked like nothing had ever happened.

The rest of the evening was a party. The women baked pies and cakes in the kitchen. Men told Uncle Morton all the big tales they could think of that he had missed. Junior then mentioned Bigfoot. Uncle Morton took a great interest in our retelling how James Ernest had been captured by Bigfoot.

"This is one of the best tall tales anyone has ever told me," Uncle Morton said.

"This is no tall tale. This is true. I was there," Susie said.

"I wouldn't expect this from you, Susie. What has happened to you since I've been gone?" Uncle Morton asked.

We laughed and laughed as Uncle Morton was filled in on all that happened while he was in the hospital. "A guy is gone for a few weeks around here, he misses a lot," he stated.

"You got that right," Junior told him.

Sheriff Cane had returned from Blaze and said he had no luck in locating the boys. The parents told him the boys were on a hunting trip and weren't sure when they would return. We knew that was a lie, unless they meant the Boys from Blaze were out hunting us.

Later that night, James Ernest and I were finally in our bunk beds. I was dead tired. It had been a long day and I was still feeling the pain from getting beaten up.

We lay there in the dark. There was no moon shining through our window. Even with my eyes open it was pitch-black inside our room. I was thinking about how good it was to have Uncle Morton back with us. I had missed him and had worried about him.

"It was really good to see Morton," James Ernest whispered in the dark.

It was almost like I was dreaming him saying it since I had just been thinking about Uncle Morton.

I leaned my head over the top bunk and whispered, "Did you say something?"

"I said it was good to see Morton back."

"Yeah."

James Ernest then asked, "What do you want to do about the Boys from Blaze?"

"What do you mean?" I asked.

"We can't let them get away with what they did to you, can we?" James Ernest said.

His comment surprised me. James Ernest was the most forgiving person I knew. He never looked for trouble or a fight.

"I was hoping Sheriff Cane would take care of it," I answered.

"He may," James Ernest said. "They just can't get away with what they did to you. I'll make sure of that."

James Ernest sounded like the big brother I'd never had, looking out for his smaller brother. I really appreciated it, but I didn't want to see more fighting. I had already decided I would stay on this side of the creek. Problem solved.

"I think we should stay on this side of the creek," I told him as I leaned over the bed.

"That won't work. We have our meetings on that side of the creek," James Ernest whispered back.

"I'll quit the Wolf Pack to stop the fighting," I said, meaning it.

"Go to sleep."

How could I sleep? My head hurt laying it on the pillow. My stomach hurt when I rolled over. I was now worried that

James Ernest would do something he shouldn't. Charley Bigfoot was outside my window somewhere, roaming around in the woods. How was a boy expected to go to sleep?

Within minutes I was sound asleep, and James Ernest slipped out the window with his rifle and was gone without my knowing.

FRIDAY, AUGUST 31

I woke up late. The sun was already shining in the window. I heard people talking inside the store. I looked down at the alarm clock on our nightstand and saw that it was nine-thirty. I couldn't believe I had slept so late. James Ernest's bed was empty. I wasn't sure if he had gone out during the night like he sometimes did and had never returned, or if he was already up and gone.

I slipped from the top bunk and put on my shorts and T-shirt and shoes and lumbered into the store. Papaw, Mamaw, and Mom were talking to Uncle Morton, Homer and Ruby, Robert Easterling, and the sheriff.

When I walked in, Robert said, "Well, if it isn't Mr. Sunshine arriving late this morning."

"Looks like something the cat dragged in," Uncle Morton added.

Ruby walked over and looked into my face and said, "That is quite a shiner."

"Looks like he was smacked with a baseball bat," Papaw told them.

"It felt like it too," I said.

"What would you like for breakfast?" Mom asked me.

This was my chance to get Mom to fix me a really good breakfast. "Biscuits and sausage gravy, home fries, and scrambled eggs," I said.

"How about either Cheerios or Sugar Pops?" Mom asked.

Mamaw came to my rescue, "I'll fix him breakfast. You stay and talk."

I followed Mamaw into the kitchen. I noticed that she had already made biscuits. She lit the burner on the stove and began making the gravy and cutting up potatoes for the home fries. I got a glass of orange juice from the fridge and watched her as she did her magic.

"Why do you think they came here to do that to you?" Mamaw asked.

"They've been mad at us ever since Russell and Silas's moonshine still was destroyed. They blame us," I explained.

"Why would they care about that?"

"They delivered the moonshine for them, so they lost out on the money they would make from the deliveries. They've been gunning for us ever since then."

"They aren't good boys," Mamaw said.

I shrugged my shoulders in agreement.

My breakfast was wonderful. Papaw's eyes lit up when he walked into the kitchen and saw what I was eating. "Looks like a breakfast for a king," he said as he grabbed a biscuit and a sausage patty.

"Where's James Ernest?" Papaw asked me after taking a big bite from his sandwich.

"I thought you would know. Did you open the store?" I asked.

"Yes. But I never saw him this morning," Papaw told me.

"He must have left during the night," I offered. I got a bad feeling in my stomach, and not because I had been punched there twice the day before.

I spent the day at home relaxing on the couch, still healing from my wounds. Papaw watched the store most of the day, and Mom went up to the lake and took orders from the fishermen. I was sure the men would rather have Mom waiting on them than me.

Tucky and Rock came to visit me toward evening. They had heard about the fight and wanted to see how I was doing. "Wow! Look at that black eye!" Tucky said as soon as he saw me on the couch. Rock quickly looked away as though the sight of my eye was gross.

"Tell us what happened," Tucky asked.

I explained what the Boys from Blaze had done and how Sheriff Cane had gone looking for them.

"That's like a headless chicken looking for corn. He's never going to find them. We'll have to get even ourselves," Tucky told me.

"I think we should do what they want. Stay away from that side of the creek," I said. "I don't want to see anyone else get hurt."

"That's going to be hard for Randy and Purty since they live on that side of the creek." Rock reasoned.

"I don't believe they count that," I said.

"Who knows what they count or even if they can count. They're ignorant people," Tucky said and then added, "I think they're just looking for a fight. If it's not that, then it will be something else."

"What do you mean?" Rock asked.

"They don't care if we're on that side of the creek. They're just looking for any reason to fight us. That's why they came to the store to beat you up—so we would come looking for revenge. And I think we should give them what they want," Tucky said. He was on a roll. This was the most I'd ever heard him say in such a short time. He seemed really upset. Everyone seemed to be more upset than I was.

I was still worried about James Ernest. We still hadn't seen him since last night. I hoped he was at the Washington's farm making baskets with Raven. Tucky and Rock left right after Tucky said, "I'm going up the see Randy and Purty. We've got to defend the Wolf Pack."

I agreed with that statement, but I also didn't want to see anyone else get hurt. I was afraid it would turn into more than just a black eye and a hurt stomach. The Boys from Blaze were a mean bunch of guys. I had to try and stop it from escalating. I went to the phone and dialed the Tuttles' phone number. Sadie, of course, answered the phone. I hung up, knowing I would never get a chance to talk to Randy or Purty.

James Ernest finally walked through the front door around nightfall. Mom had just put the 'Closed' sign on the door, and the last fisherman had pulled out of the gravel lot. Janie and I were sitting on the couch watching *The Flintstones* when James Ernest entered. He flopped onto the other end of the couch and began watching the show with us. I looked at him. I couldn't tell anything by looking at him. He was always the same.

Mom came into the room and said hello to James Ernest and then went back out to the porch where Sheriff Cane was sitting and waiting for her return. I looked up at Mom as she was saying hello to James Ernest expecting her to say something about his disappearance—but nothing. I knew what kind of trouble I'd be in if I disappeared for that length of time, and he got a friendly hello.

Later, James Ernest announced he was tired and was going to bed. I followed him into our bedroom. I climbed to the top bunk while he took off his clothes and slipped under his sheet. I didn't ask him where he had been. I figured he would tell me if he wanted me to know. I was dying to know.

I began telling him about my visit from Rock and Tucky. "Tucky is all fired up about getting revenge. He even went up to the Tuttle's house to talk them into it. I don't want someone else getting hurt."

James Ernest listened in silence. I thought maybe he had already fallen asleep.

"Are you awake?" I asked as I leaned over the top bunk.

"Yes," he said, half scaring me. I was almost sure he was asleep.

"I don't think they'll bother us anymore," James Ernest finally said.

"Why do you say that?" My first thought was, *What did he do?*

"Okay, I went to Blaze last night and paid Hiram a visit."

"You did what!" I yelled out.

Mom came to the door and said, "Are you guys okay in there?"

"Yes, we're fine," James Ernest answered.

I heard Mom walk away from the door.

"Last night I left here around midnight and walked up to Blaze. I decided I needed to talk to Hiram," James Ernest began his tale.

"I bet that went over well."

"I slipped into his bedroom."

I interrupted his story by saying, "You did what? How?"

"The back door was unlocked and all the lights were off, so I went in and made my way to where I thought his bedroom would be. But it ended up being his sister's room. I left that room and the second bedroom I checked was his and his brother's."

"You didn't really do this?" I questioned his story and his sanity.

"I woke him up."

"How did you keep him from screaming? I'd been screaming my head off and pooping my shorts."

"I don't know about his shorts, but I clamped my hand over his mouth and nose to wake him. It's amazing how quickly they wake up when they can't breathe."

I didn't know what to say, so I just listened.

"I told him, 'Don't say a word and listen. You will never bother or do anything to the Wolf Pack again, and if you ever touch Timmy again you had better get right with Jesus because it will be the last thing you ever do. We don't want trouble but we won't put up with your harassment either. I can slip in here any time I want and you will never know until it's too late. The next time I wake you in the middle of the night it won't be to warn you.' I then took out my large knife and stabbed his pillow right next to his left ear."

James Ernest had a large Bowie knife that he hung from his belt when he hiked at night, which he used to whittle handles for baskets.

"I then asked him if he understood and agreed and he nodded his head yes. I then told him I would never be back if he agreed and kept his word. He nodded yes again. I then left and went to the next house."

I was now sitting up in bed. I was shaking with excitement and fear at the same time. "I can't believe you did this. Whose house did you go to next?" I asked.

"I ended up going to all of their houses. Each one was about the same. Each one of the Boys from Blaze was scared out of his wits. I think our battle with them is over," James Ernest said.

It didn't surprise me that he was able to sneak into each bedroom without being caught. It did surprise me that he had done it. I knew he had done it for me. James Ernest was furious inside about the Boys from Blaze beating me up five on one. There were many reasons why I felt James Ernest was the coolest, neatest, smartest person I had ever met. This last thing was just another reason I felt that way.

I lay there in the dark thinking about what he had done. I couldn't imagine how frightened the Boys from Blaze were when they awoke with James Ernest's hand over their mouths. I would probably up and die if I awoke and saw Hiram standing over me in the middle of the night. Then I decided I had to be dreaming this. Surely James Ernest really hadn't snuck into five houses during the night.

I leaned over the bed to ask James Ernest if I had been asleep, but he was sound asleep.

I couldn't fall back to sleep, so I laid there awake looking out the window into the dark, hoping Hiram was fast asleep in his own bed.

17 THE PROPOSITION

It seemed the morning came as soon as I had fallen to sleep. I walked into the store due to the knocking on the front door. Sam Kendrick and Phillip Satch were banging on the door wanting bait and to pay for their fishing. I opened the door and took their abuse as they paid me. I met them on the back porch and gave them the chicken livers and night crawlers. They were sure they were missing the best fishing of the day. As I stood there watching them walk to the lake mumbling about my laziness I heard the roosters crow at the Tuttle farm. Boy, am I lazy, just beat the roosters up.

When I got back inside the store Sam Johnson and Fred Wilson were waiting for me and it started all over again. I stood in front of them with my black swollen eye and all I could hear was blah, blah, blah.

"I've got to beat Mud up to his favorite spot," Fred complained.

I told him, "He's already up there."

This made Fred almost blow his top. He looked out the front door and said, "But, but I don't see his truck."

"I'm just messing with you, like you're always messing with me," I said.

"You ain't worth a plug nickel," Fred told me.

"Maybe not, but I can out-fish Mud McCobb without stealing his favorite fishing spot," I told him. Sam Johnson began laughing. Fred started mumbling to himself. I met them on the back porch and gave them their bait. When I got back to the store I saw Papaw's green pickup truck come into the gravel lot.

He came into the store, followed closely by Mud McCobb and Louis Lewis.

"That eye is looking a lot better," Louis said, and then he and Mud laughed.

"Fred Wilson is already here, and he's taking your favorite spot."

Mud stopped laughing and I thought I heard a couple of cuss words come from his mouth as Mom entered the store. Mud turned red and took off his cap and greeted Mom. He and Louis then quickly turned, exited the store, and headed to the back porch. Papaw went to get them their bait.

"It's September now," Mom said.

"It is?" I asked.

"You'll be starting school in a couple of days."

"Don't remind me."

"You like school, don't you?" Mom said.

"Not as much as summer."

"I'd say you've had a pretty full summer. It's time to get some learning done. I want to see straight A's this year," Mom threatened. I was afraid that what she wanted and what she would see would be two different things.

Did she think she was talking to James Ernest or Susie? Straight A's, maybe straight C's. I was an average student and

I knew it. I knew I would probably get an A in arithmetic, and on the rest I struggled, which averaged to a C. Mom said I didn't apply myself. I thought I knew what that meant, but I didn't know how to do it. Although I knew how to apply my clothes and how to apply food to my mouth. I didn't know how to apply smarts to my head.

That afternoon Mom and Jane went up to help Mamaw at the farm. Papaw was still at the store. I had made many trips to the lake and back with orders from the fishermen wanting more bait and snacks and drinks. And they called me lazy! I was standing near the pop cooler when the phone rang. I hurried to pick it up hoping it was Susie wanting to do something that evening.

"Hello. This is Timmy," I said into the phone.

"Hey, we need to talk," the voice said.

I had no idea who was talking on the other end. It was a good thing he wasn't talking to Sadie or the twins. They would set him straight in a hurry about telephone manners. I even thought about it except the voice sounded somewhat familiar.

"Who is this?" I asked.

"This is Hiram."

I froze with the phone pressed against my ear. I had no idea what to say. He was definitely the last person on earth I thought would be calling me. I quickly debated whether to hang up or talk to him. I stretched the phone cord around the door frame and into the living room so Papaw wouldn't hear our conversation.

Finally I said, "Okay." I figured he meant he wanted to talk to me.

"Can you and your gang meet us tonight at the cabin where you guys always camp?"

"But that's on the western side of Licking Creek. You told us to stay out of there," I said.

"That's okay. We just want to meet and talk," Hiram said.

"What time?" I asked.

"Around nine," he answered.

"I don't know. We have church in the morning and Mom won't want me out late," I told him.

I heard him chuckle and then he abruptly stopped and said, "Whatever time works for you guys."

"How do we know this isn't an ambush or something?"

"We swear. We'll leave our guns and weapons at home. You guys do the same. We just want to talk."

"I'll have to talk to the other guys and get back to you," I told him.

"Call me back at this number." He then began rattling off his number.

I told him to wait until I had a pencil and some paper. I went into the store. Papaw gave me a look as though he knew something was going on. It was a good thing he was waiting on a customer. I wrote down Hiram's number and said, "I'll call back when I have news."

He hung up without saying bye, which I thought was rude, but what else would I expect from Hiram? I was scared about meeting the Boys from Blaze at the cabin. It didn't sound like a good idea to me. I needed to see what the others thought.

I had no way of getting in touch with everyone. James Ernest was probably at the Washingtons, and they didn't have a phone. Neither did the Key family, and I was tied up for the afternoon at the store. How was I supposed to talk to everyone?

175

I walked back into the store. Papaw was handing the customer his change. The lady thanked him and left. Papaw looked at me and asked, "Who was on the phone?"

This was a tricky situation. I never wanted to lie to Papaw, but I couldn't see where telling him the truth would be a good thing. Telling him would probably be the end of the meeting, which, I guess, could be a good thing. But if I couldn't talk to the guys there would be no meeting anyway.

"It was Hiram," I blurted out.

Papaw looked at me as though I was lying. I couldn't believe I was telling the truth either.

"What did he want?"

I told Papaw everything. I explained my dilemma. Papaw stood and listened without butting in. Did I even want to go to this meeting?

Papaw asked, "Do you want to go to this meeting?"

I shrugged my shoulders because I was truly torn as to what I wanted to do.

"Well, isn't Randy the leader of the Pack? I'd start by calling him and seeing what he wants to do. Then we'll call Betty and have her come back to the store if we need to. I'll drive you to find the other members."

Papaw was great.

I picked up the phone and dialed the Tuttles' number. A miracle happened. Sadie didn't answer the phone, Mrs. Tuttle did.

"Hi, this is Timmy."

For the next five minutes I didn't say a word as I listened to Loraine ramble on and on about anything and everything she could think of. She started out talking about me getting beaten up and went on to school starting on Tuesday and then on to how she was looking forward to the trees turning color and how early the roosters crowed that morning and on and on.

Finally she said, "It was nice of you to call. You sure don't talk much. Tell your mom I said hello."

"Mrs. Tuttle, may I talk to Randy?"

"Oh, is that why you called? You should have said something. I thought it was a little strange that you called me. I was wondering why..."

"Mrs. Tuttle," I yelled into the phone, "is Randy there?"

"Yes. He's watching *Wide World of Sports*. I can't believe that guy fell off that ski-jump thingy..."

"May I talk to him?" I screamed a little too loud.

"Of course, all you have to do is ask." I then heard her say, "Randy, it's for you."

I then explained everything to Randy. After I finished he said, "That's unbelievable."

"I agree. Should we go?"

"I think we should. We should all go together," Randy said.

"I'll make sure everyone else can come. Where should we meet?" I asked.

"Let's meet up here, and we'll leave around eight."

"I'll call you if it falls apart," I told Randy.

We hung up and Papaw took the phone and called Mom. Thirty minutes later Mom, Janie, and Mamaw walked into the store.

Mom looked at me and Papaw and asked, "So what's going on?"

I quickly looked at Papaw for help. He looked at me and then answered, "The boys are having an emergency meeting tonight and we need to tell the others about it."

I wasn't the brightest bulb in the house, but even I didn't think that was going to fly.

"What kind of emergency meeting? What's does that mean?" Mom questioned.

I was questioning it myself. I looked at Papaw again, and he looked like he was in over his head. I tried to bail him out.

"We need to have one last meeting before school starts. We're not camping out. I'll be ready for church in the morning."

"Where is this meeting going to be?"

Uh-oh! Mom knew the Boys from Blaze did not want us near the cabin. I was going to have to lie again. "We're going to have it in the barn at the Tuttles' farm." I came up with that idea at the last moment. I looked at Papaw, and he looked relieved. He was also in over his head. If this went bad he would be taking all the blame for not stopping it.

"We'll be back in a little while," I said and motioned for Papaw to follow me.

I heard Mom say, "There's something going on," as we walked down the porch steps.

We first drove to the Washington farm. We found James Ernest, Raven and Junior in his garden. They were picking some late-blooming vegetables from his second crop. We all stood around the bed of the truck as I explained to them what was going on. I figured I might as well tell Raven because I knew James Ernest shared everything with her anyway.

Raven didn't like the thought of us meeting with the Boys from Blaze at the cabin in the dark. I wasn't crazy about the idea either, but I kept it to myself. It was four-thirty then. James Ernest said he and Junior would be back at the store by seven. He said if Junior wasn't allowed to go we would go without him.

We next drove to the Key clan's house. When Papaw turned into the driveway Mr. Buck Key came out of the house followed by the entire clan. It reminded me all these clowns climbing out of a small car on TV I'd seem once. They just kept coming, one after another. It was hard to believe so many had been inside. Papaw got out and made his way to the filled porch as I motioned for Tucky.

"What's up?"

I explained what was going on.

"You want me to bring my big brothers, Monk and Chuck? They don't mind a good fight."

"No. Hopefully there won't be any fighting."

"Then why are we going? Don't we owe them a good whupping after what they did to you?" Tucky said.

"We're hoping to just talk things out, I think."

"That doesn't sound like much fun," Tucky said.

"We're to leave from the Tuttle's at eight. Are you in?" I asked.

"Of course I'm in. Wolf Pack forever!" he screamed out.

Everyone on the porch looked toward him. He was dancing around like a crazed cow on loco weed.

Papaw and I made a hasty retreat and backed out the driveway. "That is one strange family," Papaw said.

"You don't know the half of it," I said.

18 THE MEETING

SATURDAY EVENING

We were all standing together in the side yard at a quarter till eight. We had no idea how the night would turn out. Junior was allowed to come. He was going to spend the night with James Ernest and me and go to church with us the next morning, if there was a next morning for us. I reminded the guys again that we were not supposed to have any weapons with us. Everyone nodded in agreement. Coty was roaming near the weeds sniffing for rabbits. Bo was perched high in a tree near the barn.

The mood was heavy as we began our walk to the cabin. Generally we would be joking and laughing, that evening we walked in silence. Even Purty was staring at his feet as we hiked. The sun had already dipped below the mountain and the twilight gray washed over me.

I stopped. "Maybe we should forget about doing this," I interrupted the silence. The other five turned mid-stride and looked back at me.

"I mean, maybe this… this isn't such a good idea. What if something really bad happens? What if they're setting us up for a surprise attack?" I asked.

"Do you really think they're going to attack us?" Junior asked.

"We'll just have to whup them like we did the last time," Purty said.

"But this time sitting on them may not work, Purty. They could be armed," I said.

Purty lifted his arms and flexed them, showing off his muscles, which were almost non-existent, and said, "I'm armed with these guns." He looked at his biceps—which were very disappointing. The rest of us began laughing, breaking the solemn mood.

"Nothing to worry about then," James Ernest said as he turned back around and continued the walk to the cabin.

We followed.

By the time we made it to the old logging trail I was ready to throw up. My stomach was doing flip-flops; I felt stuff coming up to my throat. I was trying my best not to let it explode. We turned left and walked toward the small trail that would then lead to the cabin. I had walked this trail many times, usually with joy and excitement, anticipation of a club meeting, or the beginning of an adventure, never with such dread and trepidation as I felt that evening.

It wasn't long before we had made it to the path. We turned right and slowed our pace, not that we were hurrying to our appointment. I felt like a turtle crossing the road while looking for a speeding truck that was racing to crush him. Bo flew down and landed on my shoulder. I nearly jumped out of my skin. Bo spread his wings trying to balance himself from my jump of fright.

The temperature was dropping. No one else was at the cabin when we finally arrived. Randy and James Ernest quickly built a fire so we wouldn't be in complete darkness.

The six of us gathered around the fire and sat on the logs while we waited for the Boys from Blaze to arrive. I was praying they wouldn't come. The dark eyes of Bo the crow shone bright with the reflection of the fire. Coty settled by my feet. No one spoke. I listened to the wood crack in the flames and I heard an owl hoot nearby. Tree frogs and crickets were singing their nature songs.

I was staring into the fire and suddenly sensed movement ahead of me. I looked up to see a figure standing about twenty feet from the fire. The other five saw my head jerk, and they looked toward the person. One by one, other boys began to appear around us. I recognized Hiram to my right. He was standing behind Purty. I then saw the boy I had fought with above Devil's Creek. He was at least a foot taller than he was then.

"We didn't think you guys would really show up," Hiram finally spoke. "We figured you were chicken."

I then noticed that one of the Boys from Blaze was holding a hoe handle in his hands. I looked at another one and saw what looked like a gun in his hand.

"You said no weapons," I yelled out.

Before I finished with the sentence all five of the boys pulled out weapons of some kind. "You're a liar," I yelled at Hiram.

Before I knew it Randy, James Ernest, and Tucky pulled rifles out from under the logs they were sitting on and slowly stood. My mouth fell open. Where did the guns come from?

I heaved vomit into the fire. The flames bounced and sizzled from my explosion.

"Looks like I'm not the only liar," Hiram coolly said back.

"You called for the meeting," Randy said as he stood and faced Hiram.

Purty and Junior slowly stood also. I was leaning over the fire, expecting a second eruption.

"Coming into our homes in the middle of the night wasn't okay," Hiram stated while the other four shouted in agreement.

"You ruined my favorite pillowcase when you stabbed it," one of the boys said.

"Duct tape should fix it," James Ernest told him.

"You trying to be smart?" Hiram said.

"A pillowcase is a small price to pay for coming into the store and ganging up on one guy. Cowardly is what I'd call it," James Ernest said.

Our other Wolf Pack members had not been told about James Ernest's visits to their houses in the middle of the night. They looked at Hiram and James Ernest, wondering what they were talking about.

"Well, we are all here now," Hiram said. "This doesn't seem very cowardly."

"Except you came with weapons," Randy told them.

"Kind of looks like you did too," Hiram said back.

"Only after we saw yours. We knew not to trust you," Randy countered.

I figured it was a fine time to let me know we were bringing weapons. Here I sat with my only weapon being a crow while others had guns, clubs, and rifles. Didn't quite seem like a fair fight.

"We could end up hurting each other or even killing a few guys. I propose we put the weapons down and come to some kind of agreement," James Ernest suggested.

"I feel lucky," Hiram stated.

"Luck isn't getting what you want. It's surviving what you don't want—and you don't want to do this," James Ernest told him.

I could see everyone thinking about that. Most everyone was trying to piece together what it meant.

Purty quickly sat back down and his log began shaking. He was shivering with fright. The mention of people dying was all he could take. I had never seen a person shake so much. He looked like a human tambourine.

Unexpectedly, out of the woods, walked another figure. "Before anyone starts shooting anyone else, I think you should put down the guns and talk." His jaw was cockeyed, and his face looked mangled, but I knew who it was—Billy Taulbee—the worse fisherman in the world, the person who kidnapped Susie and me.

Coty began running toward Billy and barking. Hiram raised his rifle and I shouted, "No, Coty, come here." Coty stopped and growled at Billy. "Come on, Coty." He reluctantly turned and came back to me.

The Boys from Blaze then lowered their guns and other weapons and Randy told them to come take a seat. Randy, James Ernest, and Tucky put their weapons back under the logs. The Wolf Pack sat on the north and east side of the fire while the Boys from Blaze sat on the south and west.

Billy Taulbee sat with the Boys from Blaze, showing where his allegiance was.

"You start," Randy said looking at Hiram.

Our gang looked like a band of Indians. We all still had our Mohawks. They looked like mountain folk, with unwashed long hair. The older boys had some form of hair on their faces. The scene looked like a powwow in the old West—perhaps getting ready to sign a treaty or go to war.

Hiram began, "You guys started this feud when you came up on the mountain looking for the moonshine still."

"The only reason we were up there was to find a way into the cave on the rock wall. We would never have known anything about the still if you hadn't trapped us inside the cave," James Ernest explained.

"Russell and Silas told us you were sent up there by the sheriff to snoop around and find the still," another of the boys said.

"We didn't know anything about the still until that day," I said.

"We told the sheriff about the still after you guys followed Russell's directions and tried to kill us," Randy chimed in.

"We didn't care nothing about the moonshine still," Purty said after he had calmed down once the weapons were put down. "We were just up there on an adventure. We just wanted to see if it was a cave."

"Was it?" one of the other younger Boys from Blaze asked.

"Yeah, it had all kinds of caves going into other caves. It was really neat, except for the getting trapped in there by you guys," Purty told them.

"Wow," was all the kid said after Purty described it.

We all looked at one another, waiting for someone to bring up some other offense.

A kid with long shaggy hair reached into the pocket of his t-shirt and pulled out a pack of cigarettes. I noticed that they were the same brand that my dad had smoked, unfiltered Camels. He took one from the pack and passed the pack on to the next Boy from Blaze who did the same. Four of the five boys began lighting up their cigarettes. Hiram then looked around and asked if we wanted one. We all shook our heads no.

"You guys too good to smoke or something?" one of their gang members asked.

"It's a club rule," I said while looking into the flames of the fire.

The kid laughed and said, "You have a rule that you can't smoke? Don't you guys raise tobacco?" He laughed again and then added, "I guess we could never join your club."

I thought, *That's not the only reason you can't join.*

One of the other Boys from Blaze then asked, "Why do you have a colored boy with you?"

The other four boys leaned over and around the fire to look closer at Junior. "He is a Negro boy," Hiram said. "Why is he here?"

"I thought the kid just had a dark tan from working in the tobacco fields," another boy said.

"He's a member of the Wolf Pack. He's our friend," I said. I then stood and added, "You got a problem with that!?" I was upset. Here we were defending ourselves to the Boys from Blaze when we hadn't done anything wrong, and now they were questioning why Junior was one of my best friends. I had had enough.

"Hey! Okay, okay! We don't have a problem with that. My family is Jewish and we get treated badly also, especially when I was younger. I got no problem with him. I actually like you guys better now," Hiram told us.

He surprised me. I slowly sat back down.

We all looked at each other for a couple of minutes.

"What else?" Randy asked.

"What's the Wolf Pack?" one of the boys asked.

James Ernest answered, "It's a club we formed to do things together. We voted Randy as the Leader of the Pack. We have meetings and plan big adventures each summer and just do things together. We have seven members including Coty. Checking out the cave above Devil's Creek was one of our adventures."

"What else have you guys done?" another of the boys asked.

"We've been on a two-day hike. We found a treasure chest in a cave once. We went on a four-day canoe trip on the Red River this past summer. We try to do fun things," Randy told them.

The Boys from Blaze looked jealous as they thought about our adventures. Apparently all they had done was fight with others and deliver moonshine.

"You should start your own club," Purty offered.

I saw a couple of them nod their heads in agreement.

"We could challenge each other to wiffle-ball and football games," I suggested, which was what I'd always wanted to do to settle our differences instead of pointing weapons at one another.

A minute later I looked at Billy Taulbee and said, "The police have been looking for you."

"I know. I've been holed up, hiding. Are you going to tell them you saw me?"

"I don't know. The sheriff is becoming my stepfather. It's tough keeping things from him."

"Your mother is marrying the sheriff?" Hiram said and laughed. The other Boys from Blaze laughed along with him.

"He's a good man," I told them, taking up for my future father.

"I couldn't imagine a worse thing happening to a boy," Hiram stated.

I wanted to jump up and hit him, but I didn't. I sat there and gave him a mean look. He finally looked away and laughed again.

"I'm tired of hiding out," Billy told us, changing the subject.

"Come turn yourself in. I don't think you'll have to do as much time as Silas and Russell. You tried to save my life. I've told them that. That means something," I said.

"You told them about that?"

"I did."

"You still have your whole life ahead of you, Billy. You don't want to hide out your entire life," James Ernest told him.

The Boys from Blaze seemed to be getting more comfortable around the campfire. Billy Taulbee came over and sat next to me. I didn't know why I always ended up feeling sorry for him. He had done nothing but be mean to me, make fun of me, lie to me, kidnap me and Susie, but I always ended up feeling sorry for him. Perhaps it was because he was such an idiot. Maybe it was because he couldn't catch a fish if his life depended on it.

Bo had been perched high in a tree during the meeting. With everyone seated he decided it was safe to swoop down and land on my shoulder. Billy Taulbee must have been scared half to death, because he stumbled off the log and ended up lying next to the fire. He looked up at Bo with fire in his eyes, which was only the reflection of the flames on his eyeballs.

"Caw! Caw!" Bo called out at Billy's disturbance. Bo's dark eyes stared at Billy as he scrambled off the ground and found a new sitting place as far away from the bird as possible. Coty looked at Billy as if he was annoyed at being disturbed by Billy's antics. The Wolf Pack and the Boys from Blaze joined together in laughing at Billy.

We talked for another thirty minutes before ending the meeting. They never apologized for the things they had done, but at least they didn't shoot us. We ended up shaking hands and agreeing to stop our feud. I knew we would never be good friends with the Boys from Blaze, their lifestyles were just too different from ours, but at least we went away better understanding each group.

The Wolf Pack walked back to the Tuttle farm in the dark. I felt as though the meeting had been a great success. We had finally settled things with the Boys from Blaze and hopefully we would have no further problems with them. Billy Taulbee said he would consider turning himself in. It was almost midnight before we entered the barnyard. The back porch light came on, and Loraine came out on the porch dressed in her nightgown with big pink rollers in her hair.

"I couldn't get a wink of sleep knowing you boys were out on this dark night. I heard coyotes howling and had all kind of images jumping around in my brain. You boys had better head on home. Is everyone okay? I certainly hope so. I sure hope your meeting was worth keeping me up till all hours. Forest has been in bed for hours. He could sleep through a hurricane, not that we have hurricanes in these parts, but if we did, he would sleep right through it."

Randy and Todd made their way around Mrs. Tuttle and into the house. The rest of us began walking around the house toward the lane. Loraine was still talking as we faded out of sight in the darkness, heading for home.

19 TRICKED

SUNDAY, SEPTEMBER 2

Mom woke us up for breakfast. I was asleep on the floor. I had given my top bunk to Junior. I heard Mamaw's voice as I dressed and then realized she was fixing breakfast when my nose picked out the aroma of frying bacon. I hurried into the kitchen and hugged Mamaw as I looked at the table filled with eggs and bacon and biscuits. A bowl of home fries was surrounded by jars of jams and milk and orange juice.

"Better wake up the others," Mamaw told me as I stared at the morning feast.

I hurried back into the bedroom and said, "Mamaw fixed breakfast."

James Ernest and Junior knew what that meant. They both jumped from their beds and quickly dressed and then headed for the outhouse. They paused in the kitchen to look at the table filled with breakfast goodies.

Within minutes the three of us were seated at the table. Janie and Papaw soon joined us to eat. Papaw said the morning prayer, thanking God for the food. I was thanking Mamaw. Mamaw and Mom went to watch the store while we ate. They would eat as soon as Papaw finished.

We three boys lingered at the table eating biscuits filled with jellies and jams and butter.

"How did your meeting go?" Mom asked, after Papaw took over the store.

"It went well," I quickly answered.

"Any problems or surprises?" Mom questioned.

Why was Mom asking us these questions? I tried to evade them the best I could and then Junior spoke without thinking, "Billy Taulbee being there was a surprise."

I wanted to bury my head or get away as soon as possible. I jumped up and turned from the table.

"Get back here!" Mom ordered.

Junior covered his face with his napkin. I wanted to cover his face with a pillow. I walked backward to my chair and took a seat.

"You guys saw Billy Taulbee and failed to mention it to us?" Mom stated. I wasn't sure if she wanted a response or not. It wasn't long before I knew for sure. "Answer, now!"

"I forgot about it this morning with all the good food. I'm not used to getting such a good breakfast, and Billy Taulbee slipped my mind," I said.

"It may be your last breakfast!" Mom yelled out. I slunk down into my chair. James Ernest and Junior did the same. It was actually hard to even see Junior's Mohawk; he was so far under the table.

Papaw entered the kitchen when he heard Billy's name. He stood and looked at the three of us slunk down into our chairs. "Is there pig grease on those chairs?"

Mom was standing over us. I guess she was trying to think of what she was going to yell next.

She looked at Papaw and said, "They saw Billy Taulbee at their meeting last night and just happened to forget to mention it to us."

"What was Billy doing there?" Papaw asked.

"He came to the meeting with the Boys from Blaze," I told them.

I thought Mom's head was going to pop off. Her face turned a darker shade of bright red. She was pulling on her hair. "Your meeting was with the Boys from Blaze? The same kids who have tried to kill you and then beat you up here in our store!"

It seemed like a great time to keep quiet.

"I think we became friends," Junior almost whispered from under the table.

"You've got to me shucking me. That's all you boys need—friends like them. Next thing I'll know, you'll be delivering liquor and kidnapping kids. What is wrong with you guys? James Ernest! I trust you to know better!" Mom almost shouted.

Mamaw kept silent. She stood in the doorway and wrung her apron in her hands. I wondered what she was thinking. She always told me I was a good boy. I wondered if she still thought that.

"We need to tell Sheriff Cane that you boys saw Billy Taulbee. He's still an outlaw. What did he say?" Papaw asked.

"He said he was thinking about turning himself in. We told him he should. Billy said he was tired of hiding. If you tell the sheriff we might lose the trust we gained with the Boys from Blaze," I answered.

"I can't believe the words I hear coming out of your mouth, Timothy Allen!"

I knew when Mom was really upset. Any time she used my full name I was in deep doo-doo. Janie had been in the living room watching TV, and she stuck her head into the kitchen, Mom pointed at her, and she quickly turned around and left.

"Go get ready for church. We leave in fifteen minutes. Apparently you boys need it a lot more than I thought."

I had never been so happy to get away from a table. When we got to the bedroom Junior looked at me and said, "Sorry, Timmy. I wasn't thinking when I said Billy's name."

"Don't worry about it," I told him.

We three were sitting in the backseat of the car waiting for Mom when the fifteen minutes were up. Mom and Mamaw and Janie slid into the front seats and we were off to church. We found the rest of the gang in our usual wooden pews. The church was crowded that Sunday. Miss Rebecca sat next to Mom, who was sitting with Sheriff Cane. Henry and Coal sat with Clayton and Monie. Uncle Morton was in a pew with Uncle Homer, Aunt Ruby, Robert, and Janice.

The Tuttle clan took up a pew near the rear of the church. This was the first Sunday I had ever seen their whole family at church. Janie was sitting with Delma and Thelma. Rhonda and her parents walked into the church at the last minute. Rhonda squeezed in between Susie and Raven. Elmer and Mary found seats near the front. It seemed as though there were always empty seats near the front.

Pastor White began the service by singing an old Shaker song. He explained the meaning of the song before he sang it. It was really neat. Susie was invited to come forward and recite the day's verses. This was a surprise. Susie calmly stood and made her way down the pew and onto the platform. I noticed that no one tried to trip her or keep her from going up.

She said, "Acts 26, verses 14 to 18." I knew she was doomed. No one could recite that many verses in front of people. She began the verses. "And when we were all fallen to the earth, I heard a voice speaking unto me, and saying in the Hebrew tongue, Saul, Saul, why persecutes thou me? It is hard for thee to kick against the pricks.

"And I said, Who art thou, Lord? And he said, I am Jesus whom thou persecutes.

"But rise, and stand upon thy feet: for I have appeared unto thee for this purpose, to make thee a minister and a witness both of these things which thou hast seen, and of those things in which I will appear unto thee;

"Delivering thee from the people, and from the Gentiles, unto whom now I send thee,

"To open their eyes, and to turn them from darkness to light, and from the power of Satan unto God, that they may receive forgiveness of sins, and the inheritance among them which are sanctified by faith that is in me."

Susie stopped and then walked off the stage. One by one the congregation began to applaud. Never had a kid recited verses in front of the church with such perfect diction and so accurately. At least I figured it was perfect. I remember what a moronic idiot I was when I tried saying verses and how I ended up saying God loved turds.

I sat up straighter as Susie retook her seat next to me. This was my girlfriend, the one who was perfect.

Pastor White proceeded to preach on Saul and the forgiveness of sins. I held hands with Susie during the sermon, therefore, I didn't quite hear everything the preacher said.

The forty-five minute sermon flew by, and then the pastor quoted a few more verses from Matthew Chapter 6.

He began, "After this manner therefore pray ye: Our Father which art in heaven, Hallowed be thy name.

"Thy kingdom come. Thy will be done on earth, as it is in heaven.

"Give us this day our daily bread.

"And forgive us our debts, as we forgive our debtors.

"And lead us not into temptation, but deliver us from evil: For thine is the kingdom, and the power, and the glory, forever, Amen.

"For if ye forgive men their trespasses, your heavenly Father will also forgive you:

"But if ye forgive not men their trespasses, neither will your Father forgive your trespasses."

Pastor White then asked the congregation if there was anyone who needed forgiveness that Sunday. He asked the people if there was someone there who needed to ask forgiveness of another person. He said now was a good time to do it. A woman whom I had never seen before went forward, and then a couple of people approached others in the church. I figured they were asking them for forgiveness. The service was just about over when it happened.

When I say it happened, I mean *it* happened. The front doors flew open to the church, and in walked Billy Taulbee. He stood by the open doors as everyone turned to look at the intruder. Tears were flowing down his face. Some folks in the church didn't have any idea who he was. I knew who he was and I was wondering what he was up to. Was he going to rob the church? Was he going to kidnap a few more people?

"I want that forgiveness!" Billy Taulbee screamed out, almost falling to his knees.

Pastor White remained calm. He stood on the platform and asked, "What forgiveness are you looking for, Billy?"

"All of it," he answered from his mangled face. "I want God to forgive me of my sin and wicked ways. I want everyone to forgive me for all that I've done. I want Susie to forgive me for kidnapping her." The congregation moaned in recognition of who this man was. "I want to beg forgiveness from Timmy, who fed me when I was hungry, who has been nothing but nice to me while I mistreated him and also kidnapped him."

"Come forward then," Pastor White told him.

Billy took a step and then said, "Is it true? Will God really forgive me of everything I've done?"

"He will if you confess your sins and believe in your heart that Jesus loves you and you turn from those sins," the pastor answered.

Most of the congregation stared in disbelief that this was happening. It was like the best movie a person could ever watch. The tension was so high that I was gripping the back of the pew as I watched the scene unfold.

Billy took another step toward the front and asked, "But will Timmy and Susie and Martin forgive me? Will the Washington family forgive me for burning down their home?"

Henry Washington stood and said, "Billy, if you're truly sorry, and I believes you are, then me and my family forgive you. God will do the same for you."

"Thank you," Billy Taulbee cried out.

Susie turned and looked at me. Did she want me to stand and forgive Billy Taulbee? I looked at her face. She was almost pleading with her eyes. I turned and looked at Billy. He then turned his head and saw me.

He walked on up the aisle and continued looking at me. He never stopped looking. "Please forgive me, Timmy. I'm so sorry." He began blubbering.

The congregation's eyes were on me. What else could I possibly do?

"I forgive you, Billy," I said. I didn't really mean it, but I figured I didn't have much of a choice but to say I did. Susie and I almost died because of him!

Billy dropped to the floor and wept. The pastor and Clayton helped him up and forward to the front where Billy asked God to forgive him amid the blubbering.

The pastor closed the service with prayer and most of the congregation went forward to greet and meet Billy Taulbee. Most of them didn't know he was also the worse fisherman in the world, not that it really mattered. The last to greet Billy was Sheriff Cane. He took a pair of handcuffs from his pocket and placed Billy's hands behind his back.

"Wait, wait!" Billy cried out. "I thought I was forgiven. What are you doing?"

"Well, Billy, the congregation and God may have forgiven you, but you still owe a debt to society. The law works differently," Sheriff Cane told him.

"But I was forgiven! This was a trick! Y'all tricked me!" Billy cried out as the sheriff walked him down the aisle. "Y'all done went and tricked me! Y'all are dirty polecats."

I can't say I was sad to see Billy taken away in handcuffs. I was sad to see how stupid he still was.

By two o'clock that afternoon the store, porch, and house was full of people wanting to talk about the church happenings. No one had ever seen such a thing. Even folks who didn't attend the morning service had heard about it and came to get a firsthand replay of the event.

Uncle Morton told of a service he had attended. "When I was a teenager, a middle-aged woman barged into the middle of the service and began confessing all her dirty, wicked sins out loud to everyone in attendance. The older women in the church were gasping and holding hankies in front of their faces and a few of the men slid down in their seats, afraid she might begin pointing a finger or naming names of the men whom she had sinned with."

The men on the porch laughed and slapped their thighs as Uncle Morton told the story.

Papaw told of one church service where a man stood up in the middle of a sermon and told the preacher he had it all wrong. "He yelled out that there was no heaven or hell because he had died two years earlier and recently had come back to life. After going on for nearly ten minutes, the deacons of the church had to lead the man out of the church and straight to a hospital. The man was nuttier than a hickory tree."

The only other time I had ever seen church interrupted was when Bo began rapping on the church window.

Sheriff Cane arrived later that day and told everyone that Billy Taulbee had been released because the county judge felt he wasn't a threat to society, and Billy agreed to show up for court on Tuesday. By the look on his face, Sheriff Cane didn't seem very happy with the decision.

"You won't see that boy again," Papaw said.

"He's probably already up in the mountains hiding in a cave," Sheriff Cane echoed.

James Ernest and I were still in trouble for not telling Mom about the meeting with the Boys from Blaze and about seeing Billy Taulbee. We were told by Mom that we could do nothing with the Wolf Pack for the next month. It didn't seem like much of a punishment since school was starting on Tuesday, and the Wolf Pack had nothing planned coming up. We had had a full summer of adventure and probably needed a break anyway.

I was kinda looking forward to school starting and getting to see Susie every day. I loved the autumn season and the changing color of the leaves. The maples and oaks of Morgan County lit up the countryside. The heat of the summer would fade away, and the fields would lie empty for the next six months. It was a good time for hunting, fishing, harvest celebrations, going on picnics, and having long walks with Susie.

Labor Day–Monday, September 3

Monday morning started early as fishermen banged on the front door. again before the roosters crowed. I jumped out of bed and was followed by James Ernest. I opened the door and the men began complaining and bellyaching about the usual things–how I was the laziest boy in the county and that I wasn't adding their total correctly, among other things.

"If the service here is so bad, why don't you guys go fish somewhere else?"

"Now that's no way to be, Timmy," Mud McCobb cried out.

"Geez, we were just teasing you," Louis Lewis followed.

"Touchy, touchy, this morning," Fred Wilson said.

"Well, all you guys do is complain about everything. Why don't you ever say 'good morning', or 'how are you doing?' You could thank me for getting up so early so you can fish."

"Okay. We understand your protest. I meant to say, good morning, Timmy. It sure is nice of you to let us give you our hard-earned money so we can be honored to fish in your lake," Fred Wilson said and then tipped his cap toward me.

James Ernest began snickering.

Louis Lewis walked toward the counter and bowed to me and said, "I beg your forgiveness. Would you honor me by letting me pay for the opportunity to fish in thou pond and a dozen of your perky royal nightcrawlers?"

"This is a lot better," I said, and then laughed along with everyone else in the store.

I then told them, "We're closing today at four because it's Labor Day. I'll come up before then to see if you need anything."

"Hopefully, we'll be long gone by then with a stringer full of catfish," Mud said.

"You may be gone, but I doubt you'll have a stringer full of fish," I teased him.

"See there, we were being all nice and everything and then you say hurtful things. I ain't never been to no such place no how," Mud rambled.

We were going to the Washington farm to celebrate Labor Day. It was the first time the Washingtons had invited everyone to their home for a party. Most everyone in the community was going to be there.

I heard Mom say that Coal was as nervous as chickens with a fox in the henhouse, but she was also excited to have her friends over.

James Ernest left the store around ten to go help the Washingtons ready their place for the party. I was busy all day with customers, taking orders at the lake, and doing chores that Mom kept finding for me to do. At three-thirty I made my last trip to the lake to tell all the fishermen we were closing and that it was their last chance to order anything. The lake was crowded with men and families, and it took over thirty minutes to take their orders and then another forty-five minutes to fill the orders and deliver the orders back to them.

We ended up not making it to the Washington's farm until after five o'clock. Coty jumped in the car and went with us. We were the last to arrive. Susie came running up to the car when Mom drove up.

"I'm glad you finally arrived," she said as she kissed me on the cheek.

We helped Mom with her covered dishes and then ran to find the other kids. They were back by the barn playing games. All the Wolf Pack members were there. Tucky and Rock had come for the party, but not the rest of their family, even though they had all been invited. They stayed to themselves mostly.

It wasn't long before the dinner bell rang and we made our way to the house. Pastor White said the blessing and Uncle Morton said a few words about how thankful he was to be out of the hospital and among his many friends. Then we ate.

There was plenty of fried chicken, ham, mashed potatoes, side dishes, collard greens, and black-eyed peas. A card table was put up to hold all the desserts. I spotted the cherry dumplings and the coconut pie.

The Washington home had furniture that was as nice as our furniture. Not that our furniture was fancy or all that new. The home was so much different from the house they had lived in that had been burnt down. They had a dining table with matching chairs now. They even had a new small TV with rabbit ears in the living room.

I couldn't imagine a nicer family than the Washingtons. They loved their community and church, and they all seemed so friendly and sweet. It was hard to think of the community without them.

Pastor White and Miss Rebecca stood during the meal and got everyone's attention by saying they had an announcement. I was afraid that the pastor was moving to a bigger church. Pastor White began, "We wanted our friends to be the first to know that we're expecting a new member in our family."

"I'm pregnant!" Miss Rebecca shouted out.

The crowd began shouting and applauding their big news.

"It's about time," Robert Easterling yelled out.

Folks laughed.

I heard Monie tell Mom, "It wouldn't have taken me that long."

Mom covered her face and laughed. Mom then rushed over to Miss Rebecca and they hugged.

After the excitement of the news and the eating was over and I was stuffed to the gills with cherry dumplings, Junior told us kids that he had something to show us. He led us back to the barn and opened the doors and led us inside to one of the cribs. I heard a whining cry as we neared. Inside a large cardboard box was the cutest beagle puppy I had ever seen. The girls began *oohing* and *aahing* at its sight. I almost did the same. Junior opened the crib door and went inside and picked up the crying pup. It soon was licking Junior's face and its tail was wagging as fast as an electric fan.

The pup was mostly black and white with brown spots above his eyes and on its paws. Its mouth was surrounded with white, making his black nose stand out. His chest and belly were white with gray spots, and his swishing tail was solid white.

"He's so cute," Susie said, stating the obvious.

"What did you name him?" I asked.

"James," Junior answered.

"That's a silly name for a dog," Tucky poked fun.

"We named him after James Ernest," Samantha explained and added, "And it is not a silly name."

"It's a fine name," Raven said.

"I was just shucking you. James is a name meant for a dog," Tucky said and laughed along with everyone else as we looked toward James Ernest.

"I think he should be called 'Sir James'. James is the name of royalty," James Ernest said.

"Dog royalty," Purty said.

Coty jumped up on Junior and tried to sniff James. Junior then put James on the ground, and Coty sniffed every part of

James and then looked up at us as though he had given his okay. He trotted off with James following right behind. Coty spent the rest of the day playing and wrestling with James when the younger kids weren't dragging James from place to place, showing him off.

Later that evening I saw James Ernest's pet deer standing by his garden. I hadn't seen it for a few days and wondered where it had gone. I took Susie's hand and led her over to the deer. The deer raised her head and watched us come toward her. She slowly walked toward us. We petted her for a while as the sun began to set. I looked toward the house and noticed that some of the families were beginning to pack up to leave.

We were turning to return to the house to say our goodbyes when, suddenly, I heard a voice call out from the woods, "Timmy, Timmy."

Susie and I stopped in our tracks and turned toward the voice. There I saw Charley standing under the shadows of the trees, holding something in his arms.

"Charley," I said in response.

Susie and I ran toward him. Susie was careful to stay behind me. She still had never met Charley and thus didn't trust him. As I got nearer, I could see that Charley was carrying a body in his huge arms. Susie stopped completely when she saw it. I slowed and walked toward him.

"I found him around a mile from here at his campsite. He was already dead. I didn't know what to do, so I brought him here," Charley explained.

The shadows were still keeping me from getting a good look at the body. When I finally got to within five feet of Charley, I looked into the ashen face and knew who the cold, dead body belonged to—Billy Taulbee.

"That's Billy Taulbee," I said out loud.

Susie screamed when she heard what I said. The crowd at the house stopped what they were doing and looked our way.

"I need to leave this body and go," Charley said anxiously.

"But you didn't do anything wrong," I reasoned. "You need to tell them where you found him. If you run the sheriff will think you killed him."

"I didn't kill him," Charley said. His face had a frightened look, and his body was twitching with panic. "I can't let all these people see me."

The crowd was coming toward us. Men and kids were running. I quickly looked into the woods and told Charley, "Hide behind those rocks over there, and I'll have the sheriff come alone to talk to you."

"You and James come with him," Charley said.

"I promise."

Charley shook his head up and down and hurriedly left after laying Billy Taulbee's body on the ground. I stood above the body of Billy Taulbee and wondered how his life had gone so wrong. It was hard to imagine that this was Billy Taulbee. We had just seen him at the meeting, and at church, and had talked to him.

I couldn't help but look at the body and feel a bit of sorrow for him. Despite the hateful and mean things he had said and done to Papaw and me, despite burning down the Washington home, and despite him kidnapping Susie and me at the store, I still had wanted him to turn his life around. I knew he had had a rough childhood and life, but not all kids who had gone through the same things as he did ended up doing the things he had done, or ended up lying dead at the edge of the woods.

James Ernest, Randy and Tucky were the first to arrive. They stood above the body and stared down at it. Sheriff Cane and Clayton arrived next. The sheriff looked at Clayton and said, "Send the kids and women back to the house."

Clayton quickly turned and motioned for everyone to stop and turn around. Purty ran through the crowd and finally made it to where we all stood.

"Jeepers, that's Billy Taulbee. Is he dead?" Purty said, although he was nearly out of breath himself.

We all stared at the body for what seemed like minutes. The sheriff then asked someone to go get something to cover up the body. James Ernest turned and ran toward the house. Papaw and Henry Washington walked up and looked down at the body. If anyone should have been happier other than me of Billy's death it would have been Henry Washington. Billy had burned down his home and almost killed his children.

But Henry looked down at his body and prayerfully said, "God, be merciful on this child." He then had tears flow from his eyes.

My future stepfather asked me and Susie, "Did you two find the body here?"

"Charley brought him here. He said he found him dead at Billy's campsite," I explained.

"Where is he now?"

"I can lead you to him. He didn't want everyone to see him."

"Take me to him," the sheriff told me.

I saw James Ernest running back with a blanket to cover the body.

"I think we should take James Ernest with us. We probably need a light. It's dark in there. Or maybe if we send everyone back to the house, he'll come to us," I suggested.

Sheriff Cane asked everyone else to go back to the house and asked Papaw to tell the others about Billy Taulbee.

They left me, James Ernest, and Sheriff Cane standing at the edge of the woods in the twilight. I then called out, "Charley, Charley, come on out. The others have left. It's just the sheriff, James Ernest, and me. The sheriff just wants to ask you a few questions."

James Ernest added, "You can trust him. He's a good man."

We then saw movement as Charley moved from behind the rocks. He looked like a monster in the darkened shadows of the twilight and woods. As he neared, I saw Sheriff Cane move backwards a couple of steps at the sight of the large figure approaching. Charley moved toward us until he was at the edge of the tree line.

"Charley, this is Sheriff Hagar Cane. This is Charley," James Ernest said to Hagar.

The sheriff offered his hand to shake. Charley ignored it.

Sheriff Cane asked him about finding the body, where he found it, what he did when he found it, and why he brought the body here.

Charley answered all the questions in as few words as possible.

"Can you lead us to the spot you found the body?" Sheriff Cane asked.

"Yes, when it's light," Charley replied.

"Do you have any idea what killed him?"

"He choked to death. His face was blue."

"How do you think he choked?" the sheriff asked.

"On a fish bone. There was a partly-eaten fish lying at his feet," Charley answered.

Could it possibly be true that Billy Taulbee, the worst fisherman in the world, had finally caught a fish and cooked it to eat, only to choke to death on one of its bones?

21 No Signs of Love

Charley agreed to lead the sheriff to the spot of Billy's camp the next morning. I really wanted to go along but knew I would have to go to school the next day.

The porch light was on, and everyone stood on the front porch, carrying on and speculating on Billy Taulbee's reason of death in the glow of the porch light. The guests had delayed going home due to the body being found. I found it hard to believe that Billy had caught a fish. I thought maybe someone had felt sorry for him and had given him a fish to eat. Apparently, they should have also filleted it for him to get rid of the bones.

Sheriff Cane addressed the crowd. "I guess everyone knows that the body is that of Billy Taulbee. I'll investigate further in the morning."

"God bless his sorry soul," Mamaw said.

"Another dead body and it's not Timmy," Delma said out loud.

"You would think sooner or later. It's another sad day," Thelma added.

"I don't want to hear nary 'nother word out of ary one of you two. Have some respect for the dead," Monie scolded.

Monie was so upset at the girls' lack of respect that she slipped right into her upbringing country talk.

I was kind of upset that the twins wanted me dead so bad. Maybe I should start sleeping with one eye open.

I looked toward Billy Taulbee lying there at the edge of the woods. He wouldn't be going to the West Liberty courthouse Tuesday morning. He wouldn't ever try to catch another fish. He wouldn't ever crack another corny joke. All that was left was going to the funeral home. I wondered if there would even be a funeral service for him. As far as I knew he didn't have any family and hardly any friends, unless you could count the Boys from Blaze as friends. But I knew they wouldn't go to his funeral.

I knew there was or had been some good in Billy Taulbee. I believed there was some good in everyone. I also believed there was some bad in everyone. I figured a person had to decide which one to get in cahoots with—the good or the bad.

Sheriff Cane and Clayton took the police cruiser over to where the body lay. In the dark I watched them load the body into the back-seat of the car. Sheriff Cane's car pulled away, and Clayton walked back to the house as folks finally broke up and headed home.

I was standing next to Susie. I reached for her hand. She turned her head toward me and said, "I can't believe he's dead, even though I saw his body."

"I know what you mean. We just saw him yesterday at church. He's definitely a person we'll never forget."

"See you at school tomorrow," she said as she leaned over and kissed me.

"Okay," I said.

211

She ran to the pickup and jumped into the truck bed.

⌒

When we got home, we each had to take a bath since we were going to school the next morning. Janie was starting school. She would be going to first grade the next morning and she was so excited. It was all she had been talking about all week. She actually thought it would be fun. Silly kid.

It was nearly eleven by the time we settled into the bunk beds. The bed felt good after the long day. I knew the morning would come soon, but I was bug-eyed due to Charley finding Billy's body.

"It's going to be different at school without any of you guys there," I said.

"Tucky will be there," James Ernest said.

"When he comes, or if he comes."

"Junior will be there."

"Oh, yeah."

"Susie will be there."

"That's the best thing about going."

"You're supposed to be going so Miss Holbrook can teach you some book learnin', you moron."

"Oh yeah," I said as I drifted off to sleep.

Tuesday, September 4

I lay there on the top bunk and stared up at the ceiling. I saw way off in the distance a soft glow past the ceiling, the roof, and the mountains. It came closer slowly and even slower. It drifted through the roof and the ceiling and hovered above me like an angel. The glow became a flowing gown whose face was covered by its hood. The hood slid off, and Billy Taulbee's glowing face looked down at me. His face didn't smile or frown at me. It just looked at me and then began circling around my bed as another glow took his place. Its hood slid off and the Tattoo Man stared at me before joining Billy Taulbee in the circle. I then noticed the glowing bodies began stacking up one after the other. Some I knew, and others I wasn't sure of. The ones I knew were people who had died during my life. One hood slid off, and it was Mrs. Robbins, and she smiled at me. The others didn't.

They all circled near the ceiling, continuing to look down at me, never taking their eyes off me. The last glow finally faced me, and the hood slid off. I screamed and began crying. Staring down at me was my dad. The man whom I had needed in my childhood but who decided that alcohol was more important to him than his son, the man who had abandoned me more times than I could remember, the man who felt I wasn't worth his time. His face stared down at me with no expression, kind of like in real life.

James Ernest had hold of me and was shaking me with all his might. Mom and Janie were in the room as Mom tried to calm me down. I was still screaming and the tears were flowing as they had never flowed from my eyes before. I couldn't stop crying.

"It's a nightmare, Timmy. You're okay," Mom was saying as I continued to cry.

James Ernest had stopped shaking me and he now was bent down holding onto Janie, who was crying, unsure what was happening to her brother. Slowly, I began to calm. I could still remember the images on the ceiling. They were still in

my mind. I could close my eyes, and they would reappear–
Billy Taulbee, the Tattoo Man, Mrs. Robbins, and my dad.

Mom had me slide off my bed and go into the kitchen.
She had Janie go back to bed. It was nearly five o'clock in the
morning. She poured me a glass of cold water from the fridge.
I took a drink.

James Ernest patted me on the shoulder and went back
to bed.

"Are you okay now?" Mom asked.

"I think so," I answered.

"That was your worst nightmare."

I swallowed hard and didn't say anything.

"You want to talk about it?" Mom asked.

I took another small drink and said, "I don't
understand Dad."

Mom looked stunned that I had brought up my dad.
"What don't you understand?"

"Why he didn't like me. Why he never had time for me.
Why he hated me," I said as I began to cry again.

Even at my young age, I knew Mom was at a loss for
words. How could she convince a son that his dad loved him
when there had been no signs of love? She probably wasn't
even convinced that he had loved her. Maybe she had the
same doubts. Until that moment I had never thought that
before. Sitting there at that table I was now sure that Mom
had the same feelings I did. She had been neglected and left
to fend for herself while he spent days and weeks on long
drinking binges. She felt just as unloved by him as I did. I was
sure of it.

I stood and wrapped by arms around my mother's neck and we both cried and sobbed, remembering the hurt we were left with. There were no real answers. We could say that Dad was addicted to alcohol, or that the demons had hold of him. But those were not real answers. I would never know how my father truly felt because he never told us. I could only go by his actions.

After a while, when the crying subsided, I then told Mom about the nightmare and whose faces I saw. She shook as she got chills up her spine when I told her the names. We sat at the table and talked about Dad and his demons, until Mom got up and began making breakfast. She fried sausage and bacon and made gravy while I cracked eggs and began scrambling them. We had never before fixed a meal together. When it was nearly ready, I went to get James Ernest and Janie up for school and told them we had a big breakfast. We feasted.

22 Good-bye to a Friend

Papaw came to the store early to take us to school. He walked into the kitchen and saw the breakfast. He started to say something but decided to leave well enough alone.

Janie rode in the front seat with Papaw and I rode in the pickup's bed. We drove to the Key house to pick up Tucky and Rock. When we got there Tucky and Rock came out followed by Chero and Adore. Adore got in the cab with Janie and the rest hopped into the back with me. I was happy to see more of the kids coming to school with us.

This would be my and Susie's last year at the one-room school. I loved the school and knew I would miss it. One thing I wouldn't miss this year was Bernice "the Skunk" Strunck. She was now going to high school with Purty. Our eighth grade in the one room school was the largest class of the eight. There was myself, Susie, Sadie, Daniel "Sugarspoon" Sugarman, Raven, Rhonda Blair, Kenny "Tucky" Key, and Rock Key. There were eight of us in the class.

Janie was in the first grade with Mark Daniel Washington and Trudy Tuttle. Sadie tried her best to get in with the other girls in our grade since Bernice was no longer there, but by the end of the first recess she was talking with Carma Delight, who was in the seventh grade.

By the end of the day Miss Holbrook looked like she was going to pull her hair out. It was enough having Delma and Thelma correcting everyone to their way of thinking—right or wrong—but you throw in Bobby Lee and Billy Tuttle, and most of us wanted to follow Miss Holbrook's lead.

Janie thought the whole day was quite entertaining. She loved school. Just before the end of the school day, Miss Holbrook gave out an envelope to the oldest child of each family represented. "Give the letter to your parents when you get home. Do not forget! And don't open the letter under any circumstances," Miss Holbrook demanded. Well, she might as well have written **"Open Now!"** across the front of the envelope after saying that.

As soon as we got out of the building and in the gravel parking lot kids began opening the letters. Delma and Thelma were going around shouting at everyone that they were not doing as instructed. I heard Sadie say, "Good riddance." Susie, Raven, and I hadn't opened ours yet, but Sugarspoon ran over to us and announced, "They're closing the school. This is the last year for Oak Hills School."

Susie and I looked at each other. The twins heard what he said and they starting bawling as Clayton drove into the school lot. I looked around and saw other kids crying, and others were laughing at the kids who were crying and calling them names like "cry-baby" or "blubber nose."

I took a seat in the back of Clayton's pickup with Susie and the Key kids. Janie and the twins were up front crying. Janie was having a sympathy cry with Delma and Thelma. I didn't say much. I would be in the last class to graduate from the one-room school. Most adults knew that it was only time before the school closed, but no one knew it would be this soon. One-room schools were closing all over the state.

Some parents took the news hard. Mrs. Tuttle called Mom and complained for fifteen straight minutes without taking a break. Mom simply told Janie that next year she would be going to a nicer school. The closing didn't affect me in any way since next year I would be going to high school anyway.

A little later Sheriff Cane drove into the gravel lot and had James Ernest in the cruiser with him. The sheriff had picked up James Ernest at the high school as it was letting out and wanted to talk to him on the way to the store about Charley.

Sheriff Cane told us that indeed Billy Taulbee had choked to death on a big fish bone that had wedged in his throat. The medical examiner confirmed it. Charley had taken Sheriff Cane to Billy's campsite, and they found the leftover bones lying on the ground next to the fire pit. He said it looked as though animals had eaten most of the fish. Sheriff Cane had asked James Ernest what all he knew about Charley. James Ernest told him everything he knew.

Sheriff Cane was concerned because Charley had locked James Ernest up in a cave and worried that Charley might be a danger to other community members. Of course James Ernest took up for Charley, and I really didn't believe he would harm anyone else, but I understood the sheriff's concerns.

Papaw was watching the store, so I fell onto the couch to relax. It had been a long day, and I was tired. Within minutes I was sound asleep. Two hours later Mom woke me up because supper was ready. We had meatloaf, mashed potatoes and peas. Janie talked the whole time about her first day at school and how much fun it was. I knew Janie would be a good student and maybe even graduate from college one day.

I was lying on the top bunk later that night. James Ernest was below me. I wasn't very sleepy after getting a two-hour nap, and I was a bit afraid to go back to sleep. I sure didn't want to have the same nightmare as the night before.

James Ernest pulled himself up to where our faces were staring into each other and he said, "I'm going to find Charley. Do you want to come?

"It's a school night."

"I know, but it might be my only chance."

"But it's a school night."

"Quit saying that. I'm going. Do whatever you want."

James Ernest slipped his pants and shirt on quietly, and I climbed down from the top bunk and began pulling on my clothes. The window was already open. James quickly took the screen out, and we slipped out of the window. He slid the window most of the way down to where Bo couldn't get in. James Ernest led the way up to the lake. Coty heard us and came running. Within minutes we were around the lake and headed up the stream. I had my flashlight in my hand, but James Ernest led the way without one.

"It's a school night. Mom will ground us forever if she catches us gone."

"You can tell her I kidnapped you and made you go along."

"Why do you have to see Charley tonight?"

"I want to say goodbye."

"What do you mean?"

He didn't answer my question. He just kept plowing along in the dark as though he had done this a thousand times before, and maybe he had.

WEDNESDAY, SEPTEMBER 5

It was now past midnight and we were almost at Charley's cave. I looked around the entrance and saw no sign of Charley. James Ernest entered the cave and, not really wanting to, I followed. Coty was right at my heels. We followed the cave back to the end. As James Ernest got deeper into the cave, he called out, "Charley, Charley."

Suddenly, my flashlight shut off, and we were pitched into total darkness. I felt something rubbing against my leg. I wanted to scream like Purty, but I held it together as I shook the flashlight until it came back on. "Thank you, God," I said. I then aimed the beam of light on my leg to see what was against it. It was only Coty. Apparently he was as scared as I was.

We made it back to where the wooden cage had been, and I shined the light further back into the cave and saw two yellow eyes peering back at us. I knew for sure it wasn't Charley. The growl in front of me sounded nothing like Charley. It also sounded nothing like him from behind me as I turned and ran as fast as I could through the cave to the entrance. Coty was right beside me, and hopefully James Ernest was behind me. Not that I wanted him to get caught, but better him than me.

He had a better fighting chance than I did. Yeah, that was what I thought.

The three of us burst through the entrance and ran on down the trail until we felt safe, not that I felt safe at any point since I had left my top bunk.

From out of the darkness I heard, "I see you met Gar."

I couldn't stop gasping for breath. "Who is Gar?" James Ernest asked.

"I found him in a trap a few days ago over on the other side of the creek and rescued him. He's a wolf. Unsure how he got to Kentucky, but he's taken a liking to me," Charley explained.

"That happens when you save an animal's life," James Ernest said.

"He couldn't chase you. I've got him tied up. What are you two doing here in the middle of the night?"

"I was worried that you may be leaving the area," James Ernest told him.

"I am."

"But why?" I asked.

"When people die, other people want someone to blame. I feel I'm that someone."

"They confirmed that Billy died like you said. There's no reason to leave," I reasoned.

"You guys have been great friends. The best I've had, but it's best for me to move on," Charley said.

James Ernest walked over to him and shook his hand and told him, "Be safe, and know that you have friends here if you ever need us." He then gave him a piece of paper. "Our phone number, if you ever need help."

Charley walked over to me and shook my hand. His hand swallowed my hand. It was like me shaking hands with a sparrow. Charley reached down and patted Coty on his head.

"Take care," James Ernest said.

Charley turned away and headed toward his cave. James Ernest headed back down the trail that led us here. I still didn't understand why Charley was leaving. The sheriff knew

221

he didn't kill Billy Taulbee. To me there was no reason why he had to go. It wasn't until years later that I began to understand his leaving.

James Ernest and I walked in silence as we made our way back to our beds. Later I was lying there staring up at the ceiling and thinking about the giant of a man whom we had mistaken as Bigfoot. He was a man who had been used and mistreated due to his lot in life, a man who now had two friends who loved and cared about him and would miss him—and isn't that all that we really want in this life, love and friendship?

I looked up at that ceiling and thought of all the love I had found in Morgan County. I had my family, my grandparents, my mom, my sister, and now, James Ernest, my brother. I had the Wolf Pack. I loved them all. I had my relatives who lived in the area, Homer and Ruby, Robert and Janice, Tammy, Dana and pretty Idell. I had my many friends at school and in the community. I had Uncle Morton—one of my favorite people on earth. I had Susie and her family, not including the twins, Delma and Thelma. I wasn't sure about Brenda. Did she still see me as the weird little kid?

I had the many fishermen as my friends—Mud, Louie, Fred and others. I had the Washington family and the Key family and the Tuttle family. I was rich in friends and love. I would never need more.

I knew that I had lost one friend whom I'd never see again. I was sure I would never see Charley again. I'm not sure he counted me as a friend, but I did, and it saddened me a little to know that he felt as though he needed to leave. In time I would learn that he and James Ernest knew best. There in the dark I wished him the best.

As scared and upset as I was when I had awoke from the nightmare last night, I was now calm and happy as I drifted off to sleep this night. I dreamed of Susie and her purty face.

23 JUST LIVE YOUR LIFE GOOD

That school year at the one-room school was the most boring and aggravating since I had moved back to Kentucky. Purty was at the high school. The twins were belittling me every moment of every day. I was told I had to set a good example. The only good thing was Susie. I got to be with her every day. The winter was long and cold. I couldn't wait for spring and then summer to come. I was so looking forward to the Wolf Pack's next adventure, but little did I know that the Wolf Pack would never be the same.

Randy took a summer job in town. Plus, he was involved in sports, so he gave up being the Leader of the Pack, to which James Ernest was elected. But James Ernest also was working so much on area farms and making baskets and trying to save money to go to college after high school that he seldom had time for meetings and no time for long adventures. Purty, Tucky, Junior, and I did a few small things in the area, but it was never the same. By the end of the summer the Wolf Pack adventures were over, even though we still called ourselves the Wolf Pack–once a member, forever the Pack!

Everything was changing that year. The Beatles became the hottest thing around. Susie and the other girls loved John, Paul, George and Ringo. On November 22, 1963 I was sitting in my new high school when we heard the news that President John F. Kennedy had been shot in Dallas. The lady teachers cried. Classmates cried. My mom cried.

Vietnam began in 1963, although it was just news on the TV and radio. The government didn't send troops until 1965. Monk and Chuck Key both volunteered in 1964 and were both sent to Vietnam in 1965. Monk was killed in battle later that year. Chuck was badly wounded and sent home in 1966.

After graduation Randy was drafted into the Marines and served a year in Vietnam. He came home missing his left arm and his hearing in his left ear. The war games I played in the woods and our fights with the Boys from Blaze and the bootleggers were turning into real-life battles in the jungles of Vietnam.

James Ernest graduated from high school and spent the next four years at Berea College in Berea, Kentucky, and therefore avoided the draft. Mom, Janie, and I attended his graduation. He was going to teach.

I was drafted into the Army in 1969 and lucked out by being sent to Germany instead of Vietnam.

Back in my junior year of high school I was sitting in my classroom when Mom suddenly appeared at the classroom door. I knew something bad had happened. I walked through the door and was hit with a ton of bricks when Mom told me that Papaw had a heart attack and died that morning. I wrapped my arms around Mom and cried. It took all the strength I had to be able to walk out of the building and get into the car. The man who had shown me how to be a man, the man who had been a true father to me, the man who had taught me right from wrong, how to fish, to catch a baseball, to enjoy life, and so many other things had died so suddenly and unexpectedly. My world suddenly turned upside down.

Only around a month later my dear Uncle Morton also died suddenly. He was my confidant, my moral compass, my friend, and my direction. I was devastated again. The only thing that got me through those days was that I knew I would one day stand in heaven with both of them, and we would talk of our days in Morgan County. I had gone forward and accepted Christ as my Savior one day at an altar call at church. I knew that in my heart I had accepted Jesus years before, but I wanted to make it official so everyone else knew. I was baptized by Pastor White at the same spot that Mom had gone under the waters next to the bridge.

James Ernest, Tucky, and I were the first in our families to graduate from high school. I was so proud of Tucky as we stood there throwing our caps into the air. Tucky became my closest friend after James Ernest went off to college. We shared so much of our teenage years together through high school. We, along with Junior, drove the gravel roads together. We hunted for squirrels, rabbits, and deer every fall and winter. We tried out for high school sports teams together.

The Washington kids had a hard time in high school. The 1960s were filled with civil-rights unrest. Battles raged in our nation between blacks and whites, especially in the south. They had to endure name-calling, bullying, and abuse in the halls of the school. The school body was divided in their support of the kids. James Ernest, Tucky, Purty and I did our best to diffuse any trouble.

Raven ended up leaving the school in the middle of her junior year because a group of boys had threatened her with unspeakable acts. She couldn't take the abuse any longer. Susie was so mad she also wanted to quit high school. Raven got her high school diploma later in the 1970s.

During October of our senior year, Susie and I took a picnic basket and went hiking to find the 'butterfly field' with Coty by our side. Bo had long ago disappeared for good. I missed him. I believe he left during my sorrow when Papaw and Uncle Morton died. I hadn't noticed for a long time. During the summer between my junior and senior years, I went back to the spot of Bo's stash. I found our missing items including the watch, silver dollar, and pocket knife. It was amazing all the shiny things Bo had collected over time.

Susie and I settled on the flat rock and spread out a blanket and opened the picnic basket. The flowers were mostly past, except for the few fall flowers that still held their blooms. But the colors of the maples and oaks were as bright and beautiful as any fall I had ever seen. The meadow was outlined with reds, yellows, oranges, and greens. I could hardly take in all the beauty. I then looked at Susie and the colors of the fall faded in comparison to the beauty who sat there before me.

Susie had grown in shape and beauty. No longer was she the cute girl with freckles and strawberry-blonde pigtails. No longer was I craving to have her lift a rock that might produce a crawdad. I was now craving the lady that small girl had become—a lady of great charm and beauty. She was a person whom everyone respected.

"I miss them," I said quietly as I took a bite of the sandwich.

"Who do you miss?"

"The Wolf Pack days."

"There were some dangerous times during those days."

"But the days were filled with anticipation and excitement. The guys were such special guys. It was almost as though those adventures were getting us ready for the war and the civil-rights movement and the disappointment and pain that come during a lifetime–except, those days were filled with happiness and fun."

"It wasn't much fun being kidnapped."

"Looking back now–it was."

"Sure, but at the time I was terrified."

"Remember when I peed on Billy Taulbee's hands?"

We both laughed as we did when it had just happened.

"I also remember when we were hidden under the rock ledge in Licking Creek with Silas on top of it, looking for us. I was shaking with fright," Susie added.

"The Wolf Pack really did save our lives that day," I said.

"James Ernest never stopped looking for us."

"He's always been my hero," I said. "I miss him."

"He's doing well at college. He'll be back."

I finished my sandwich and stretched out on the rock, placing my head on Susie's lap. I looked up at the heavenly blue sky. Susie leaned down and kissed me on the lips.

"I also had Papaw and Uncle Morton during those years," I added.

"I know you miss them terribly."

"I do. I don't want to let them down. I can't disappoint them."

"What do you mean?"

"They believed I was being tested for something great in my life. But I'm just a normal guy. They believed in me."

"They still do. I think they're still watching over you. You can't let them down. Just live your life good."

I don't believe any wiser words were ever spoken than those five words Susie spoke that day. 'Just live your life good.' I took those words and applied them to my heart. I wanted to live my life well. I didn't want to look back when I became an old man and think that I had wasted my days and years. Also, I wanted to be good. I wanted to be the type of man about whom others would say, "He's a good man."

We heard commotion and saw a large buck and three deer run into the field. We sat motionless, watching as the deer pranced for the buck. The birds sang as the butterflies and dragonflies circled our heads.

24 THE REUNION

After talking to Susie about having a reunion of the Wolf Pack and friends from our youth, she spent the next few months finding addresses and phone numbers and tracking down everyone. She sent out invitations. She explained that she hadn't put RSVP on the invites because she wanted to be surprised by all who'd show up.

We decided to have the reunion at the farm under the eight tall oak trees that still stood off the front of Mamaw and Papaw's old farmhouse. The weather that morning was perfect. The day reminded me of the October day that Susie and I spent years ago in that butterfly field.

As I helped ready the place for the reunion, I couldn't help but wonder what some of the people I hadn't seen in years would look like. I also wondered if anyone would come. I did know that those who still lived in the area would be there, but would others come from around the state and out of state? The reunion was to begin at noon; it was now eleven.

I heard crunching gravel at the top of the hill and saw the car of James Ernest and Raven descend the hill toward the house. James Ernest and Raven had married after he graduated from college–amid great controversy. They still lived on the farm that Coal and Henry had lived on. James Ernest had begun teaching in Morgan County, and quite a few parents were very upset when it was learned he was marrying a black girl. The thing that saved him was the love his students had for him. He has since taught fourth, fifth and sixth grade kids every year. Raven went to college after James Ernest began teaching and also became a teacher. They had a wonderful life together, and we remained as brothers. They had three children, two beautiful girls, Emily Sparrow and Erin Crow, and a boy, Eddie Hawk.

I met the car as it parked at the side of the barn. I hugged Raven and punched James Ernest on the arm. I then helped them carry dishes of food toward the house.

"Where's your wife?" Raven asked.

"She's not going to be here. Sickness," I said and smiled.

Just then the kitchen screen door opened, and Susie came out onto the porch with a huge smile on her face.

Raven gave me a mean look and said, "There she is, you scoundrel."

"Must have been a miracle," I said and laughed.

Susie married me the June of our high school graduation. We raised five kids, three girls and two boys, on the farm where Papaw died. Two of our girls were twins. We tried our best to keep them as far away from Delma and Thelma as possible. Our oldest child was a boy whom we named, Martin Clay. He ended up marrying James Ernest and Raven's oldest daughter, Emily Sparrow. They gave us three beautiful grandchildren that the four of us took turns spoiling.

Mamaw lived with us on the farm until she died years later. After her death we tore the old farmhouse down and built a bigger home for our growing family.

Mom and Hagar were married and later moved to West Liberty after I graduated from high school. They were so happy together.

Next to arrive from Lexington was Randy. He was alone. His wife died of cancer five years earlier. Randy had owned a sports and outdoor store in Lexington since his return from Vietnam. It was a job he could do with only one arm. James Ernest and I both hugged Randy in greeting. It was good to see him. We had stayed in touch over the years and visited every so often.

"I brought an Apple Stack Cake. An old-fashioned bakery down the street still makes them," Randy told us.

"Looks great," James Ernest said.

"As long as it's not potato waffles I'm okay with it," I said, and all three of us laughed.

Following closely behind was Todd Tuttle. He drove all the way up to the trees in his new silver Lexus. I was sure glad to see Purty. What kind of reunion could we have without him?

He stepped out of the car and gave a big smile. "How do you like it?" he asked, pointing to the car.

"I like you better," I told him and hugged him.

Purty became a music-video producer in the 1970s. He had also dabbled in the movie business at times. He lived in Nashville with his third wife. The women seemed to like his money a lot more than they liked his weirdness. But the weirdness was what made him great at his job to earn the money he had. His third wife must have decided not to come, because Purty drove up alone.

"I couldn't believe it when I got the invitation. The Wolf Pack together again! You guys look old," Purty announced.

We laughed at him as we always had. "We're not as young as we once were," James Ernest agreed. "But we're not as old as we're going to be."

"Still as profound as ever," Purty said and laughed.

I was fifty-six and could feel the life of a farmer in my bones. Besides farming the land, we also raised cattle, and Susie had opened an antique store in town after the kids were grown and gone. Plus, I had been elected mayor twenty years earlier. I was ready for a rest.

Raven and Susie came out of the house to greet Randy and Todd. Raven asked Purty, "You still running around naked?"

"Only when I'm chasing my young wife around the house," Purty said and grinned.

"No wonder she's running," Raven cut and everyone laughed.

"Just like the old days." Purty laughed along.

"Is Junior coming?" Randy asked Raven.

Junior stuck it out through high school and became a great running back in high school. He got a football scholarship to Michigan State University. He starred there until tearing up his knee during his senior year, ruining his chance to play in the pros. He graduated from MSU and went on to a great job with Ford Motor Company in Detroit.

He had married a girl from college and had eight kids. He and his wife, Tonya, were the next to drive down the lane. Junior exited his car with a grand grin on his face. I ran as quickly as I could to hug him and welcome him to our home. I then hugged Tonya and said, "So glad you could come. Welcome."

"I was so excited when we got the invitation, I bounced around the house for days," Junior told me.

"That's the truth. I don't think I'd ever seen him that excited. Even on our wedding day."

"I was just scared that day," Junior said and smiled. He then asked, "Is Mom and Dad here yet?"

"Not yet," I answered. "Are they coming?"

"Told me they were. Dad wanted to drive down separately. Said they wanted to take their time and reminisce."

Junior had managed to get his dad a job at Ford on the production line after he was hired. Henry couldn't see himself working at the quarry forever. Plus, he knew the quarry would be shutting down soon, and he was right. Not long after he moved north, the quarry did close down, and a lot of folks in the area lost their jobs. James Ernest and Raven bought the farm and still lived there.

A few minutes later Tucky and Sadie arrived. Tucky had finally convinced Sadie to date him steady during their senior year of high school. They were the strangest combination I had ever seen together, but it worked. They were still married all these years later. Sadie had given up her dream of being famous and wealthy, and Tucky had quit eating road kill—a good give-and-take.

Sadie had even become good friends with Susie and Raven over the years. Tucky had moved to Morehead and worked for the State of Kentucky in the Game and Wildlife Division. He was in charge of making sure hunters were killing only what they were allowed to kill. So far no otters had been harmed under his watch.

Sadie was still a stunning woman at fifty-six, even though some of it had to do with a few cosmetic procedures, not that I would ever mention it. Susie and Raven also had retained their natural good looks at their age. We were three lucky guys.

In 1971, Pastor White and Miss Rebecca moved their son and daughter to Lexington when a large church called him to pastor. Pastor White knew it was what God wanted, but it wasn't what his heart wanted. He loved the people and church here in Morgan County and hated leaving them. But the members of the church convinced him that even though they hated to see him leave, they also felt it was God's will. The members knew he could affect so many more lives in Lexington than at the small Morgan County church. Randy and his family attended the church.

They were the next to arrive. Pastor White, retired now, and Miss Rebecca were greeted warmly by everyone who was already there. Bobby Lee and his wife, and Marie and her husband were in the car behind them. Miss Rebecca had named their little girl Marie, after my mother, who was named Betty Marie.

My mother died years earlier, and Sheriff Cane died a few years later. Monie and Clayton were still alive and living on the adjoining farm. They were the next to arrive. Following closely behind them were Delma and Thelma, now my sisters-in-law, with their husbands. Folks continued to arrive during the afternoon. Dana and pretty Idell visited. Tammy was there with her mother, Janice Easterling.

Rhonda and her husband came. Henry and Coal arrived later after taking their time. Henry and Clayton hugged for what seemed like five minutes.

Francis Tuttle also arrived after flying in from California and renting a car at the Lexington airport. Samantha Washington drove in from Columbus, Ohio. Rock Key came from Louisville.

We had not been able to find an address for Bernice Strunck, who had moved from Morgan County during her junior year of high school. She had not kept in touch with anyone that we knew of, including Sadie. Daniel Sugarman had died in a rock-climbing accident while he was in college.

The porch was filled. The house was filled. The shady ground under the giant oaks was filled with conversations and glad tidings and talk of days past. I could not have been happier with the turnout, or from seeing all my good friends. I spent the day moving from one group to another, trying to be a good host and gathering news from each person.

I made my way over to Henry and Coal. They were sitting with Monie at a picnic table. Coal hugged me in greeting and said, "It is so good to be back. Thank you for having this. I miss everyone every day."

"You two became such a big influence in my life."

Henry threw his hands toward me and said, "Come on."

"Really. You were. I watched how you took on your disappointments and continued to smile and praise God. I loved the way you never let things affect your love and living. You always bounced back stronger."

"It was a lot easier due to the people of this community," Henry said.

"And most of that was because of you, Timmy." I loved that Coal still called me Timmy, even when I was fifty-six years old.

"Me? What did I do?"

"I remember that summer day when you dared to come visit us. You looked like you had just seen monsters under your bed. You stood there with your arms at your side, your eyes wide open, looking at the strange sight of a colored family living in that old pitiful house. I'm surprised you didn't wet yourself. I first thought you were going to turn and high-tail it back to the store. But no, you stood right there and talked to us. You even shook my hand and came up to the porch and told us about everything. In your nervousness you went on-and-on."

"I didn't talk that much. And when I shook your hand I remember trying to sneak a peek at my hand to see if your darkness came off in my hand."

"I saw you look at your hand. You were so nervous, but you stayed. You began talking, and you went on and on just like Loraine Tuttle, bless her soul."

"Well, maybe."

"You were the one who gave me the faith that we had found a special place. Because of you, we were given food and clothes, and the kids were able to go to school and get educated. You were such a blessing."

"Coal thanked God for you and asked Him to watch over you every night after that," Henry told me.

I sat there at that table, and tears filled my eyes. I moved over next to Coal and gently hugged her. "I knew someone had to be praying for me."

"Let me tell you a secret. You had a lot of folks praying for you. We all knew God had plans for you, and we also knew you needed protecting. That Wolf Pack was something."

"Scared us to death when you asked Junior to become a member," Henry added.

"But you let him go on the canoe trip and you let him join the Pack," I said.

"There was no telling that boy he couldn't. You should have seen his eyes. He was so happy and excited. It gave him so much confidence, just like when you took him fishing. All of that led to him being able to do what he did on the football field. Without that confidence he never would have tried out for a team. He even told us that when he decided to do it," Coal told me.

"You and James Ernest have been the best things that ever happened to this family," Henry said.

"No. I don't accept that because I watched how strong you and Coal were and how much respect I had for the both of you. If anything, we made each other better. That's the way life is supposed to be. The strength and gifts of each person making another person stronger and better," I said.

"You're right," Coal said, and Henry, who was now in his eighties, shook his head in agreement.

James Ernest made his way over and said, "Hi, Mom and Dad." We all smiled.

I later walked away from talking to them, thanking God for putting the Washington family in my life. I saw Randy standing alone under the oaks. I hurried over to where he stood.

"It's really good to see you again, Randy. How have you been?" I asked.

"I've been good. I miss Cindy most days. But I guess that's to be expected."

"I'm sure. She was a good woman."

"A good wife," Randy said.

"How are your kids?'

"They're fine. I'm going to be a grandpa soon. We all get together every Sunday afternoon."

"Congratulations. There's nothing better than being a grandfather." Susie and I already had three grandchildren. Our son Ernest T. had two children, both boys, and one of our daughters, Lauren Raven, had a daughter.

"Let's go get something to eat."

I noticed my sister, Janie, talking with Delma and Thelma. I decided to detour around them. Janie ended up marrying Bobby Lee, Miss Rebecca's son, and moving to North Carolina. The food was all spread out on tables off the porch, and we invited everyone to gather for the blessing. Pastor White and Miss Rebecca were talking with Monie and Clayton, and I asked Pastor White to say grace.

"Lord, it is so good to see everyone again. I thank you. I'm thankful for this community and for Timmy and Susie for bringing us together once again. How you have blessed us, and now we ask you to bless us again as we fellowship today. Bless this food. Thank you for dying for us. We love you. And all the people said, Amen."

"Amen."

"Everything looks delicious. I warn you though; I would stay away from whatever the twins brought. Dig in," I told everyone. The twins shot me dirty looks. I was looking forward to the cherry dumplings that Susie made.

"Looks like you should stay away from all the food," Delma shot back.

"Maybe eat a salad," Thelma added.

I knew I had asked for the ribbing. What was a gathering without being insulted by the twins? The twins refused to be part of the ceremony when Susie and I were married, which didn't bother me at all, and then they didn't talk to Susie for six months afterward due to being so upset with her. It was like a six-month-long honeymoon.

They campaigned against me when I ran for mayor, certain that if I was victorious, the town would fall into ruin.

Later in the day we decided to set up horseshoe pits. Delma and Thelma just happened to walk by. Purty asked them, "Do you two want to join us?"

"You want us to play that dumb game?" Delma quipped as they both frowned.

"No. We wanted to use your necks as the stakes," I offered.

"You're as rude as ever," Delma said.

"What Susie ever saw in you I'll never know," Thelma followed.

"Had to have been slim pickins' back then," Delma told her as they walked away.

We all laughed as we started our match. I had sent special invitations to the members of the Wolf Pack to spend the night camping out with me. Their wives were invited to spend the night in the house with Susie. They all accepted. I built a fire pit below the house in the woods and put up a large tent that would sleep all six of us.

As darkness drew near, James Ernest and I set up a surprise for everyone to top off the day. We had gone together and bought a supply of fireworks. We fired up the first one without telling anyone and it flew high into the sky and exploded in red and white colors. Everyone hurried to find a spot to watch the fireworks as the streaks rose toward the man in the moon. We had different colors and designs and drew many "*oohs*" and "*aahs*" from the crowd. The show lasted around thirty minutes and ended with much applause and cheers.

We shook hands with guests as they began to leave after the show. It seemed as though everyone had such a good time they didn't want to leave. Everyone said we should get together each year. I thought it was a good idea. Henry and Coal were spending the night with Clayton and Monie. Other folks were spending the night with other families in the area. A few were heading home.

25   The Last Wolf Pack Meeting

Susie, Raven, Sadie, and Tonya waved and called out, "See you in the morning."

"You boys be safe," Raven yelled to us as we walked through the field with flashlights. The women laughed at the sight of six old men limping and struggling as we walked away. We all were carrying sleeping bags strapped to our backs. I suddenly felt thirteen again. My right knee felt better than it had in years. Purty began singing, "Zip-a-dee-doo-dah," as we hiked toward our campground. We started laughing at him, but soon we joined him in song.

The campsite that I picked out sat on top of a large cliff which overlooked Devil's Creek. Minutes later we entered the woods and followed a path. Years ago Susie and I had sat at the same spot and exchanged one of our first kisses. It seemed like decades ago, but it also seemed like yesterday.

"Are we almost there?" Purty asked.

"Why? Are you getting tired like in the old days?" James Ernest asked him.

"I never got tired. I always led the Wolf Pack," Purty shot back.

We all turned to look at Purty.

"Old age has taken his memory," Randy said.

"Poor thing," I added.

"Remember our two-day hike to Blaze when I led almost the entire way?" Purty defended.

"That was only because you were so anxious to kiss the big-butt rock that was on the map," James Ernest explained. "And you had poison ivy so bad you couldn't stop moving."

I hadn't thought of the poison ivy in years, and I began laughing and couldn't stop. I was remembering the mud James Ernest talked Purty into applying to the affected skin.

Finally, we came to the spot that I had cleared. The tent almost glowed in the full moon. Randy and James Ernest began making a fire. I had already cut limbs off the downed trees for marshmallows. I had placed a cooler in the tent filled with soft drinks and there was a bag with marshmallows. Instead of rolling logs around the fire I had placed six lawn chairs for us to sit on.

"Now this is the life," Randy said as he took a seat in one of the chairs.

Finally we all took a seat and then noticed that Purty was missing.

"Where is Purty?" I asked, looking around.

"He must be marking the trees," James Ernest said.

"What?" Tucky asked.

"You've never heard this story?" I asked.

"I don't think so."

"We were on up the creek from where we are now, on top of the ridge, just like this, and we were surrounded by the Boys from Blaze. It ended up in a big fist fight. Afterward Purty went around trying to pee on the trees to mark the area as ours."

"How many trees did he end up peeing on?" Junior asked.

"Ten," Purty said as he walked back into the campground.

"Ten! You managed to pee on two," James Ernest said.

"It was at least ten, maybe more. I was celebrating our victory by letting them know they couldn't come into our woods and take on the Wolf Pack," Purty exaggerated.

"You do realize we weren't really wolves," I said and laughed.

Purty ripped open the marshmallows and placed three on his stick and began roasting them. It felt like a real Wolf Pack meeting again. It could have been 1962 again.

"I want to thank you guys for being such great friends. I couldn't have had more fun than I did once I moved back to Kentucky. We had quite a ride. We were quite a unique cast of characters," I told them.

"Yes, we were," Randy said. "There were a lot of memorable tales."

"You guys saved my and Susie's life when we were kidnapped. They were going to kill us after they got the money."

"You really think so?" Junior asked.

"They had to if they were going to get away with the kidnapping. Billy Taulbee was supposed to blindfold us and tie our hands behind our backs, but he forgot about tying our hands. I reached up and pulled the blindfold off and saw them. After that there was no way they could get away with their plan. I heard them say they were going to dump our bodies in a deep hollow."

"Did they ever get out of prison?" Purty asked.

'Yes. Silas and his wife moved away as soon as he was released. Russell's wife died while he was in prison. He only lived a few years after being released," I told them.

"How they thought they were going to get away with it I'll never know," Randy said.

"I remember all the booby traps they hit when they were searching for us in the creek. And I remember hearing the "*kerplunk*" sound when Purty drilled Silas with the sling-shot."

"I was an ace marksman with a sling-shot. I hit him twice, once in the head and again in the chest," Purty bragged.

"You were," I affirmed. "But then someone shot Silas in the leg with a rifle."

"Who shot him?" Tucky asked.

"Randy did," James Ernest answered.

"I couldn't believe I was shooting a person. I had his chest in my sights, but dropped it to his leg and fired. I didn't want to kill him unless I had to," Randy said.

"You three were my heroes that day," I said.

"That was the most exciting day of my life," James Ernest stated.

"Even more exciting than the day you tied the Bottom Brothers up in their truck and then we were locked up in the basement by their mother?" Junior asked.

"Yes, even more exciting than that. But that had to be the funniest memory I have of a Wolf Pack adventure. Seeing Purty hopping on the floor thinking he was a toad, I thought I would laugh for months."

We all began laughing again.

"First he thought he was a wolf, peeing on trees, and then a toad, hopping on the kitchen floor. Back then your brains were as scarce as hen's teeth," Tucky said and laughed.

"I didn't really think she had turned me into a frog. I was just going along," Purty tried convincing us. We weren't having any of that, and we continued laughing.

"Just like when you climbed up in the tree to protect yourself from the lightning," Tucky cried out.

I laughed harder than I had in forty years.

After the laughter died down Purty said, "I'm glad I could entertain you guys."

"You definitely did that, and you still are," James Ernest said as Purty put three more marshmallows on his stick.

It grew quiet around the fire as I suspected each of us was drawn into thoughts back to our Wolf Pack days.

Randy asked, "Tim, how many times do you think you could have died or almost died?"

I began thinking back on all the adventures. "Twice, when I was trapped in the cave."

"Twice?" Junior questioned.

"I didn't think anyone would ever find me, and I didn't think I'd ever find a way out and then, secondly, when I tried to swim out I almost drowned."

"Swim out?" Purty questioned.

"Save that question. I'll show you tomorrow. I thought I was going to be killed by the Tattoo Man three or four times. When he trapped me in the store, when I was hiding in the rag bed, and when he swung a large stick at my head. Oh yeah, also when he shot at my face as he was climbing out. When I was trapped inside the burning trailer I thought I was dead. I guess we all thought we might die when we were trapped in the cave above Devil's Creek. I almost died when Silas shot at us, but Billy Taulbee jumped in front of Susie and me. I thought we might die in the creek when they were trying to kill us. I thought we were going to die on that homemade bobsled track we made. I thought I was dead twice when the two men robbed the store and then took me, and also when the Boys from Blaze came to the store and beat me up."

"Man, that bobsled hill was fun," Junior said.

We all looked at Junior and laughed.

I continued with the times I thought I could have died, "I was scared of what the Bottom Brothers might do if they caught us after James Ernest tied them up and bent their rifles. I thought the witch was going to kill us. And I was afraid we could have died by the hands of Bigfoot when we were attempting to find James Ernest. Plus, there have been run-ins with bears, mountain lions, and coyotes."

"But you survived it all," Tucky said.

"Only with the help of some great friends and the good Lord above," I stated.

"Amen," sounded around the campfire.

"I thought James Ernest was going to die at the hands of Bigfoot," I said as I stirred the fire with a small log.

"That was the strangest thing we ever came across," Tucky said.

"I certainly never thought I'd see James Ernest locked up in a cage," Purty added.

"Did you think he was going to kill you?" Randy asked.

"I thought he was going to either eat the deer or me. No, actually, I never did think he would kill me. At the time I felt he locked me up because he was scared and didn't know what to do with me. Later, he told me that I was the first person to track him down and get that close to him," James Ernest answered.

"I wonder what happened to him," Tucky said.

We all shook our heads with no answers.

"I think about him every time I read an article in the paper about a Bigfoot sighting or a picture of Bigfoot on the Internet," I said.

"Yeah, I do too," Randy said.

"You think there really is such a thing as Bigfoot?" Junior asked.

"I don't think so," Purty said.

Just before Purty continued James Ernest said, "In my wanderings at night through the woods I've seen him twice."

"Who? Charley?" Junior asked.

"No. Bigfoot," James Ernest answered.

I dropped my stirring log into the fire and fell back into my chair. Junior's eyes widened. Purty stopped with his mouth still open as he had begun to speak. Randy and Tucky turned toward James Ernest. No one said anything, waiting for James Ernest to continue, but he just stared into the fire flames.

Finally, moments later, I asked, "You saw Bigfoot twice?"

James Ernest looked at us as if he was studying whether or not to tell us.

"C'mon, man, you've got to tell us," Purty begged.

"I was sixteen the first time, and I was up on the cliff near the spot where we fought the Boys from Blaze, near the moonshine still." He pointed into the dark, but we knew he was pointing to the other side of Devil's Creek. "I saw him bent down on a trail. It looked like he was eating something. He sensed I was behind him and he quickly turned to see me. He straightened up and lumbered away. He looked just like some of the pictures I've seen. I walked up to where he had been and found rabbit fur, bones, and guts scattered on the trail."

"You're kidding," Tucky said.

"No, he's not, Tucky. Keep going," I said.

"I know it sounds crazy. That's why I never told anyone about them. The second time was a few years ago. I went out one night to catch some frogs and I saw a large figure bent over at Licking Creek. I watched him for nearly ten minutes. He never knew I was watching. He looked the same as the other one I had seen."

"What was he doing?" I asked.

"He had been eating frogs. Then he washed his face in the water, and he got up and moved on down the creek."

"Are you sure neither of them was Charley?" Tucky asked.

"No, it wasn't Charley. Its face was more animal-like. Charley had a long beard. Bigfoot didn't. Bigfoot wasn't as tall as Charley either, and was a lot broader and stronger looking."

We sat in silence for a while before Purty asked, "What else haven't you told us about?"

"We'd be a hundred by the time I told you everything I haven't told you about," James Ernest said and laughed.

"As Gomer would say, sur-prise, sur-prise, sur-prise! You're always surprising us," Tucky said.

"I have a surprise for most of you in the morning," I told the guys.

"What now? Did you see little purple people?" Randy asked.

"It's something I've kept a secret for forty-six years. I've only told three other people. I'll show you in the morning," I explained.

"Who else have you showed this secret to?" Tucky asked.

"That's all I'm saying for now."

I found another large stick and began stoking the fire again. The temperatures were falling the later it got. I placed a couple more logs into the fire.

"We've been pretty fortunate in our lives," Randy said.

"We're only missing a couple of parts," James Ernest said and smiled at Randy. Randy looked to where his left arm used to hang.

"Nothing I can't do without," Randy said. "It probably would have just gotten me in trouble."

"We're thankful for your service and sacrifice," Junior told him. "You too, Tim."

Randy and I both said, "Thanks."

"Since school, what's the most surprising thing that's happened to each of us?" Randy asked.

"That's easy for me," I started. "Sadie marrying Tucky."

Everyone laughed, even Tucky.

"I always thought Sadie would head to Hollywood after school. She wanted that glamorous life, and she ends up with Tucky," I explained.

"I had other qualities she liked," Tucky said and smiled.

"What? The best road-kills in Kentucky?" James Ernest said, and we all laughed.

"I was most surprised when James Ernest and Raven got married. I knew they loved each other, but boy, that was a gutsy thing to do, especially at that time in our country's history," Tucky said.

"I was never so proud of two people," I said.

"It wasn't an easy decision," James Ernest began explaining. "I was scared for Raven and for myself, I guess. But Raven was the best girl I'd ever known and I loved her so much. I couldn't bear the thought of not marrying her. We wanted our marriage to be an example of what our country could be, the same way our community was back then."

"We all wanted the two of you to get married, but I sure didn't know if you would," Tucky said.

"We're all glad you did," Randy said.

"I was surprised when Junior didn't win the Heisman Trophy or play in the pros. Your injury saddened me for years," Randy said.

"My knee never did heal right. I could run straight ahead well enough, but I couldn't cut like a running back needed to. I think if I could have played one more game my senior year I may have had a chance to win the trophy," Junior told us.

"You must have been disappointed," Purty said.

"Not really. I felt blessed to have gotten a free education, a college degree, and then I got a wonderful job and a great wife. Dad had always taught me to work for the things I wanted and to accept the things I couldn't change. It could be God's perfect plan. I was blessed."

I knew Junior was right. So many times man's hopes and prayers aren't the plan of God, and we had to be faithful enough to accept it.

"I was surprised that Randy didn't marry Brenda," Junior said, turning the attention to someone else.

"I was too," Purty said. "He pined for her all the time through high school."

"I don't know what happened. It seemed as though it wasn't meant to be. We dated some, I was drafted and soon after, she met the guy she married. We never had an understanding that she would wait for me or anything. It worked out for the best for both of us."

"I was surprised and am still surprised that you, Purty, could find three different women to marry you," James Ernest said. We all started laughing.

"I guess that is surprising. I guess the money helps with that. I wish I had what you guys have, the love of your life. I always wanted one person to share my life and money with. I've had a good life, but I never found my true love."

"Why didn't your wife come with you this weekend?" I asked.

"I'm ashamed to say, but we're in the middle of a divorce," Purty said with his head bowed.

"I'm sorry to hear that. There's still time to find your true love," James Ernest told him.

"Maybe, but I guess everyone's not meant to be lucky in love," Purty said. Purty had tried all through high school to get Rhonda to date him, without any success. He was so hurt by her rejection, and I think it followed him during his life. It had to be hard to think of someone as your 'one true love' and be so utterly ignored.

"That leaves Timmy. What has surprised us about his life?" Junior asked.

"We all knew he'd marry Susie and be happy," Purty said.

"We knew he'd never leave Morgan County," Tucky added.

"I guess, though, I was a little surprised when he became mayor. But everyone knew who he was, and he was the sheriff's stepson," Randy said.

"But everyone liked Timmy, except for the twins, who campaigned against him," James Ernest said.

"We're getting along a little better these days," I said and laughed.

It was beginning to get very late. The full moon had passed over our heads and was beginning its descent. Our time around the campfire had felt like it did forty years previous. We laughed, made fun of each other, and Purty even erupted a couple of times, scattering us. Just like old times. I hated to see the meeting end, but due to our age, I could tell that everyone was beginning to tire.

"What do you say we get some shut-eye? The ladies are going to have breakfast ready at nine in the morning," I said.

James Ernest hopped up from his chair and placed his hand above the dying embers, and we all followed his lead. We place our hands on top of one another and Randy said, "Seven times in memory of Coty."

We roared in the night sky, "Wolf Pack, Wolf Pack, Wolf Pack, Wolf Pack, Wolf Pack, Wolf Pack, Wolf Pack, Forever the Pack," and then we howled as we had never howled before. I wondered if we woke the women in the house.

We slowly made our way into the tent and slipped into our sleeping bags.

"When was the last time you guys were in a tent?" I asked, once everyone was settled.

"Quite a while," Randy said.

"Not since our last time in high school," Purty told us.

"You're kidding."

"I had no children, and it seems as though young wealthy women don't much care for tents and sleeping bags," Purty explained.

"Tomorrow will be our next adventure," I said.

We talked for a while and then the tent began to grow silent. I whispered into the dark, "I love you guys."

"Shut up and go to sleep," James Ernest said.

The other four men laughed long and hard.

26 FOREVER THE PACK!

We awoke the next morning to the sound of singing birds and chirping squirrels in the trees above and around us. I awoke before the alarm on my cell phone went off. It was seven-thirty. I slipped out of my sleeping bag and unzipped the tent. A beautiful blue early-morning sky greeted me as I looked up and through the colorful limbs and falling leaves. I walked over to the ledge of the cliff overlooking Devil's Creek and remembered the day I let the Wolf Pack talk me into hanging over the edge to see the cave opening below.

It seemed my adrenaline boiled through my body as I thought about what a thrill it was to hang over the cliff, trusting my life to two of my Wolf Pack brothers. I would have trusted them with anything, even my life. I knew I should have trusted them with the secret of the Indian cave, but I hadn't. This morning, that would change.

I heard steps behind me and looked back to see James Ernest nearing.

He stopped beside me and looked down toward the creek. "We had a lot of good times in those waters."

"We certainly did," I said. "I was just thinking of the day you and Randy held my legs over the ledge."

"We did some crazy things," James Ernest said.

"Some purty stupid ideas," I agreed.

"But they made our childhood awfully special."

"Yes, they did."

Suddenly, we heard screaming from the tent. We knew instantly who it was. The tent was shaking and moving, looking like it might come down any moment. Unexpectedly, we saw a filled sleeping bag being rolled from the end of the tent with a screaming Purty still inside. The other three Wolf Pack members had rolled Purty out of the tent.

"He refused to get up, and then he farted. God-awful smell," Tucky explained.

Purty's head had been zipped up in the bag and the drawstring pulled up tight, making him breath in his own expulsions.

He finally was able to undo the string and slip from the bag and he stood in front of us in nothing but bikini briefs.

We shook our heads in disbelief.

"What? Body heat. The less clothing you wear in a sleeping bag the more heat your body gives off," Purty said.

"Please put on some clothes," I begged.

⌒

Raven, Susie, Tonya, and Sadie stood waiting for us as we approached the overhanging porch.

"I see you guys survived again," Susie said.

"Not without a few scary moments," Randy said, looking at Purty.

"What did Purty do this time?" Susie asked.

"The usual," Junior answered.

"Smelled up the tent again?" Raven said.

"Hey, a guy can change in forty years," Purty defended.

We all laughed, because we knew he would never change. I for one never wanted him to.

"Breakfast is ready. C'mon in and get it, before I throw it to the hogs," Susie directed and threatened.

The girls had prepared a breakfast fit for a king. We all dug in and filled our stomachs with eggs, biscuits and gravy, bacon and sausage, jams, and pancakes. I wondered if my plan for the guys to swim into the cave would work after eating. We might all sink.

"We need to leave our wallets and other valuables here," I told the guys.

As the guys emptied their pockets and placed their watches and cell phones on the table, Randy asked, "What are you girls going to do while we're gone?"

"We have two four-wheelers, and we've built a trail through the woods. I think we're taking a trip to see the fall colors and the cliffs while you boys are gone," Susie said.

"We'll be a couple of hours," I said as I got up from the table.

"Have fun. We will," Sadie said.

I walked over and kissed Susie goodbye.

"Ooh." "Yuck." "Gross." Those were some of the comments we got from my immature friends.

I jumped into the cab of my Ford pickup. Junior took shotgun, and the other four hopped into the back bed. I said, "I wonder how long it's been since they've been in the back of a pickup truck," as I drove up the gravel lane.

"Maybe forty years," Junior guessed. "Is it even legal these days?"

"I think only in Morgan County." We both laughed

After a two- to three- minute drive, I pulled into the empty gravel lot below the dam of Papaw's pay lake. As I opened my door everyone began jumping from the pickup.

"Where are we going?" Tucky asked.

"Around the lake," I answered.

James Ernest led the way as I brought up the rear. My mind raced back to the days when we walked so many times to the swimming hole and I imagined all of us still with Mohawk haircuts and thin bodies from all the chores we did. Now most of us were heavier. I sported a goatee. Randy and Tucky both had mustaches. Purty sported a five-day beard, which I assumed he kept the same length all the time. None of us had Mohawks any longer, and Junior and Randy both were lacking much hair on their heads at all.

We walked over the last rise on the west side of the lake, and I said, "Right there, leaning against that tree, is where Susie and I first saw the Tattoo Man."

The store had been knocked down long ago, and the ownership of the land had gone to different owners over the past forty years. Susie and I ended up with the land five years ago. I wanted the land as a memento of my grandparents and my childhood.

I began retelling the story of the Tattoo Man as we walked. By the time we got to the swimming hole I was telling them about how I lured the Tattoo Man up the hill toward the cave. We walked around the swimming hole, which I would now bring my grandchildren to swim, and took them to the trail that led up the hill. James Ernest led them up to the cave entrance.

James Ernest and I lifted the large metal plate, which now protected children from falling into the earth, and I explained how I escaped from the cave and how the Tattoo Man died in the cave.

"You swam out of the cave and into the swimming hole?" Tucky repeated in disbelief.

"How did you do that?" Junior asked.

"That's why I brought you here, to show you how and to show you what's in the cave," I answered.

"What's in the cave?" Purty blurted out.

James Ernest and I slid the heavy lid back over the entrance, and I said, "Let's hike back to the swimming hole, unless any of you want to jump over the ledge and into the swimming hole."

We watched as Purty headed for the edge. He pulled up short and turned and smiled. "I'm not quite as crazy as I used to be."

We were stunned when Randy suddenly yelled out, "Forever the Pack." And he ran toward the ledge and jumped. We hurried to the edge and looked over to see him rise from the waters below with his arm raised in triumph. Behind us I heard, "Last one in is a rotten egg." Junior ran past us and flew off the ledge and down into the water.

"I think the Leader of the Pack has spoken," Tucky said as he backed up. He then ran and did a somersault off the cliff and into the pool below. Junior and Randy applauded his daringness from below.

I was next. I was ten again. I never thought a thing about my bad right knee and tender back as I jumped from the cliff. James Ernest followed, leaving only Purty on top of the cliff. Forty years before he jumped from the cliff to prove to himself that he was brave and to prove to his father that he was brave. Today, he stood up on top, wondering if he really had anyone left in his life he needed to prove anything to. I believed he had himself.

I know it took all his strength and courage to jump off that cliff at his advanced age. The five of us held on to the edge of the pool and gazed up at the sky, hoping he still had it in him. Junior began to chant, "Purty! Purty!"

Soon we all were chanting his name, "Purty! Purty! Purty!"

I didn't think he would do it. I started to look toward the trail to see if he had hiked down the path when I heard, "Geronimo," and saw fifty-seven-year-old Purty fly off the ledge without a stitch of clothing on, his clothing floating in the air. He tumbled down through the air and into the swimming hole, followed by his clothes. It was the most graceless jump I had ever seen, but also the best. We whooped and hollered for him for the next five minutes. At that moment in time I believed we all thought we had time-traveled back to our years together in our youth. I hadn't felt that much excitement since my children's births.

"Purty, you beat all," Tucky said as he swam over and rubbed Purty's head. They embraced as only two members of the Wolf Pack could.

Once everyone had calmed down I told the guys about the underwater entryway into the cave. "Randy, can you swim okay underwater?" He nodded yes, so I told Junior and Randy to follow me. Purty and Tucky were to follow James Ernest after we were inside.

I dove down and swam underwater. I looked back to see bodies following. I finally popped up inside the cave. A couple of seconds later Junior was beside me and then Randy. We stood in waist–high water on the rock floor and waited for James Ernest to enter. He soon was standing beside us and then Tucky popped up. After a long ten seconds went by, Purty finally came up out of the water. It was much too dark inside for the guys to see the Indian drawings on the wall. A couple of days earlier James Ernest and I had brought a lantern into the cave in a waterproof bag and placed it in front of the wall.

"This cave is what I've kept a secret for so long. And this," I said as I flicked the battery-powered lantern on and turned it all the way up.

After spending close to an hour inside the cave we swam back out. Purty put his clothes back on and we walked back to the truck as though we had just completed another amazing adventure.

I drove down the now rutted and potholed gravel road toward the quarry. I paused at Pastor White and Miss Rebecca's old house and then again at the now over-grown lot where Henry and Coal had made their first home before having it burnt to the ground. Junior stared at the spot with tears forming in his eyes.

"There's where I first met you," he said. "That changed my life."

"It changed my life also. I love you, man," I said. He kept staring out the window. I knew his thoughts went back to those days long ago.

I stopped along Licking Creek at the spot where Russell and Silas and the Wolf Pack had our shoot-out. I stopped the truck and got out of the cab. Everyone else emptied and we walked down the bank to the creek.

We explained to Tucky and Junior what and where it all happened that night. I showed them the rock we had hid under. Purty showed them the spot he had stood when he plunked Silas with the slingshot.

"Susie and I were sure Coty had been killed and we were going to be next," I said.

"We couldn't have had a better seventh member of the Wolf Pack than Coty. He risked his life for us so many times," James Ernest said.

"He was a great dog," Randy said.

"Even to this day I miss him," I said. "I've had other good dogs that I loved, but he was special. There has to be a place in heaven for him."

"When we all meet again in heaven, we'll still be the Wolf Pack," James Ernest said.

We all looked at one another, as though we all had the same thought at the same time. We all threw an arm toward the sky and yelled out:

"Forever the Pack!"

Epilogue

2015

That evening in 2005, as we stood around the cars and said our goodbyes, we agreed to come together every year. Purty was the first to open his car's door. He turned and looked at the other five of us and said, "You know, someone ought to write a book about our adventures." We all laughed.

I waved to each one of my friends as they drove away. I put my arm around Susie and we quietly walked toward our home. The weekend was special to both of us. It sparked us. It fueled us. It restored our memory of our youth. It caused us to recount our blessings, and it made me want to try my hand at writing. We entered the house, and I went straight to my den and turned on the computer. I stared at the first blank page, wondering if I was up to the task. I prayed, asking God to give me the words and the memory for the task. "Use me," I asked Him.

I then typed:

TIM CALLAHAN

Saturday, June 13, 1959

How could I, a nine-year-old boy, end up in the bottom of a Kentucky cavern with no way out that I could see and no hope of being rescued?

Well, I'll tell you.

I'm still typing.
The End

Dear Readers,

From what started out as a way to honor my grandparents, and to have a new hobby, writing turned out to be a tremendous blessing. I appreciate each and every one of you who has read the "Kentucky Summers" series and gone on all the adventures of Timmy and his friends with me.

I never dreamed that the books would end up being read in schools from elementary classrooms to college classes, or that I would make so many new friends with fellow authors and faithful readers of my books. I honestly do consider you as friends. I've had families drive through Morgan County on State Route 711 to see the places I've described in the books. I've heard amazing stories from readers about how the books have either affected them or others in a good way, or cost them sleep from staying up late to finish a book.

Thank you for all the kind e-mails and for reading my writings. *Forever the Pack* is the last book in the series. I wanted to end the books while the kids were still at a somewhat innocent age. I do, however, have plans to write one or two books of short stories about the characters of "*Kentucky Summers*".

I want to thank the real characters for letting me use them in the books. They were people I knew growing up. (I've included a list of real characters and fictional characters at the end of the novel.) Even though the characters are real, it doesn't mean that everything about them in the books are real. For example: the twins were real, but they weren't really that mean. Could anyone have been that crabby?

I've both laughed and cried as I've written and then reread the books. The characters, even the fictional ones, have become so close and personal to me that it saddens me to have completed the series. My hope is that the books become special to those who read them and will one day be passed down to a child's child or to a grandchild in the future and that the characters will remain alive long after I'm not.

I hope the books have brought you enjoyment and that you've grown closer to those you've shared the books with. I pray that the careful message of Christ in the books perhaps brought someone to a personal relationship with my Lord.

Please feel free to e-mail me at, timcal21@ yahoo.com, or call me with comments or questions concerning the books or writing. I'm always willing to answer all. You can find more information on my website: www. timcallahan.net

I especially need to thank three ladies who I owe so much to. Donna Elam, Shirley Jones and Peggy Cramer have been so instrumental in the writing and editing of this series and my website. Thank you for your help and love of the books. I am so blessed to call you friends.

Even though, at the end of the series none of the boys became preachers, or great singers, or famous people, I believe most of them still did great things in God's eyes. Living a life of service and having love for others is what I believe God expects from His children.

'Just live your life good.'

Blessings & keep reading,
Author Tim Callahan

REAL CHARACTERS OF THE
KENTUCKY SUMMERS SERIES

1. **Timmy**—Main character and author of the *Kentucky Summers Series* novels. Son of Delbert and Betty Callahan.

   Enters—book 1, chapter 1, page 17

2. **Mom (Betty)**—Betty Marie Callahan (Collins), mother of Timmy and Janie.

   Enters—book 1, chapter 1, page 27
   Lived: 5/22/1928-4/19/1994

3. **Dad (Delbert)**—Delbert Lee Callahan, father of Timmy and Janie.

   Husband of Betty.
   Enters—book 1, chapter 2, page 31
   Lived: 3/25/1926-9/19/1980

4. **Janie**—Cora Jane Callahan, Sister of Timmy.

   Enters—book 1, chapter 1, page 21

5. **Mamaw**—Cora Collins (Easterling), Grandmother of Timmy and Janie.

   Wife of Martin Collins. Mother of Betty, Ola, Ruth and Helen.
   Enters—Book 1, Chapter 1, Page 20
   Lived: 11/30/1900-8/31/1982

6. **Papaw**—Thomas Martin Collins, Grandfather of Timmy and Janie.

   Husband of Cora Collins. Father of Betty, Ola, Ruth & Helen
   Enters—book 1, chapter 1, page 2 Lived: 11/30/1898—1/26/1967

7. **Homer Easterling**—Brother of Mamaw. Husband of Ruby.

   Enters—book 1, chapter 6, page 82
   Lived: 11/8/1906-10/20/1982

8. **Ruby Easterling (Swim)**—Wife of Homer.

   Enters—book 1, chapter 6, page 82
   Lived: 11/5/1909-7/19/2008

9. **Uncle Morton Collins**—In book he is Papaw's brother. In real life he was Papaw's Uncle. Explanation of how he went blind is in book 1, chapter 5, page 67.

   Enters—book 1, chapter 5, page 63.
   Lived: 5/18/1896-1/28/1967

10. **Clayton Perry (Collins)**—I changed family name in book from Collins to Perry. (Explanation—I wanted Susie to be Timmy's girlfriend in books, so since they were actually related to me (Collins), I had to change their last name.) Husband of Monie. Father of Brenda, Donna (Susie), Delma and Thelma.

    Enters—book 1, chapter 1, page 23. Lived: 8/21/1925-5/22/1998

11. **Monie Perry** (Real last name was Collins. Maiden name–DeHart)Husband to Clayton. Mother of Brenda, Donna (Susie), Delma and Thelma.

    Enters—book 1, chapter 6, page 75
    Lived: 11/8/1925-11/21/2013

12. **Brenda Lucille Perry** (Real last name was Collins, married name Whitt.) Oldest daughter of Clayton and Monie. .

    Enters—book 1, chapter 6, page 80.

13. **Susie Perry** (Real name was Donna Jean Collins, married name Elam.) Second oldest daughter of Clayton and Monie.

    Enters—book 1, chapter 1, page 24.

14. **Delma May Perry** (Real name was Delma May Collins, married name Whitt.) Twin daughter of Clayton and Monie. Twin sister of Thelma.

    Enters—book 1, chapter 6, page 75.

15. **Thelma Fay Perry** (Real name was Thelma Fay Collins, married name Haney.) Twin daughter of Clayton and Monie. Twin sister of Delma.

    Enters—book 1, chapter 6, page 75.

16. **Robert Henry Easterling**–Husband of Janice. Father of Dana and Tammy. In real life he was the older brother of James Ernest.

    Enters—book 1, chapter 5, page 68. Lived: 3/10/1941—4/8/2008

17. **Janice Lamar Easterling** (Easterling)—Wife of Robert & mother of Dana and Tammy.

    Enters—book 1, chapter 5, page 68.

18. **Dana R Easterling**—Son of Robert & Janice.

    Enters—book 1, chapter 8, page 96.

19. **Tammy Lynn Easterling** (Now Gibson.)—Daughter of Robert and Janice.

    Enters–book 1, chapter 8, page 96.

20. **Idell (Now Easterling.)**–Known in the books as Pretty Idell. Wife of Dana.

    Enters–book 1, chapter 8, page 96.

21. **Billy Easterling**—Fisherman, Enters book 1, chapter 6, page 81

22. Roy Collins—Fisherman, Enters book 1, chapter 6, page 81

Lived: 1904–1975

23. Aunt Mildred Collins—Wife of Kenneth, Sister of Mamaw

Had two daughters—Sandy and Phyllis
Enters—book 1, chapter 8, page 96
Lived: 9/12/1924-5/13/2013

24. Kenneth Collins—Husband of Mildred, Brother of Papaw, Husband of Mildred

Father of Sandy and Phyllis Enters book 1, chapter 8, page 96
Lived: 4/23/1921-7/5/1984

25. Phyllis Collins—Daughter of Kenneth & Mildred

Enters—book 1, chapter 8, page 96
Lived: 5/15/1949-8/30/1984

26. Aunt Ola Mae Perry (Collins)—Daughter of Mamaw & Papaw, Mom's oldest sister.

Enters—book 1, chapter 14, page 170 Lived: 2/20/1919-7/8/2000

27. Uncle Corbett H. Perry—Married to Ola. Enters—book 1, chapter 14, page 170

Lived: 6/29/1915-5/20/1996

28. **Vernita Perry**—Daughter of Ola and Corbett. Enters—book 1, chapter 14, page 170

29. **Janet Perry**–Daughter of Ola and Corbett. Enters— book 1, chapter 14, page 170

30. **Thomas (Tommy) Perry**—Son of Ola and Corbett. Enters—book 1, chapter 14, page 171

    Lived: 6/22/1944-10/28/1979

31. **Aunt Helen Leukardt (Collins)**—Daughter of Mamaw & Papaw, Mom's Sister.

    Step-mother of King. Enters—book 1, chapter 16, page 185

32. **Uncle Bill Leukardt**–Husband of Aunt Helen. Father of King

    Enters—book 1, chapter 16, page 185 Lived: 10/17/1919-7/2/1988

33. **King Leukardt**—Son of Bill and Helen. Enters–book 1, chapter 16, page 185

34. **Aunt Ruth Johnson (Collins)**–Daughter of Mamaw & Papaw, Mom's Sister.

    Mother of Jenny, Judy, and Joe Junior.
    Enters—book 1, chapter 16, page 185 Lived: 1/24/1924-7/18/2012

35. Uncle Joe Johnson—Husband of Ruth. Enters–book 1, chapter 16, page 185

Father of Jenny, Judy and Joe Junior.
Lived: 5/29/1923-2/27/1987

36. Joe Johnson Jr.—Son of Joe & Ruth. Enters–book 1, chapter 16, page 185

37. Jenny Johnson—Daughter of Joe & Ruth. Enters– book 1, chapter 16, page 185

38. Judy Johnson—Youngest Daughter of Joe & Ruth. Enters–book 1, chapter 16, page 185

39. Dudley Lykins—Enters—book 3, chapter 9, page 89

40. Larry Lykins—Enters—book 3, chapter 9, page 89

41. Mrs. Eleanor Holbrook—Teacher at Oak Hills one-room school.

Lived—12/26/1937—9/12/2014   Enters—book   3, chapter 9, page 86

42. Ulysses Perry—Enters—book 6, chapter 7, page 81
Lived: 7/12/1924—3/16/1997

43. Uncle Jack Perry—Dad's step-brother. Enters—book 8, chapter 4

44. Rhonda Blair—Enters—book 4, chapter 7, page 72

45. Elmer Blair—Enters–book 4, chapter 7, page 72

Lived: 3/24/1916—5/20/1976

46. Mary Blair–Enters–book 4, chapter 7, page 72

Lived: 4/3/1920—3/6/2005

47. Geraldine Perry (married name Brown)–Sister of Uncle Jackie Perry

Enters—book 2, chapter 10, page 120

Lived: 2/8/1927-8/29/1991

Fictional Characters

1. **James Ernest** (Last name never mentioned.)–(I used the name of a real person James Ernest Easterling–but the character is fictional.) Timmy's best friend. Enters—book 1, chapter 2, page 35

2. **Miss Morgan**—Teacher at one-room school. Enters—book 1, chapter 1, page 29

3. **Mr. Engle**—Bee-keeper who lived in Wrigley. Enters—book 1, chapter 2, page 32

4. **Sam Kendrick**—Fisherman who caught the largest catfish ever from the pay lake. Enters—book 1, chapter 2, page 37

5. **Sam Johnson**—Fisherman. Enters—book 1, chapter 3, page 42

6. **Phillip Satch**—Fisherman who played tug-of-war with Uncle Morton. Enters—book 1, chapter 5, page 62

7. **Mrs. Natalie Robbins**—94-year-old neighbor who was from dead in book 1, chapter 7, book 84. Enters—book 1, chapter 3, page 40

8. **John Robbins**—Husband of Natalie. First mentioned—book 1, chapter 8, page 94

9. **James Ernest's Father**—Mentioned—Book 3, Chapter 22, Page 218.

10. **Anna Mae**—James Ernest's mother. Enters—book 2, chapter 4, page 46

11. **Settis Ann**—Neighbor lady who babysit James Ernest when he was a child. Enters—book 3, chapter 22, page 216

12. **George Williams**—County prosecuting attorney in Henry Washington's trial. Enters—book 3, chapter 27, page 278

13. **Judge Horton Hinkle**—Judge for trial. Enters—book 3, chapter 27, page 278

14. **Lawrence Kash**—Henry Washington's lawyer. Enters—book 3, chapter 26, page 273

15. **Nurse Charlene**—Nurse at Morehead hospital. Enters—book 3, chapter 25, page 260

16. **Doctor Baker**—Doctor at Morehead hospital. Enters—book 3, chapter 25, page 261

17. **Dr. Green**—Veterinarian. Enters—book 2, chapter 8, page 105

18. **Fred Wilson**—Fisherman. Enters—book 1, chapter 5, page 62

19. **Roger Smuckatilly**—Mailman. Enters—book 1, chapter 3, page 46

20. **Lily Smuckatilly**—Wife of Roger Smuckatilly Enters—book 2, chapter 13, page 158

21. **Mrs. Taylor**—Schoolteacher in Ohio. Enters—book 2, chapter 1, page 13

22. **Billy Taulbee**—Worst fisherman in the world and bully. Enters—book 1, chapter 5, page 62

23. **Bobby Lewis**—Billy Taulbee's short friend. Enters—book 1, chapter 5, page 62 Readers learn his name book 3, chapter 17, page 164

24. **Jackson Halsey**–Billy Taulbee's tall friend. Enters—book 1, chapter 5, page 62 Readers learn his name book 3, chapter 20, page 192

25. **Preacher Flack Black**—Pastor of Oak Hills Church. Enters—book 1, chapter 6, page 72 Announces he is leaving church book 2, chapter 9

26. **Mrs. Black**—Pastor's wife. Enters—book 1, chapter 15, page 174

27. **Sheriff Grizzle**—West Liberty Sheriff. Enters—book 1, chapter 7, page 91

28. **Deputy Tom Stewart**—Enters—book 1, chapter 22, page 266

29. **Deputy Art Law**–Enters—book 1, chapter 22, page 266

30. **Mr. Ken Harney**—Banker in West Liberty. Enters—book 1, chapter 8, page 95

31. **George "Razor" McGill**—Barber in West Liberty. Enters—book 1, chapter 10, page 111

32. **Daniel Sugarman**—Known as "Sugarspoon" or "Spoon". Friend in Timmy's class. Enters—book 1, chapter 10, page 116

33. **Mrs. Sugarman**—Daniel's overprotective mother. Enters–book 1, chapter 10, page 119

34. **Mr. Gateway**—Singer at church. Enters—book 1, chapter 11, page 127

35. **Mrs. Gateway**—Singer at church. Enters—book 1, chapter 11, page 127

36. **Sara Gateway**–4 year old daughter. Enters—book 1, chapter 11, page 127

37. **Mr. Cobb**—Owner of General Store in West Liberty. Enters—book 1, chapter 13, page 153

38. Large Larry—Helped Pastor Black with Mrs. Robbins farm auction. Enters—book 1, chapter 14, page 161

39. Harry the Mouse—Brother of Large Larry. Helped Pastor Black with Mrs. Robbins farm auction. Enters—book 1, chapter 14, page 161

40. The Tattoo Man 'Franklin Boone'—Readers learn his real name in book 6, chapter 16, page 174. Enters— book 1, chapter 12, page 135

41. Forest Tuttle—Father who bought Mrs. Robbins farm at the auction. Enters—book 1, chapter 15, page 178

42. Loraine Tuttle—Wife of Forest. Enters—book 1, chapter 15, page 178

43. Randy Tuttle—Oldest son of Forest & Loraine. Enters—book 1, chapter 15, page 178

44. Todd "Purty" Tuttle–Son of Forest & Loraine. Enters—book 1, chapter 15, page 178

45. Sadie Tuttle—Oldest daughter of Forest & Loraine. Enters—book 1, chapter 15, page 179

46. Francis Tuttle–Daughter of Forest & Loraine. Enters—book 1, chapter 15, page 179

47. Billy Tuttle—Youngest son of Forest & Loraine. Enters—book 1, chapter 15, page 179

48. Trudy Tuttle–Youngest daughter of Forest & Loraine. Enters—book 1, chapter 15, page 179

49. Pastor Bartholomew Walker White—New Pastor of Oak Hills Church. Enters—book 2, chapter 11, page 130

50. Miss Rebecca Simmons—Works at West Liberty bank. Becomes Pastor White's wife. Enters—book 2,chapter 6, page 69

51. Bobby Lee Simmons—Son of Miss Rebecca. Enters—book 2, chapter 6, page 69

52. Ed Norris—Owner of Ed's Fish Farm, fish delivery for pay lake. Enters—book 1, chapter 20, page 245

53. Aunt Elizabeth—Loraine Tuttle's sister. Enters—book 2, chapter 7, page 85

54. Uncle Sid Tuttle—Forest Tuttle's brother. Enters—book 2, chapter 7, page 87

55. 2 Trail hikers—Had hiked the trail up to the Blaze cemetery and back. Gave Timmy the map. Enters—book 2, chapter 11, page 135

56. Izzie Sargent—Girl at Wednesday's kids night at church. Enters—book 2, chapter 15, page 186

57. Mrs. Hazel Roberts—Teacher at Wed. kids night. Enters—book 2, chapter 15, page 187

58. **Hiram**—Leader of Boys from Blaze. Enters—book 2, chapter 15, page 188

59. **Hiram's younger brother**–Enters—book 4, chapter 4, page 39

60. **Henrietta**—Girl from Blaze. Enters—book 2, chapter 16, page 192

61. **Trent**—Dana's best man at wedding. Enters—book 2, chapter 25, page 311

62. **Ernest Eli Smith**—1st grader at one-room school. Enters—book 3, chapter 9, page 89

63. **Anita Jones**—8th grader at one-room school. Enters— book 3, chapter 9, page 90

64. **Claude Fox**–8th grader at one-room school. Enters— book 3, chapter 9, page 91

65. **Coal Washington**—Wife of Henry Washington. Enters—book 3, chapter 5, page 52

66. **Henry Washington**—Husband of Coal. Enters— book 3, chapter 7, page 65

67. **Raven Washington**—Oldest daughter of Coal and Henry. Enters–book 3, chapter 5, page 51

68. **Henry Washington Junior**—Oldest son of Coal and Henry. Enters–book 3, chapter 5, page 52

69. **Samantha Washington**—Second oldest daughter of Coal and Henry. Enters–book 3, chapter 5, page 52

70. **Mark Daniel Washington**–Second oldest son of Coal and Henry. Enters–book 3, chapter 5, page 53

71. **Virginia Chapman**—7th grader at one-room school. Brown hair to her waist. Enters—book 3, chapter 9, page 91

72. **Bernice "Skunk" Strunck**–7th grader at one-room school. Best friend of Sadie Tuttle. Kissed Tucky in outhouse. Enters—book 3, chapter 9, page 91

73. **Oscar Coffey**—5th grader at one-room school. Ugly kid with big ears and nose, always picking it. Enters—book 3, chapter 9, page 91

74. **Lulu Adams**—1st grader at one-room school. Enters—book 3, chapter 12, page 125

75. **Lisa Green**—5th grader at one-room school. Niece of Dr. Green, the veterinarian. Enters—book 3, chapter 10, page 104

76. **Johnny Hobbs**—First grader at one-room school. Enters—book 3, chapter 12, page 126

77. **"Big Mack"**—Seven-foot-tall pitcher for Mt. Sterling's all-black baseball team. Enters—book 3, chapter 16, page 161

78. **Harold "Pepper Face"**—Robber #1 who Timmy shoots in face with rock salt. Enters—book 4, chapter 7, page 75

79. **Mack**—Robber #2 with dark hair & thin moustache. Enters—book 4, chapter 7, page 75

80. **Mud McCobb**—Truck driver at quarry. Fisherman at pay-lake. Enters—book 4, chapter 7, page 78

81. **Jesse Moore**—Fisherman at pay-lake. Enters—book 4, chapter 7, page 78

82. **Louis Lewis**—Truck driver at quarry. Fisherman at pay-lake. Enters—book 4, chapter 7, page 78

83. **Sheriff Hagar Cane**—New sheriff. Becomes Timmy's step-father. Plays fiddle. Enters—book 4, chapter 7, page 78

84. **Russell**—Bootlegger & moonshiner & kidnapper. Enters—book 4, chapter 14, page 154

85. **Silas**–Bootlegger & moonshiner & kidnapper. Enters—book 4, chapter 14, page 154

86. **Buck Key**—Long beard to his waist, chews & spits tobacco. Enters—book 6, chapter 8, page 89

87. **Winona Key**—Wife of Buck, mother of 8 kids. Enters—book 6, chapter 18, page 206

88. Monk Key—Oldest son of Key family. Enters—book 6, chapter 18, page 206

89. Chuck Key—Second son of Key family. Enters—book 6, chapter 18, page 206

90. Sugar Cook Key—Oldest daughter of Key family. Enters—book 6, chapter 18, page 206

91. Chero Key—Third daughter of key family. Enters—book 6, chapter 18, page 206

92. Kenny Tuck Key "Tucky"—Third son and twin of Rock. Haircut—Mohawk and mullet. Enters—book 6, chapter 12, page 120

93. Rock Key—Second daughter and twin of Kenny. Enters—book 6, chapter 12, page 120

94. Adore Key—Fourth daughter of Key family. Enters—book 6, chapter 12, page 120

95. Luck Key—Fourth son of key family. Enters—book 6, chapter 12, page 120

96. Rubert Hatchet—One of the Bottom brothers. Enters—book 7, chapter 12, page 124

97. Luther Hatchet—Other half of Bottom brothers. Enters—book 7, chapter 12, page 124

98. Old Fisherman on Red River—unnamed. Enters—book 7, chapter 12, page 128

99. Clifford Brown—Lived on farm near Red River. Enters–book 7, chapter 14, page 149

100. Margaret Brown—Wife of Clifford. Made BLT's for Wolf Pack. Enters–book 7, chapter 14, page 149

101. Ophelia—One of three skinny dip girls. Enters—book 7, chapter 18, page 204

102. Mary Jane–One of three skinny dip girls. Enters—book 7, chapter 18, page 204

103. Valentine–One of three skinny dip girls. Enters—book 7, chapter 18, page 204

104. Lydia Boggs—Kidnap victim. Enters—book 7, chapter 20, page 228

105. Claude—Husband of black fishing couple on river. Enters—book 7, chapter 20, page 215

106. Hattie—Wife of Claude. Enters—book 7, chapter 20, page 215

107. Zelda Hatchet—Kidnapper and self-claimed witch. Also known as Zerelda Samuel. Mother of Bottom brothers. Enters—book 7, chapter 20, page 224

108. **Frank**—Bigoted owner of restaurant. Enters—book 7, chapter 22, page 252

109. **Derek Clouse**—West Liberty Deputy. Enters—book 8, chapter 9, page 89

110. **Linny Stutts**–West Liberty Deputy. Enters—book 8, chapter 9, page 89

111. **Charley**—Big Foot. Enters—book 8, chapter 4

112. **Tonya Washington**—Junior's wife. Enters—Book 8, Chapter 24

113. **Marie White**—Pastor White and Miss Rebecca's daughter. Enters—book 8, chapter 24

114. **Emily Sparrow**—James Ernest & Raven's daughter. Enters—book 8, chapter 24

115. **Erin Crow**—Second daughter of James Ernest & Raven. Enters—book 8, chapter 24

116. **Eddie Hawk**—Son of James Ernest & Raven. Enters—book 8, chapter 24

117. **Martin Clay**—Son of Timmy and Susie. Married to Emily Sparrow. Enters—book 8, chapter 24

118. **Cindy Tuttle**—Wife of Randy Tuttle. Enters—book 8, chapter 24

119. **Ernest T.**—Second son of Timmy & Susie. Enters—book 8, chapter 24

120. **Lauren Raven**—Daughter of Timmy & Susie Enters—book 8, chapter 24

Animals in Kentucky Summers

1. **Leo**—Papaw's Yellow Lab. Enters—book 1, chapter 1, page 17

2. **Mr. Perry**—Susie's horse. Enters—book 1, chapter 6, page 77

3. **4 goats**—Billy, Nanny, Billy Jr. & Nancy. Enters—book 1, chapter 15, page 179

4. **Coty**—Timmy's part coyote dog. Enters—book 2, chapter 8, page 92

5. **Bo "The Crow"**—The black crow who landed on Timmy's shoulder one day. Enters—book 6, chapter 2, page 33

6. **Honeycomb**–Papaw's mule. Enters—book 7, chapter 5, page 54

7. **James**—Junior's Beagle. Enters—book 8, chapter 20

8. **Gar**—Charley's pet wolf. Enters—book 8, chapter 22

9. **Yearling deer**–James Ernest's pet deer. Enters—book 8, chapter 7

listen|imagine|view|experience

AUDIO BOOK DOWNLOAD INCLUDED WITH THIS BOOK!

In your hands you hold a complete digital entertainment package. In addition to the paper version, you receive a free download of the audio version of this book. Simply use the code listed below when visiting our website. Once downloaded to your computer, you can listen to the book through your computer's speakers, burn it to an audio CD or save the file to your portable music device (such as Apple's popular iPod) and listen on the go!

How to get your free audio book digital download:

1. Visit www.tatepublishing.com and click on the e|LIVE logo on the home page.
2. Enter the following coupon code:
   3998-e665-4b76-ad19-ad1a-b7ed-a4dc-9fa0
3. Download the audio book from your e|LIVE digital locker and begin enjoying your new digital entertainment package today!

CPSIA information can be obtained
at www.ICGtesting.com
Printed in the USA
LVOW01s1213300916
506773LV00021B/66/P